C. B. Lyall grew up in Stockton-on-Tees, England. Since then, she has lived in India, Belgium, Hong Kong, and the USA. She currently resides in the Hudson Valley, north of New York, with her husband. She has three adult sons and one grandson.

For Nick, Alex, Anthony, Gregory, and Logan.
With love.

C. B. Lyall

# THE VIRUS OF BEAUTY

## WILF GILVARY SERIES

### BOOK 1

AUSTIN MACAULEY PUBLISHERS™

LONDON • CAMBRIDGE • NEW YORK • SHARJAH

**Copyright © C. B. Lyall (2019)**

**Ordering Information:**
Quantity sales: special discounts are available on quantity purchases by corporations, associations, and others. For details, contact the publisher at the address below.

**Publisher's Cataloging-in-Publication data**
Lyall, C. B.
The Virus of Beauty: Wilf Gilvary Series – Book 1

ISBN 9781643780658 (Paperback)
ISBN 9781643780665 (Hardback)
ISBN 9781643780672 (Kindle e-book)
ISBN 9781645366799 (ePub e-book)

Library of Congress Control Number: 2019935034

The main category of the book — Young Adult Fiction / Fantasy / Wizards & Witches

www.austinmacauley.com/us

First Published (2019)
Austin Macauley Publishers LLC
40 Wall Street, 28th Floor
New York, NY 10005
USA

mail-usa@austinmacauley.com
+1 (646) 5125767

This book could never have been written without the encouragement and support of a number of people. Thank you to the Production USA team at Austin Macauley Publishers LLC for their help and professionalism.

The talented writers in our writing group: Jean Huff, Gregory French, Kim Greene-Liebowitz, Elyse Pollack, and Anne Foley. The instructors at Sarah Lawrence College's Writing Institute: Pat Dunn, Jimin Han, and Wendy Townsend. The YA class: Rebecca Adams, Alison Cooper-Mulin, Claire Hansen, Laura Sinko, and Suzanne Ste. Therese. Barbara Solomon Josselsohn and the Friday group at the Scarsdale Library. The helpful feedback from Brooke Lea Foster, Reyna Marder Gentin, and Rosana Szabatura.

Thanks to Julia Pennock for being a loyal reader and my favorite sister. To my sons: Alex, Anthony, and Gregory, for their love and support. To my parents, Keith and Chris Browell. Finally, to my husband, Nick, for all the encouragement, belief, and support.

Thank you.

# Table of Contents

# Chapter One
# Shattered Destiny

Wilf waited in bed until he could no longer hear his father's footsteps on the stairs of their Hong Kong apartment. If he was lucky, he could sneak out and avoid another confrontation.

The shooting star tattoo on the back of his right hand pulsed. He scrunched his eyes. Beads of sweat collected on his forehead and trickled down his face. The pain became impossible to ignore, and he cracked open his eyes.

A long, trembling sigh escaped him. For the second time this week, his bedroom had transformed overnight from orderly to resembling the aftermath of a major typhoon's direct hit.

He shivered from the sweat cooling on his body and the cold room. Grabbing a towel, he headed for the shower.

Water coursed over him.

It had to be Myra messing his room during the night. He tried to remember what he'd done recently to upset his stepsister, but nothing unusual came to mind.

He stepped out of the shower, dried, and wrapped a towel around his waist.

Whatever it was, he'd better find out soon and apologize.

"You're late," Myra said as he emerged from the steam-filled bathroom.

"I know." He took a deep breath. "Myra."

She disappeared down the stairs, towards the kitchen.

He padded along the landing, turned into his room, and stopped. A knot tightened in his stomach. She'd done it again. His room had magically been tidied. She'd even laid out his clothes on the bed. He threw them on the floor. This was control on an unhealthy level.

She had no right to enter his room, let alone clear it up. If he wanted his room to resemble a catastrophe, why should she interfere?

11

He picked up the white shirt and dark-gray pants off the floor. He hated South Island School's uniform. Next year, he'd be free to wear whatever he wanted, the privilege of being an upperclassman.

He shoved textbooks, binders, and his soccer kit into a backpack. Collecting his wallet from the nightstand, he checked inside for his Octopus card. *Shit.* It wasn't there.

He picked up yesterday's cargo shorts and checked all the pockets. It wasn't possible he'd lost it so soon. His father would explode.

He tore the room apart looking for the card. Bedding lay heaped on the rug, and schoolbooks covered the mattress where he'd shaken each one. Gnawing the skin around his fingernails, he glanced over at the bedroom door.

He needed that card. Coach would check he had it. If he didn't, he'd have to clear up after soccer practice, and then he'd be late for school, which would put him in detention. Not to mention that the stupid thing was the only way to register attendance and pay for lunch and the bus home.

He repacked his backpack and ran down to the kitchen.

"Have you seen my Octopus card?"

"No." Myra stepped away from the fridge. "You haven't…?"

He threw his backpack under the table, grabbed a hand towel, and took the stairs two at a time.

Standing on the street, in front of the store, he swallowed trying to ease his dry throat.

There was only one place left to search: under the counter, and his father would already be at work in the basement workshop. It was either risk his father going ballistic or having the rest of his day ruined. With a bit of luck, his father would be busy on a call or in the middle of some experimental magic.

Opening the store door slowly, he grabbed the doorbell clangor with the hand towel to stop it from jingling. He guided the door closed, dulling the Hong Kong street noise, until he heard the click of the lock. Tossing the towel aside, he crept into his family's gift store, trying to avoid the floorboards that creaked. He stopped at the counter and listened. No sound came from the basement. The card had to be underneath. He pulled out bags and paper. A coin bounced onto the floor. Wilf froze and waited for a creak on the workshop stairs. Nothing. He continued until the shelf was bare. The shooting star tattoo on the back of his hand burned.

Perhaps he'd dropped the card. It could have fallen out of his pocket. He spun around and wove his way between the shelves, scouring the floor.

The tattoo pulsed. He shoved the hand into the pocket of his pants and continued threading his way through the store's cluttered shelves of t-shirts, Laughing Buddhas, shot glasses, and Happy Cats. The sinking feeling grew in his stomach as hope faded.

A piercing pain shot up his arm.

"What the…?"

A rumbling groan echoed around the store. He glanced towards the alcove housing the Mage's Crystal. His eyes widened as the mirrored surface glowed red. A loud crack pierced the air like a ball smashing through a window. He ran for the supply closet and forced his six-foot body inside.

Quartz exploded across the room from the Crystal's center.

He felt a whoosh of air next to his ear as he slammed the door shut. He switched on the closet light and stepped backward into brooms and mop handles that banged the back of his head. A large piece of polished quartz, still vibrating from its violent impact with the wall, reflected the shock in his gray eyes.

Thuds echoed in the tiny room from projectiles impaling the door. He touched his ear, but seeing no blood on his fingers, exhaled. That had been too close.

Several seconds of silence passed before he braved stepping outside. Crystal fragments, lying over the shelves and floor, filled the store with colliding rainbows as sunlight hit the debris. Wilf blinked rapidly. Half-buried crystal daggers covered the closet's wooden door. All he'd done was glance in the crystal's direction, but his father would blame him for this disaster.

"Wilf, is that you?" Reginald's shout was followed by a creaking sound from the basement stairs.

Wilf bolted for the front door. His shoes crunched the broken glass. He jerked open the door and the bell gave a traitorous jingle. He shot out of the store and back into their living quarters. He barged into the kitchen.

"What's happened?" Myra asked, putting down the bread knife.

He threw himself onto a chair, poured cornflakes and milk into a bowl, and shoveled a spoonful into his mouth.

"Wilf," Myra said, her voice taking on the adult tone she'd started using 2 years ago, when she turned 18. "I take it you didn't find your card in the store."

"It wasn't me," he mumbled through his mouthful of cereal. "But I'll be blamed. Tell him I was here, having breakfast."

"Why am I covering for you again?" she asked, folding her arms and trying to look more imposing than her five-feet, two-inch height would allow.

Wilf's spoon leaped from his hand and splashed into the bowl at the first heavy footstep on the stairs.

The faucet stopped dripping and the clock held its next tick. The small kitchen in the Gilvarys' Hong Kong apartment held its breath.

The kitchen door flew open. His father stood there, shaking with rage. After a moment, Reginald thrust his hands into the pockets of his beige pants.

"You've shattered the Mage's Crystal." His lips formed a thin line on his angular face. "It's been in our family for generations."

Wilf half-expected the green tiled walls to be sucked in with the force of his father's inhale.

"Why don't you ever accuse her?" He pointed at Myra.

"Because your stepsister has control of her magic, unlike you." His father stood over him. "Besides, all the shards have your image on them."

"It would take magic to break it. I don't use magic; therefore, it can't have been me." Wilf reached under his chair, trying to locate his backpack. "I'm late for soccer practice."

"Soccer practice. Soccer practice…" Veins stood out in Reginald's neck. "I've let this foolishness go on for far too long. You're almost 16. You can't avoid magical training any longer."

"I told you. It wasn't me. Perhaps the humidity caused it to crack. How should I know?" He pushed his bowl away and reached further under the chair, trying to locate his bag.

"It's a magical artifact, as you pointed out. It can adapt." The small mirror on Reginald's wrist lit up and pinged. "Bat's blood. Of all the times… I have to take this call. I forbid you to leave until I return. This isn't finished." Reginald paused at the door. He waved his hand and the ruby at the center of his wizard's ring flashed. Wilf's soccer ball and cleats flew out of the room and down the stairs. "I think you might need this." The ring flashed again and an Octopus Card appeared on the table.

The door slammed shut behind Reginald with enough force to rattle the crockery stacked on the open shelves.

Wilf clenched his fists.

"That won't stop me," he shouted at the closed door while shoving the card into his wallet.

"He's worried about you," Myra said, wriggling her fingers. The dirty dishes flew across the room and clattered into the sink.

"No, he isn't. He stole my card so he could take my kit." Wilf pushed his chair away and grabbed his bag. "He always wants to control me."

"I think you're misjudging him," Myra said. "You know I'm on your side, but…"

"Didn't hear you supporting me."

"You didn't give me a chance." She pushed her short blonde hair behind her ears. "Besides, you get that 'closed for business' look on your face and stop paying attention whenever anyone mentions magic." Her soft voice produced a wave of calm in the room. "He's being very patient."

"Well, his patience just ran out," he scowled. "And stop it with the damned magic. I know you're trying to use a calming spell on me."

Myra shrugged as the dishes rinsed themselves and then hopped into the dishwasher. Her ice-blue eyes held his. "You're a wizard, whether you like it or not. Regardless of what happened to your mother."

He folded his arms across his chest. "I don't need magic here, and I never will. I'm perfectly happy in Hong Kong as a Normal." He kicked the chair under the table. "I'm late," he said, stuffing a water bottle into the backpack's mesh pocket.

"But Reginald said you were to stay."

"I heard him."

Wilf ran down the narrow stairs to the street, slamming the front door behind him.

The crystal had to shatter while he was in the store. The charms had probably worn thin, but his father wouldn't have considered that first. No, it was another excuse for his father to rant about Wilf, soccer, and magic. It always was with him.

Even when he'd been offered a place at The Academy, and a chance to play soccer in a Premier League team's youth program in England, magic had prevented him. His father had declared it was too risky having an untrained wizard out in the world on his own, and that he felt the only responsible cause of action was to refuse permission. It always came back to magic ruining Wilf's life. Why couldn't he have been born to Normal parents?

He tightened the backpack's straps and started jogging up Tai Wang Street. The sweet vanilla and musk smell of the incense burner at the Hung Shing Taoist Temple wafted over him as he turned into the swirling mass of the morning rush hour on Queen's Road East. He pressed forward by dodging and weaving his way through any narrow gap he could find in the crowd, as if he were dribbling a ball around plastic practice cones.

The jostling throng of business people in their smart suits, together with shop workers pouring out from packed double-decker buses, would have made a snail complain about the pace of forward momentum along the street. Wilf hunched his shoulders and cut between two women. The air, thick enough to taste, was the usual blend of pollution, dust, drains, humidity, and molding vegetation. But at this time of day, it also carried the sweet smell of baked goods, congee, and chowmein.

The lights at the Hopewell Centre crossing changed. Wilf charged across the road and managed to whirl around a tattooed, muscular man struggling with his heavily-laden wooden trolley.

"You're late," Enzo said, leaning against the bamboo scaffolding enclosing the sidewalk. "Another couple of minutes and I'd have left." His friend had inherited his Italian father's dark, curly hair and olive skin, but his almond-shaped, hazel eyes came from his Chinese mother. Wilf hadn't inherited any of his mother's Chinese characteristics. He was his father's double, an all-Anglo-Saxon mixture with dark hair and gray eyes.

"Tell me something I don't know. I'm lucky to be here at all."

"Your old man at you again?"

Wilf nodded and cut hard to his left, around a group of tourists blocking the street. In heavily-accented English, their guide explained the history and architectural value of the blue house with its wrought-iron balconies, old-style wooden staircases, and no flushing water.

Wilf stormed forward with Enzo flanking his right wing.

"Tunnel or dragon?" Wilf asked, pausing at the end of the street.

"Dragon. We should pay our respects for the luck we had in last night's match," Enzo said, heading down Morrison Hill to the giant golden dragon that guarded the entrance to Causeway Bay. Its Feng Shui purpose was to make people feel happy and safe.

"That wasn't luck, it was pure skill." Wilf reached over to stroke the dragon's nose.

"A bicycle-kick goal from that angle? Pure wizardry." Enzo turned to watch a group of chattering girls walk past.

Wilf gasped as his tattoo tingled. He glanced quickly at his friend, and then followed his gaze. "Ahhh... the beautiful Emma. You know she'll never acknowledge your existence, don't you?"

"I can dream."

"Waste of time. Come on. Coach is going to bench us for the rest of the season if we're late again."

"He might bench me, but never his superstar player," Enzo said, punching Wilf on the arm.

"You're full of it," he said, crossing at the lights under the busy flyover.

"Race you." Enzo flew past him.

"Hey," Wilf yelled, drew level, and then overtook his friend. He charged into Hong Kong Football Club with Enzo at his heels.

Coach stood with a clipboard in his hand as they entered the locker room. "Good of you two to join us this morning."

Wilf and Enzo waved their Octopus cards at Coach.

"Sorry, Coach," Wilf said, pulling his practice strip out of his bag. "Oh, no! I've left my cleats at home." He wasn't about to admit that his father had confiscated them

"Look through the lost and found for a pair," Coach said. "Then, give me five laps of the field to help you remember next time."

Wilf dug through the box and unearthed a sorry-looking old pair. He filled the toes with tissue to stop them rubbing up and down on his heels. Then, he headed past the stands holding a group of giggling girls.

"Great goal last night, Wilf," several of the girls shouted.

"Ahhh… Thanks," he said and grinned. His smile disappeared as he noticed Amy glaring at him. It had been a month since they'd broken up, and she was still stalking him. He tripped over the edge of the ramp.

"You're going to do some serious damage in those clown cleats," Enzo said, jogging ahead. "This could be my big chance."

Wilf prayed the cleats would stay on his feet, especially during goal practice. He'd no wish to knock out the goalie.

He ran out onto the field to start his laps. The rest of the team was doing warm-up sprints through the rows of practice cones.

The argument with his father kept filtering through his thoughts even as he lined up balls to take a few practice shots at the goal. His father needed to accept that he was never going into the family business.

"Wilf?"

The goalie's voice drifted away and a silence engulfed him. A small cloud of dust floated across the pitch in his direction. It swirled and shimmered around him. His father's voice contained a note of sorrow as it whispered in Wilf's head, "I'm sorry. I hope you'll understand it's for your own protection."

Small flashes of heat and power zapped him. His father's large, ornate ring appeared on Wilf's right ring finger, spun round three times, and shrunk to fit. The cloud rose above him in a plume. A rift opened in the sky as his father's essence ascended, and then it closed with a green flash.

"You all right?" the goalie asked. "You look kind of weird."

Wilf stared at the red, glowing ruby at the center of the wizard ring. His father had evaporated. Died. That wasn't possible.

He charged across the pitch towards the exit.

"Where the hell do you think you're going?" Coach yelled. "If you leave now, Wilf Gilvary, you're not playing in the championship."

Wilf was already through the gate.

# Chapter Two
## Gift Store

Myra stood in front of Wilf, talking, lecturing really, on how they couldn't keep living in Hong Kong.

Wilf zoned her out and stared at his red, swollen finger. This morning, he'd stood in the bathroom with soap, ice, and oil balanced on the sink.

He'd held the ice in his hand until it was numb and his finger shrunk. The ring slid up to his knuckle. He smiled and pulled hard.

"Fuck!" he shouted as the ruby flashed. A bolt of energy arched from the ring to heat the flesh of his finger. His tattoo tingled and its color deepened.

Next, he'd taken oil and slathered it over the ring and his finger, massaging it until he couldn't hold the bottle any longer. The ring moved up to his knuckle with ease, until the ruby sent another bolt. The oil disappeared and the ring shrunk to cut into his flesh.

"Damn it to hell." He picked up the soap and the ring flashed a warning at him. The shooting star tattoo on his hand pulsed. It looked as angry as he felt. His stomach knotted in revulsion.

"I bet you're really happy about this," he shouted at the ceiling. "You've no right to force magic on me." He threw the soap at the wall and it smashed. His father's last thought must have been to make Wilf's life miserable.

He stood shaking his head at the mirror. He tried to push thoughts of Reginald to the back of his mind, but a gnawing guilt that somehow this was his fault began to take root.

"Are you listening at all?" Myra asked.

Sighing, he spun the small carousel that stood on the counter. It whirled, jangling the metal key rings together and several flew off.

She narrowed her eyes and glared at him.

He picked up the key rings and hung them back on the carousel.

"I said, you're only 15," she emphasized every word.

"I'm almost 16."

"Still a child in the eyes of the law. And now that Reginald has evaporated…"

"He's dead." Wilf swallowed the lump in his throat. "My father died while I was playing soccer."

Myra took a deep breath. "I know you're upset. But his magical energy will have returned to the Source. We don't die, not like Normals." She went to place her hand on his arm, but he flinched away. "Our only option is to go and live in the Magical Realm. It's where we belong."

"Not again." In the last 2 days, she'd mentioned leaving for Kureyamage at least 20 times, although it felt like a 100. "I'd rather make my bed in the gutter and eat out of garbage cans than be forced to live there."

"You're delusional. There's no way you could survive here on your own. You'd end up having to use your magic."

"I'm never going to use it… again."

Myra gave a bark of dismissive laughter. "I don't have time for this now. You've made me late for my tour group." She headed into the restroom at the back of the store. "This isn't finished."

Taking a ball out of his soccer bag, he bounced it a few times. He glanced towards the closet hiding the entrance to his father's workshop. Only a few days ago, the sound of the ball would have brought his father storming up the stairs. He gave himself a mental shake. The noise wouldn't annoy his father anymore. Part of him wished it could.

He dribbled the ball down the only wide aisle in the store and then began juggling it from one foot to the other.

His father and Myra had never understood how he felt about soccer and being accepted by the team, no longer any different from his classmates. He focused on the ball, trying to block all the other thoughts racing through his head.

He stalled the ball between his ankles and knees. Then flicked it up onto his head and wove around, balancing it on the center of his forehead.

He loved doing ball tricks. They gave him a sense of control, especially now, when his whole life seemed like it was falling apart.

If only he could have shared his love for the game with his father. Perhaps then Reginald would have appreciated how much practice it took to master soccer skills, but his father had refused to attend any of Wilf's matches. There was always a new project that needed to be finished. Being a father came a long way down Reginald's list of priorities. A wizard first and foremost, he'd never understood why Wilf hadn't had the same passion. Wilf couldn't remember the last time he'd talked to his father, rather than argue with him. Probably before his mother's accident, but that was a taboo subject between them. Never to be mentioned.

"Wilf!"

The ball plunged off his forehead. He lunged, hoping to catch it before it landed on the shelf of plates, mugs, and Laughing Buddhas. The ball came to a stop in mid-air above the shelf and floated there. He reached for it, but it leaped towards the ceiling, hurled across the store, and slammed into the trashcan with a loud hissing noise.

"No." Wilf tore across the store. "Damn it, Myra. Coach won't give me any more free ones." He took the deflated ball out of the trashcan and let out a sigh of relief. At least she hadn't shredded it this time.

"Then, you should take more care not to get it trashed." She stood in front of him with her hands in the pockets of her knee-length, khaki shorts. The front of her white t-shirt bore the slogan: *'Enjoy your spell in Hong Kong with Myra Tours'*.

He wiped sweat from his fuzzy top lip and then rubbed his hand down his black shorts.

"You know the team won the League last night," Wilf tucked the deflated ball under the counter, out of Myra's reach. "Coach will be picking the squad for the championship in Singapore. It's really important I make evening practice."

"There's more to life than soccer." Myra opened her backpack and checked its contents.

"Not to me," Wilf said. He could feel the heat rising in his cheeks.

"You should be thinking about your exams instead of kicking that ball around," Myra said, glancing up. "My tour guides pay the bills, and that means you need to take care of the store. Singapore isn't happening." She turned her back on him.

Wilf pointed at her. "You could have saved some money on printing. Your slogan stinks."

"Stop being childish." She put an aluminum water bottle into the bag's side pocket. "I'm going up to the Chi Lin Nunnery and Nan Lian Gardens with a group from that cruise liner that came in last night."

"How long will that take?" Tourist season in Hong Kong sucked. The streets were already crowded enough, but the influx of people who wandered lost around the Mass Transit Railway, held up buses, and took all the taxis made the city impossible to navigate.

"All afternoon, but that doesn't make a difference to you, because you'll be minding the store." Myra slung her backpack over her shoulder and took a deep breath. "Fine, I'll spell it out for you. First, we visit the Nunnery, then the Gardens, tea at the vegetarian restaurant, and finally, we take the MTR from Diamond Hill." She put on her wide, peaked cap. "I'll make it back around five."

"But I need to leave at 3:30." Wilf followed her to the door. "Myra, you can't do this to me. You'll get me thrown off the team at this rate."

"You're still on about soccer? Forget it." She took a step towards him and grabbed his right hand. "This ring is our passport to Kureyamage. If you would only use it, life could be so much better."

Wilf pulled his hand free and stuffed it into his pocket. He glared at Myra.

"Thought not." She slammed the shop door behind her.

He looked down at the goosebumps covering his arm. Kureyamage, the wizard-controlled city in the Magical Realm, the very name made his skin creep.

He paced around the store like a substitute warming up along the sidelines.

If she wanted to go to the Magical Realm so badly, then she should go. He could manage on his own. Enzo's family, or maybe Coach, would take him in. Then, he could play all the time. Magic would be out of his life forever.

The ring flashed. There had to be a way of removing the revolting thing. He crossed over to the counter and pulled out the deflated soccer ball. Cradling it in his arms, he sat down on the metal stool and swung its front legs off the ground until his back rested against the wall.

He needed to get out of the store. He stared over at the alcove hiding the remnants of the shattered Mage Crystal.

"This is all your fault," he yelled, remembering his 13th birthday.

He'd locked eyes with Myra as his father had stepped towards him. "Fantastic. A magical father and son moment," he'd whispered to her as Reginald propelled him towards the alcove. The four-foot crystal had sat on its rosewood stand. It reminded Wilf of half a rotten, hard-boiled egg with its gray albumen and black yolk. The crystal's gray oval surface changed into throbbing bands of different colors as they approached. The black center turned to mirrored glass that reflected the store's interior.

"Stand up straight," Reginald had said, resting his hands on Wilf's shoulders. Wilf shifted his feet and watched his father's reflection. The intense gray eyes had held his.

"Place your right hand on the crystal's center," Reginald said, before beginning an incantation. Wilf's hand touched the warm surface and it misted over. A small pinprick of light began to spread out from the heart of the crystal until an image of Wilf standing alone appeared. He was taller, older, and wore a full-length black robe. The image moved, and his right hand poked out of the folds of the robe, revealing a red shooting star etched on its back.

Wilf bit his lip against the pain searing through his hand. The faint outline of a wizard's shooting star appeared. He blinked away tears as he pulled back his hand and cradled it.

"Excellent." Reginald took his hands off Wilf's shoulders. "I knew this nonsense of refusing to perform magic couldn't last. And look, not only will you be a wizard, but a Rod Wizard. Congratulations, my boy. Your mother would have been so proud if she'd lived to see this day…"

Wilf shuddered and took a step away from his father.

"Another Red Wizard in the Gilvary family," Reginald continued.

A tingling ran up Wilf's spine as the star tattoo started to fade on his mirrored image. He turned to see if his father had noticed the change, but Reginald wasn't paying attention. He'd strutted over to Griselda and Myra. Wilf glanced back, but his image shattered. Jagged pieces spread across the crystal's surface. The surface misted over and then cleared, showing his 13-year-old self, looking shocked. It darkened, all images vanishing.

Wilf tried to take a deep breath, but his lungs refused to work. He staggered forward. His right hand came into contact with the crystal's surface. An image sprang to life of Wilf's six-year-old self with his right arm outstretched, screaming noiselessly. He recoiled from the crystal. His whole body shook as the image faded. The surface darkened once more.

"You're wrong," Wilf said, his voice filled with loathing.

"We've always been Red Wizards," Reginald said, standing in front of Griselda with his back to Wilf.

"It's not true," Wilf said.

"What did you say?"

Wilf looked at his father's smiling face. Pride shone in Reginald's eyes.

"The crystal's wrong," Wilf said.

"You have your tattoo. It's obviously your destiny to be a Red Wizard." Reginald furrowed his forehead and drew his eyebrows together. "How can that be wrong?"

"It's some kind of trick." Wilf's whole body trembled. He balled his fists until his fingernails dug into his palms. "You stopped watching too soon. The crystal… I shattered… It shattered me."

"Nonsense," Reginald snapped. "The red shooting star is clearly marked on your hand. Shattered, indeed. If this is another attempt to avoid magic lessons…" Reginald took a step forward, but Wilf dodged his father's outstretched hand and ran from the store. That was the last time he could remember his father being proud of him.

The air-conditioning unit vibrated loudly into life again. Wilf gulped down the lump in his throat. Tears slid down his cheeks, but he dashed them away.

He took out his phone and checked the time. He wasn't going to miss practice today, no matter what Myra said. He'd deal with any fallout later, but he couldn't spend time alone in the store. There were too many memories he didn't want to relive.

# Chapter Three
## Ermentrude Arrives

A loud croak sounded from the bell above the shop door, instead of its usual soft, musical jingle.

Wilf hadn't expected anyone to venture down the narrow street to the store. Pulling the clean Newcastle United shirt down over his head, he crossed the back of the store, while running his fingers through his close-cropped hair, trying to smooth it back into place. The stool's legs grated over the wooden floorboards as Wilf pulled it out and sat down. He nudged his deflated ball to the far edge of the counter.

A woman stomped down the central aisle towards him. He glanced at the purple silk slippers she wore. Shoes that delicate shouldn't sound like soccer cleats marching across a metal basement hatch. She stopped at the counter.

His gaze lifted from the woman's feet to her face. Her leaden complexion and doughy face were enough to make him recoil. But the enormous wart at the end of her long, beaked nose was his undoing. He gasped.

The woman pinched in her lips and her eyes flared. Wilf took in the rest of her appearance from the severity of her hair bun to the red carpetbag, the size of a professional tennis player's racket bag, slung over her shoulder. He furrowed his brow. She reminded him of someone, but he couldn't quite remember whom.

"Beautiful, isn't it? Not many are blessed with a wart of such magnitude," she said.

The hairs on his arms all stood to attention at the sound of her scratchy voice. He looked at the blackened nails poking out from the ends of her fingerless gloves. Thankfully, she wasn't offering to shake hands.

"Have we met?"

"Not that I can recall," she said.

"That's a terrible sore throat you have." He tried to avoid meeting her hypnotic, brown eyes. They seemed like mud pools wanting to suck him into their fathomless depths.

"Sore throat?"

His stool rocked of its own volition and forced him to stand.

"Ermentrude Wakefield is the name." She glanced around the small store. "You may call me Witch Wakefield."

Wilf stepped back, braced against the wall, and shoved his ringed hand into his pocket. His heart raced. The Wizard Council had dispatched this witch to collect him. Well, it didn't make any difference who they sent. He wasn't leaving Hong Kong.

"Now, I don't normally deal with wizards…" her face wrinkled the way Myra's did when she took his soccer kit out of its bag for washing. "…But this time I have to. So, show me the rest of the place. We'll need your father's journal, and then we'll be on our way. There's sure to be a portal nearby we can use. I can't abide taking passengers on my broom. Although, I'd rather not have to use the warehouse portals up in Sha Tin, but if needs must…"

"There's been some mistake." Wilf could hear the panic in his own voice. "I'm not a wizard. That was my father. He died—I mean evaporated—a few weeks ago."

Her shadow leaned forward. It always surprised him how a witch could command her shadow. Griselda's had a permanent lean before she left. "I don't have time for games with a junior wizard." She pointed at his pocket. "What are you hiding?"

"Nothing."

Ermentrude stared him down before turning to survey the store. There wasn't much to investigate. It was possible, with a few steps in both directions, to touch a wall. The small counter, protecting Wilf, stood in the middle of the back wall.

"Where's the workshop?" Ermentrude said.

"Workshop? This is it," he said, waving his left arm. "Except for a closet, through that door." He pointed at the paint-chipped, two-paneled door behind him. "And a washroom through the other." The workshop had disappeared; even Myra hadn't been able to find the way in. He'd heard her knocking on all the walls in the store closet, but to no avail. The entrance vanished the moment his father evaporated.

Ermentrude wriggled her fingers towards the main door. It locked, the sign flipped to 'Closed', and the shutters came down with a clatter.

"Hey. You can't do that."

"I'm not talking about what Normals can see." She took off her jacket and hung it on the wall next to the counter. "I want to see the wizard workshop located within these premises." She glanced around warily, as if checking that no one else was listening.

"This is a gift store."

Ermentrude rubbed her square chin. Wilf winced at the wire-brush-raking-over-metal-studs sound coming from the bristles.

"I've always thought wizards were a stubborn lot," she sneered. "But most don't act habitually stupid." She reached across the counter, grabbed him by his Newcastle United shirt, and pulled him across the wooden surface. "I'm sure your father taught you that a witch's facial appearance corresponds to the amount of power she wields. Your idea of beauty, in my case, fled screaming a long time ago. My features are a direct warning not to misjudge my ability or temperament." She let him go, and he fell back against the wall, knocking the stool over. Her jacket inched away from him.

Ermentrude paced and the displays crowded into a corner to give her room. "I wish they'd sent someone else. Why do I always get the hopeless cases? There isn't time for this. I should be…" She stopped in front of Wilf. "Well, we'd better get started, since they did send me, and I'm here." She raised her fingers at him and wriggled them. "Where was the workshop before it disappeared?"

"That closet," Wilf said, pointing. The words sprung from him in a gush before he could stop them.

Ermentrude pushed past him and stepped into the closet.

Wilf followed and peered around at the empty shelves. The store was in a perfect location for a wizard's consultancy but not so good for the passing tourist trade.

"Typical," Ermentrude said. "Hiding in plain sight. So like a wizard." She raised her hand, tapped the back wall, and then caught Wilf's right hand. "So you do have your father's ring," she said, placing Wilf's hand on a black wood knot.

"Just a minute…" He tried to pull away, but Ermentrude held his hand in a firm grip.

Groans sounded from deep within the wall, and the knot expanded into a yawning, black hole. The air shimmered, and a staircase with a carved handrail popped into place.

"Look at the workmanship." She ran her hand over the runes around the entrance. "You don't see skill like that anymore."

Wilf raised his foot to step over the threshold, but Ermentrude knocked him back.

"Don't you know anything at all about decent magic?" she asked, and tutted, "What do the runes say?"

He watched the symbols shimmering into existence around the entrance. "Umm, how should I know?"

"Run your fingers over them, and then tell me what comes into your mind."

He'd always thought magic folk were half-mad. This particular witch was fully certifiable. "No," he said. "You're not tricking me into performing any type of magic."

Ermentrude's bag lifted its handles off her shoulder, placed itself on the floor, and opened. A scream jumped out and hit Wilf full in the face.

"Torturing my patience is never a good idea."

His ears rang from the deafening noise.

"Think of it more as a ritual than real magic." She softened the pitch of her voice. "It's very important that I get into that workshop. You've heard of the Pulch Virus that's attacking witch magic?"

"No." He shook his head.

"Your father's been trying to develop a vaccine to prevent the Virus. He contacted us on the day he evaporated, saying he'd made a breakthrough." Ermentrude took a step closer to Wilf. "I'm here to collect Reginald's journal; it's the only record of his findings."

Sweat poured out of Wilf as the hot waves of Ermentrude's frustration hit him.

"Do you want a large number of deaths on your conscience?"

"There must be another way." Wilf wiped the sweat away before it ran into his eyes.

"Why don't you do this little thing for me, and then you can go back to playing with your ball?"

A whoosh of air inflated the ball on the counter. It bounced on the wooden surface and then dropped to the floor.

Wilf's throat tightened as he tried to drag air into his lungs. The thought of using magic always had this suffocating effect on him. He placed his hands on the wall for support. Ermentrude didn't care what happened to him. He couldn't breathe.

"I'm not performing any kind of ritual, or magic, or any other way you want to describe it," Wilf said, and coughed. He needed water.

"But this is nonsense. You're probably already using magic," Ermentrude said, producing a water bottle with a wriggle of her fingers. She held it out to him. "Do you excel in class well beyond your classmates?"

"No," Wilf said, eyeing the bottle with both longing and disgust.

"What about sport?" The soccer ball rolled over, stopped by his feet, and bounced up and down like an excited puppy. "Are you exceptional there?"

Wilf sucked air in through his gritted teeth. "I practice a lot."

"There you are," Ermentrude said. "You've tapped into your magic to outperform. We all do it."

"I don't use magic." Wilf retreated a few steps from Ermentrude and the ball. "How dare you accuse me of cheating? I'm naturally good at soccer. Everyone says so."

"Do they know you have magical ability?"

"Of course they don't."

"I rest my case," Ermentrude said. "Oh, I'm not saying you're doing it on purpose. I can believe you never intended to, but it's part of who you are. If you want something badly enough, it's natural to use everything at your disposal. You have magic…"

"I know the rules."

Ermentrude laughed so hard she doubled over. Tears ran down her face. "That's a good one. You refuse to use magic, but you know the rules." She wiped her face on a lace handkerchief that appeared in her hand. "It's been at least 40 years since I heard that one used and someone believing it."

She shook her head. All mirth expunged from her face. "Now, you look here, Wizard Wilf. Whether you deny it or not, you're a wizard. I don't know why your father allowed you to go around in ignorance; presumably, he thought you'd come around when you'd passed through the trying years. Although, seeing as you're a wizard, I'm not exactly sure when that is."

"You're telling me I don't have a choice?"

"Just about as much as deciding what color your eyes are, initially, because you can certainly change them later on, if only temporarily," Ermentrude said, and smiled.

He hoped she didn't think her smile was reassuring.

"You're a danger to yourself and others, not being trained. Magic will start to leak out. Who knows what you might do."

This had to be a trick. Although, if Ermentrude was correct, it might explain why his father had become more insistent he learn magic over the past year.

Wilf glanced around the small closet, then down the staircase leading into darkness, and finally at his soccer ball.

Perhaps, Reginald had known all along that Wilf used magic every time he played soccer; and Myra probably also knew. She'd become so emphatic about them departing for Kureyamage. If she was afraid he could be dangerous without training, then perhaps she was trying to save him.

The alarm sounded on his phone. He needed to leave for practice.

"If I open the workshop, you'll take Dad's journal and leave?" Wilf asked.

"I can guarantee that once that book is in my hand, I'm out of here," she said, and smiled.

Wilf wished she'd stop smiling; it wasn't helping.

"Swear it," Wilf said.

"Well, I don't rightly hold with folk going around swearing, but just this once," Ermentrude said. "I bloody well promise to leave as soon as I have the journal."

"That's not quite... But it will do." Wilf ran his fingers over the runes and waited for inspiration. Nothing happened. He turned to Ermentrude.

"A little patience," she said.

The ring's ruby flared and his voice became the low monotone his father used when incanting spells. "A drop of blood on the second and fourth rune, and then step left foot first." Wilf shivered as the shooting star on his hand pulsed.

"Blood rituals. You wizards are so dramatic. Well, don't just stand there quivering like newly-made bat jelly. I said ritual, not blood fest." Ermentrude produced a jeweled hatpin and held it out towards him. "Get on with it."

"My blood? Won't yours do?" He stared at the sharp, eight-inch-long pin.

"It's a transfer ritual. It will only need to be done once, but it must be a blood relative."

"But..."

Ermentrude stabbed his finger. A bead of blood bubbled up.

Wilf could feel the rest of his blood leaving his head and racing for that small opening.

"Oh, no, you don't," she said.

Ermentrude's voice drifted through the increased drumming sound in his ears. His hand moved onto the second and fourth runes. Mesmerized, he watched the blood dripping from his finger until, with a loud "Tut" from Ermentrude, a bandage covered the wound.

"Now remember, left foot first," she said.

Through his bleared vision, he witnessed the last of his willpower run screaming for the door. He stepped forward and a rush of energy surrounded him. When the air stilled, he turned to look at Ermentrude.

"Good." Her expression resembled that of a cat that's caught its first mouse. "Let's check out your inheritance."

# Chapter Four
# The Virus

Katryna hurried along the dimly lit corridor. Its dark, stained carpet and peeling paint reflected the building's location. This wasn't a part of town she usually visited. The balconies and entrance might have a view of the market square, but at the back of the building pulsed the Veil. The swirling gray mist had separated and protected the witches of Mathowytch from the citizens of Kureyamage for over 14 years.

She unlocked the door of a studio apartment crowded with chintzy, overstuffed furniture. A cat lay sprawled along the back of the sofa, in the sunlight, licking his paws. She wrinkled her nose at the smell of cat and decay. Flies buzzed around the cat's dirty food bowl, and she zapped them, hoping the frail, old witch wouldn't be upset with her use of magic.

Griselda lay in a fetal position, whimpering on the bed. Katryna sat down next to her in a wooden, high-backed chair. She reached to rub Griselda's back, but then pulled back. It might not be safe to touch the old witch.

"Can I get you something to eat?"

Griselda shook her head and remained facing the wall.

There seemed to be very little Katryna could do. Perhaps that was why Ermentrude had forgotten to add Griselda's name to the list of new cases to visit. However, her mother had been distracted before she left. Ermentrude might be amongst the city's most powerful witches, but she always made time to visit the sick whenever she could. Her mother's hard outer shell hid a soft center of community spirit. The problem was, Ermentrude expected her daughter to pick up the slack whenever she disappeared on a new, urgent assignment for the Witch Council.

Katryna could still hear her mother's scratchy voice.

"Won't be long," Ermentrude had said, placing her bag on the floor. "Do me a big favor, would you? Pop in and see the witches on the list. You don't have to stay long, but it gives them hope."

"Must I? What if I catch the virus?"

"Don't be silly. It's not airborne, that much we know." Ermentrude stopped packing. "All I'm asking is you give a quick glance from the door to see if they need anything. Don't venture too close, and then you'll feel perfectly safe. If I thought you'd be in danger, I wouldn't ask you to visit."

"Why can't we be like everyone else? Lock our door and ignore them?"

"Is that how you'd like to be treated if you contracted the virus?"

Katryna shook her head.

"Thought not." Her mother wriggled her fingers, and her belongings started to pack themselves into the yawning depths of her traveling bag.

"But what if my friends find out I've been visiting witches with the virus? They probably won't come near me." Katryna could hear the mild panic in her own voice. "I might even be suspended from school."

"Don't let your imagination run away with you. Now, enough of your nonsense. I really must fly, Darling. Love you." Ermentrude's bag jumped into her pocket. She gave Katryna a quick hug and then picked up her broom, travel permit card and left.

That had been two days ago, the last time anyone had heard from Ermentrude.

Katryna ambled over to the kitchen, opening and banging shut a few cupboard doors, searching for a glass.

Griselda groaned and rolled over on the bed. Katryna stopped. The old witch seemed bereft of all power. Her cheeks were sunken, and there wasn't one wart on her heart-shaped face. Her nose even had a button-like appearance, which was unnatural in a witch. There were even a few waves to her long, gray hair. It must be devastating to become that pretty.

"Who are you? What do you want?"

"I'm Katryna Wakefield, Ermentrude's daughter." She offered the glass of water. "Try to take a few sips."

"That renegade witch's offspring," Griselda muttered. "Your lot is the cause of all this misery."

"What?" Ermentrude was one of the founders of Mathowytch, and Katryna was proud of her mother's role in the capture of the city.

"If it wasn't for them, there wouldn't be a virus," Griselda said.

"It's the wizards who created the virus. Everyone knows that."

"If the witches hadn't occupied Mathowytch, the virus wouldn't have been needed," Griselda said.

"Well, if the wizards had allowed witches to serve on the ruling council…" Katryna trailed off and took a deep breath to calm herself. She shouldn't argue with the sick witch.

She glanced at the door, itching to leave the stuffy apartment. Now she understood why her mother had left Griselda's name off the visiting list. The witch didn't want company. This had been a mistake.

The sun-shaped clock on the wall flashed ten times. Casting class would be starting, and the finals were in three weeks. She dug her compact mirror out of her pocket and opened the screen.

"Admiring your ugly face, are you, and that rake-thin body? Not a single curl in your dull, straw hair. Bet you're glad you don't look like me."

"I was messaging my teacher that I'll be late." She smiled at Griselda, hit send, and replaced the mirror into her skirt pocket.

"That's right, show off that grin. Not many witches your age already have a fine covering of darkness across their teeth. I bet you strut with pride at your long, hooked nose and impressive collection of warts. How old are you? 16? And promising to be one of the most powerful witches of our time."

"Griselda…"

"Your mother and her kind will kill us all." Griselda's deep breath turned into a racking cough. When it stopped, she lay exhausted on the bed. "It's the Wizard Council's right to rule." Her words were hardly audible.

"Bat's blood," Katryna muttered. "You're upsetting yourself. Try not to think about it." She picked the glass up again. "Here, please try to take a sip of water."

Griselda knocked the glass out of her hand. "Your father took my son from me."

"My father? He evaporated years ago."

"Lies. Nothing but lies." Griselda lifted her head and her blue, faded eyes blazed.

"What do you mean?" Katryna asked.

"That nasty, manipulating wizard is alive in Kureyamage. Your mother shouldn't have run away from him."

"You must be confusing him with someone else. My father has always been described as a wonderful man who evaporated before he should have."

Griselda ignored her. "He had me follow Ermentrude. I saw her sneaking through the Resistance's tunnels when she escaped with you to Mathowytch." She struggled to rise onto her elbow.

The witches' conjuring of secret tunnels underground while the wizards had been occupied with the fabrication of the new city was Katryna's favorite story in history class.

"Wait! You followed her? Why would you agree to that?" Katryna asked.

"I told you, Hywel has my son, Theimus. He knew Ermentrude was up to no good, but he never suspected the truth." She gave a dry laugh that turned into a cough. "He was too busy making all these arrangements to move to Mathowytch, the grand new city for the ruling wizard class. By the time he realized what was going on, Ermentrude and her suffragette witches had occupied it first."

"But he wasn't one of the wizards who jailed and tortured the witches' leaders. Mom told me he always supported her."

This wasn't right. The virus was confusing Griselda. Katryna understood why the Wizard Council wanted to leave the old, gothic buildings of Kureyamage. Its narrow, twisted streets looked dark and menacing in all the images she'd seen. She couldn't imagine living there. Mathowytch was so different. The tall glass buildings were elegant and each one had a unique and charming public space to meet friends. Every witch she'd met supported the action to occupy.

Her dream was to one day serve on a united ruling council. There would be no need for the Veil, and everyone could move freely. Perhaps, she might meet a wizard as caring and loving as Ermentrude had described Hywel. Griselda was obviously losing her grip on reality.

"It should have been impossible for the witches to organize, overcome the guards, and capture Mathowytch." Griselda's bony chest heaved at the effort of speaking.

"What...?" She turned back at the witch's words.

Griselda stared into the distance. "The guards raised the alarm, but it was too late... I watched the witches stand shoulder-to-shoulder and join their magic together." She stopped to draw in a loud, shallow breath.

"You watched and didn't help?"

"It was as if they'd become one giant witch. Akuna directed the magic, and the Veil was created." Griselda stared unfocused at the ceiling, and then closed her eyes.

Katryna leaned forward.

Griselda's voice became little more than a whisper. "It flowed up from the ground like a thin, gray fog, and then... as if someone had flicked a switch... an opaque wall surrounded the city... All sight and sound from Mathowytch disappeared... It's the most amazing magic I've ever seen." Griselda fell silent.

"It must have been wonderful." She'd always wished she'd seen the raising of the Veil.

"Wonderful? It's an abomination," Griselda said, grabbing Katryna's arm.

"You agree with the wizards that we're 'enemies of the realm'—'traitors'?" She tried to pull free.

"You are traitors. If they'd left the city alone, then the virus wouldn't have been necessary. Those witches have destroyed everything. Why did Reginald send me to this terrible, hateful city to die?"

"Ouch! Griselda, let go. You're hurting me." She didn't want to use magic on the poor woman, but Griselda's fingernails felt like needles puncturing her skin. She raised her other hand, but the old witch let go as another coughing spasm ripped through her bony frame.

No one died. They evaporated. However, Griselda was actually talking about dying. But if she no longer had any magic...

Katryna took out her compact mirror again. She should tell someone.

"Call your father and ask him about my Theimus. Tell him you need to visit... before it's too late." Griselda pointed a bony finger at the compact.

"He evaporated and you know it," Katryna shouted.

The old witch rocked her head from side to side. "I want to see my boy one more time."

"Calm down. This can't be good for you."

A patch of color blotched the dry, white skin of Griselda's cheek. She rose onto her elbow again. "I don't know why Ermentrude told you he'd evaporated, but it's a lie. Ask her when you see her." Griselda fell back onto the bed and closed her eyes. "I miss my son." Tears ran down her face.

Katryna hurried out onto the balcony. Sounds blared from the street below. Taking several deep breathes, she watched the flow of traffic around the square. Vendors and customers of the outdoor market looked like busy worker ants rushing around.

She dropped into a white, plastic chair and flicked open her compact mirror. Runes and numbers appeared when she swiped the screen. The Council's emergency sequence appeared.

"Witch Council Emergency Center. How may we assist?" an operator said.

"I'm here with Griselda Picton. I think she might be dying."

"Dying?" The screen flickered. "Who is this?"

"Katryna Wakefield."

"Well, Katryna Wakefield, how old are you?" the operator asked. "Witches don't die, Sweetie. They evaporate. I suggest you find your mother, or a senior witch, and have them relax… whoever it was you said is evaporating."

"There is no one else here," she said. "Griselda has the virus, and I don't think she has enough magic left to evaporate. I think I need to speak to whoever is dealing with this problem."

"Oh! Why didn't you say that in the first place?" the operator said. "I'll put you through to Degula Spack. She's the Councilor for Health, Science, and Security."

Katryna tapped her black nails on the balcony's railing as she waited for the mirror to be answered.

"You've reached the mirror of Degula Spack," the recorded image of Degula said. "I'm sorry I missed your image. Please leave a message if you want."

"Em… I'm Katryna Wakefield, Ermentrude's daughter," she said. "I'm here alone with Griselda Picton, who… em… has the virus. She's talking about dying. I'm not sure she has enough magic left to evaporate. Please tell me what to do. My image is Wakefield 24. This is very urgent. So please hurry. Bye."

With sweating palms she closed the compact and replaced it. She took a deep breath to calm her racing heart before stepping through the sliding doors. The smell of illness was a full nasal assault. If only she could leave the door open, but the cat would probably waste one of its lives jumping off the balcony.

"Myra. Is that you? I hoped you'd come. Help your brother. Promise me you won't leave him with Hywel." Griselda started to sob quietly and then fell silent.

Katryna watched the witch's chest rise and fall in an erratic rhythm. A rattling sound accompanied each inhale. Pulling out her compact again, she thumbed through all the contacts, but she didn't know who else to call.

The apartment door flew open. Four witches from the Executrix Squad marched into the room. Their black uniforms and dull, metallic buttons made them seem more like shadows.

"Name?" one of the guards asked, standing by the door.

"Katryna Wakefield."

"And that?" The guard pointed at Griselda.

"Griselda Picton."

"Good. This is the right place." The guard nodded to the others. They moved cautiously over to the bed, placing masks over their faces. "We'll take it from here. Leave."

"What about her familiar?"

The cat came out from behind the sofa and stopped by the front door. He turned, arched his back, and hissed. Katryna stepped back, feeling slightly rattled by the large black cat's malevolence.

"My orders are to deal with one Griselda Picton. They say nothing about a mangy cat," the guard said.

The cat hissed again, then ran from the apartment. The white patch near his tail disappearing around the corner was the last Katryna hoped she would see of him.

"Where are you taking Griselda? My mother will want to know."

"Quarantine," the guard said. "Why are you still here?"

She tried to swallow the lump in her throat, but her mouth was too dry.

The guard held the door for her and then slammed it shut, leaving her alone in the corridor. Charms covered the walls surrounding the door to Griselda's apartment. The smell of fresh spray paint and brimstone filled the air.

Katryna moved slowly down the narrow corridor. Her arm itched, and she pulled up the sleeve to scratch the skin around a red welt.

Her heart beat loudly. She'd been infected. No. She gave a half-hearted laugh. It had to be a fleabite. The cat's charm must have needed reapplying. She took out the list from her pocket and removed Griselda's name from the bottom of it with a wriggle of her fingers.

# Chapter Five
# The Workshop

Wilf descended the flight of stone steps and entered a long, narrow room. Globes ramped up to full brightness, revealing shelves lining three walls. In the center of the room stood a long wooden table with two carved rosewood chairs at one end.

"Well, this is badly stocked." Ermentrude pushed past him. "This is typical of my dad. Only he would make me go through a ritual for an empty workshop."

"There has to be another step." She ran her fingers over the table's rough surface. "I've never met a wizard stronger than Reginald. He's right to take precautions, as you never know... Did I mention that I knew your mother, Yan Shuai?"

"Leave my mother out of this." Wilf met her gaze and hoped she hadn't heard the tremble in his voice.

Ermentrude made a sucking noise through her teeth. "I can understand how you must have been a great disappointment to Reginald." She stood next to him. "It would have been an enormous blow to his pride. A son like you."

"You'll have to do better than that. I've heard it all before." Wilf's fingers traced a deep scratch on the table's surface.

She sighed. "I can't believe Reginald would go to all the trouble of a blood ritual and runes to leave nothing here." She resumed her pacing. "I don't suppose he had a wand?"

"Does any wizard still use one of those antiques?"

"No, not really, but Reginald was old-school, and it would have been a start." A note of desperation crept into her voice. "I must find his journal."

"Is the virus that bad?"

"It's worse. A witch gradually loses her power, until she can't perform any kind of magic. And the side effect is that the poor witch will become, what this realm calls..." Ermentrude lowered her voice to a whisper, "beautiful." She grimaced in revulsion.

"But where did it come from?"

"Wizards. There's a power struggle going on between the Wizard Council and the Witch Council over equal representation and power sharing. Negotiates were at a stalemate, and then the virus appeared."

"You're saying the wizards want to wipe out all witch magic?"

"Oh, no. They wanted to curtail our powers; make us reliant once again on the wizards. But it appears the virus has mutated and the Wizard Council lost control."

"That's bad," Wilf said.

She put her hand on his arm. "I'm glad I arrived here first. I don't think it will be long before they send a wizard to search for your father's journal."

Wilf shuddered.

Ermentrude stroked the bristles on her chin. "Have you ever had an aura test?"

"A what?"

"An aura test," she said, pronouncing every syllable. "It's how we check a person's magical quality. It doesn't hurt. Aren't you curious?"

"No."

"It would show the strength of your magic. The greater the hue, the more potential you possess. So... if you're not a wizard, as you protest, it will confirm it."

Wilf glimpsed at the wizard mark on the back of his hand. He knew he had magic but wasn't in the least curious about how much.

Ermentrude hadn't waited for his approval. Her bag jumped onto the table and yawned open. A vial rose out of it and floated above him.

"I never agreed..." He backed into the table.

The cork jumped out of the upended vial. A shimmering silver mist poured over Wilf until it covered his entire body. He'd expected dampness, but the mist felt warm and comforting. It changed from silver into a wide band of red at the bottom, which became gold at the top. The mist twisted around his body from his feet to the top of his head.

"Well, I never," she said in a hushed tone.

The mist swirled around him, and then rose in a cloud until it touched the ceiling. It hung above him for a few seconds, and then floated through the wall as if on a gentle breeze.

"In all my years I've never witnessed a two-colored band. I've heard of them in histories and prophecies, but I've never actually seen one." She twirled the white hairs on her chin. "The real question is, why did Reginald hide you from the council?"

Wilf finally remembered to close his mouth.

She dusted her sleeves. "It's a wonder there haven't been accidents. Perhaps Reginald hadn't realized how dangerous you are?" She studied him for a few moments. "Were you with your father when he expired?"

Wilf stared at his hand. "No."

"Then how did you get the ring?"

"It found me." He twisted the offensive object.

Ermentrude ran her finger along her hooked nose.

A trickle of sweat ran down Wilf's back. The room seemed to lean in closer, waiting. He cowered under her stare. Even the dust stopped dancing in the globe light.

She let out her breath, slowly. "It must have something to do with you not accepting that ring," she said. "That will be it. You need…"

"But I don't want to be a wizard." Even to Wilf, his voice sounded like a sulky child's.

"Wilf Gilvary, you're a wizard, and your community needs you." Ermentrude stood toe to toe with him. "You need to stop yelling and stamping your foot like an ungrateful brat. Accept the ring and what it represents."

At no time had she raised her voice, but Wilf felt it ringing in both his ears. It would be so easy to allow her to take control. But he wasn't about to abandon his principles.

"What are you afraid of?" Ermentrude whispered into his ear.

He edged away, out of her reach.

"Nothing," he said. "I hate magic, that's all."

"Hmmm…" Ermentrude rose in the air and sat down on the edge of the table. "You're dangerous, you know. You have one year, possibly two. Then one morning, you'll wake up and discover the nightmare you had last night was real. Magic will ooze out from you while you're sleeping and atrocities will happen simply because you don't have the training to control your power. Then, the Council will be forced to step in to eradicate your magic. I've seen it before."

"It's possible to remove a person's magic?" Wilf asked.

This could be the answer. He would ask the Council to eradicate his magic. This explained why his father hadn't let him speak to any of the visiting wizards.

"Oh, yes," Ermentrude said. "Along with their life."

He leaned against the table for support as his legs buckled. He couldn't escape his magic.

"I'm sorry," she said, placing a hand on his shoulder.

He flinched and backed away from her touch.

She could be right about performing magic in his sleep. Last week, Myra had made a bean curd stew, even though she knew he hated the stuff. He'd opened the fridge the next morning and the odor of rotting food made him gag. "What's that smell?"

"My stew," Myra said. "It's managed to grow a layer of fungus overnight." Her voice held a note of accusation.

"Nothing to do with me," he said, holding up his hands in a surrender motion.

"Hmm," she said, picking up the container and dumping the stew into the trash.

He'd thought he'd had a lucky break. But then there were the morning devastations of his room…

Wilf held out his ringed hand. "Why don't you wrap me up in some spell and force me?"

Ermentrude shook her head. "How would that make you accept your magic?" She stepped back. "This is a decision you have to make and be willing to commit to."

A tear trickled down his cheek. He'd fought so hard to escape this life, and it had been for nothing. Reginald had been playing games with him, knowing all along that at some point Wilf would have to accept his magic, or die. He couldn't believe his father would have gone that far.

Wilf balled his fist and sniffed, fighting to hold the floodgates in place on his tears. He refused to cry. But it seemed he had no choice about magic. He half-heartedly yanked at the ring on his finger.

"It's there until evaporation," Ermentrude said. "I suppose Myra Picton has supported this illusion. She's working for the wizards, you know."

"Myra?"

"Has she been searching for the journal?"

He nodded. He couldn't take many more blows today. Myra had always said she was on his side.

"She won't need you." Ermentrude patted her bun. "Although, it's possible she might receive a large bounty for bringing an untrained wizard to the Council."

"I don't believe you."

"Has she been trying to convince you to leave here and go with her to Kureyamage?"

Wilf's face felt on fire.

"I'm sure her motives are for your own good," Ermentrude said. "But Griselda is now living in Mathowytch. So, it seems strange her daughter would rather be in Kureyamage."

"Dad didn't say what had happened to Griselda, only that she was sick and needed to return to the Magical Realm."

"The virus," Ermentrude mouthed. "You can help to save her if we can locate that journal. It would be nice if she had someone with her. She didn't look at all well when I left."

Wilf twirled the ring around his finger. Griselda had always been kind to him, especially when his father's berating had been particularly vicious. She even attended a few of his soccer matches. He couldn't refuse if he was the only way to find the journal and save her.

Ermentrude tapped her fingers on the table. "Just clasp your hands together and say you accept the life of magic and wizardry." She smiled and nodded at him. "Easy as that."

His hands came together as if they belonged to someone else. He didn't have the energy to fight anymore.

"I accept the life of magic and wizardry." His voice sounded as hollow as he felt. He rubbed the ruby at the center of the ring's engravings. The wizard's tattoo etched deeper into his skin and pain raged up his right arm.

A white-robed figure took shape in the center of the room. Its features were bleared and out of focus. The deep voice of his father burst from it. "It's about time you did something right. Since you've discovered the workshop and have chosen the path of magic, I leave all this to you." A globe appeared in the figure's outstretched hand.

Wilf clenched his jaw.

"I pass on to you my name. You may now be addressed as Wizard Gilvary," his father's voice continued like a pre-recorded message. "Good luck, my boy." The apparition went to throw the globe in the air but paused. It came closer to Wilf. "One day, you'll understand. Don't think too badly of me. I did try to spare you, but there's no denying magic or destiny." He sent the globe spinning towards the ceiling.

"Father, wait." He needed answers. "Don't leave me like this," he yelled at the fading apparition, tears streaming down his face.

The globe cast a white glow over the workshop. It spun, faster and faster, its light increasing in intensity. A sound like gentle drops

43

of water rapidly increased to become more like a black rainstorm lashing against the walls. The globe shattered, sending blazing light into every corner of the room.

Wilf covered his eyes. There was a loud pop, and the room plunged into darkness. He let out a loud sob.

"Wizards," Ermentrude said, producing her own globe. "Always have to put on a show. Why can't they just leave a document like everyone else?"

A paper tissue appeared in Wilf's hand and he blew his nose. The wall globes sprang back to life. Shelves were filled with jars, herbs, vials, claws, and tails. Wilf didn't want to ever know what some of the other jars contained.

On the other side of the room, there stood a metal bench, sink, and laboratory equipment, including a centrifuge, incubator, and autoclave.

A book expanded from a mote of dust in the middle of the workbench. Three golden clasps secured it. The binding was made of thick, scarlet leather. In black embossed letters, the title proclaimed it as *The Complete Works of the Gilvary Wizards*. A rune, in the shape of a backward 'Z', shimmered below the title.

"A sizel," Ermentrude said. "Your family rune is the symbol for the sun."

"My what?" Wilf's whole body trembled. He didn't think he could cope with any more surprises today.

"The rune that identifies with you. Seems quite appropriate, I must say."

"What are you talking about?"

"That particular rune means…" Her voice took on the tone of a fortuneteller gazing into a crystal ball. "There are new opportunities awaiting you, if only you can let go of the outdated beliefs and desires you currently hold."

Wilf wanted to wipe the smug expression off Ermentrude's face, but he didn't have the energy.

"I'm a wizard." His voice sounded devoid of emotion.

"You were already a wizard. Now you've accepted it," Ermentrude said. "Come and open the book."

Wilf folded his arms.

"Don't you realize lives are at stake? Which means I don't have the time or patience to deal with a truculent child." She pointed her fingers at him. "You can either open the book of your own free will or…"

Wilf placed his ringed finger on the rune and the clasps snapped open. The pages fluttered over to the middle of the book. '*The Wizard Wilf Gilvary's Section*' floated above the empty page.

"What are you waiting for? You have the journal—leave," he said.

Ermentrude turned to the front of the book. "We've time to glance through Reginald's section first." She gave him a witchy smile. "Find the formula and see if we need any ingredients from here."

He flicked through the pages. They all seemed empty.

Inscribed on the first page was a dedication.

"How could he?" she shouted. Thin strands of white smoke spiraled in the air from her tight hair bun.

Words began to appear:

'*As your ability increases, the pages will become visible to you, and you alone. At the current time, it has been deemed appropriate that you be limited to this dedication page. Good luck.*'

Ermentrude picked up the book and stowed it in her bag.

"What are you doing?" Wilf asked.

"Putting it someplace where I won't be tempted to hurl it across the room, stamp on it, and then rip it to shreds. At a time like this, to put such a spell on vital information! It's good he's evaporated, or I'd... Well, I'm sorry. I shouldn't speak like that about your father."

"He had a way of bringing those emotions out in people."

Ermentrude sighed. "It's a waste to leave all this behind, but it can't be helped." She gestured for Wilf to follow her as she headed towards the steps. "We need to set off immediately."

"I'm not going with you."

"There's no time to dawdle. We'll put all this back where it came from and be on our way."

"Are you listening to me? I'm not going anywhere."

"What?" Ermentrude stopped and slowly turned around. Her shadow leaned towards him and grew, until it loomed over him.

"I don't know how to put this back," he stammered. "Don't expect me to give any more blood for those stones." He clutched his hand behind his back.

"I hope that isn't a sample of your deductive reasoning," Ermentrude said, folding her arms in front of her. "The blood ritual is only needed once, to establish ownership." She continued up the steps, out of view.

The globes dimmed and started to extinguish, one by one, with a popping sound. Wilf ran to follow her as the workshop plunged into darkness.

Ermentrude nodded encouragement.

He placed his hand on the second and fourth runes. Nothing happened. But it had taken time before, so he stood and waited. He heard a tapping sound from behind him. It grew louder, and he detected a definite angry beat to it. He spun around.

"What?" he asked.

"It won't be the same pattern to close. A door doesn't open in the same direction. You pull one way when you open it and push another when you close it. So it stands to reason, as this is a doorway…" She waited, looking expectantly at him.

"I should…?"

"Use a different code. Any code. Just make it quick, and something you'll remember," she said.

He placed his hand on the first and third. Nothing.

He heard a grating sound behind him.

His stool had dragged itself over to Ermentrude. She tutted and dismissed it back to the counter. "Try laying your hand on longer."

He closed his eyes, took a deep breath, and let his hand rest on the runes. They gave a sucking sound, and the entrance closed in on itself until only the original black wooden knot remained.

He made a silent vow never to open the place again. Wilf rubbed his sweating palms down his shorts.

"That took you longer than a demented cat trying to catch a mouse. Now, what do you need to do around here before we can leave?" Ermentrude asked.

"How many times do I have to tell you that I'm not going with you?"

Ermentrude wandered up and down the aisle.

"What are you doing?" Wilf asked.

"I'm looking for my broom," Ermentrude said, from behind a rack of postcards. "It likes to rest against a wall when it's not in use."

Key rings jangled as Ermentrude bumped a rack. Her steps echoed around the store. She reappeared with her broom in hand.

"Proper transportation. Nothing like being on a broom and riding the Magical Thermals." Her jacket floated over to her and she slipped right into it. "I hate taking passengers, but you won't be able to locate your father's portal. And even if you knew where it was, I doubt you could use it." She glared at him. "You'd better sit perfectly still, and don't you dare grab onto me."

"I'm not..." Wilf's mouth snapped shut.

Ermentrude stopped wriggling her fingers at him. "I need you to listen to me. The Realm can't survive without you and the journal. Are you really going to be responsible for its collapse? Hundreds of wizards and witches will perish if we don't find that formula soon. You can't learn magic here. You have to travel." She wriggled her fingers again. "I won't force you. But the next magical person to arrive here will be a wizard, and they won't be so understanding." Her bag shrank to the size of a small wallet and jumped into her pocket.

He glanced around the store until his eyes rested on the soccer ball. Coach would be furious. He'd probably never let Wilf play again, but the team would manage. However, according to Ermentrude, the Magical Realm wouldn't survive without him. He couldn't refuse.

"I need to text Myra," he said.

"No need. That's already been dealt with," Ermentrude smiled. "I've left her a message."

"A message?" Wilf picked up his backpack and placed his deflated soccer ball inside.

"More an invitation to join us. I'm sure we'll see her soon." She held out her broom. "Shall we?"

# Chapter Six
## Myra Returns

Myra couldn't wait to leave the hot, steamy weather of Hong Kong for the joys of air conditioning. The cruise liner group she'd taken around the Nan Lian Gardens had added to her frustration. They'd wandered off on their own, or chatted vociferously, while she explained the place's history. She'd been tempted to use magic on them and make them the most well-behaved tour group of all time.

Her feet dragged as she negotiated the noisy crowds on Queen's Road East. An umbrella, being used as a sun shield, almost poked her in the eye. She clenched her jaw and wriggled her fingers.

A gust of wind plucked the umbrella out of the woman's hand and sent it spinning into the path of a double-decker bus. Myra smiled at the mangled spines of steel and nylon. A little magic was necessary now and again. The quiet sanctuary of Tai Wang Street engulfed her as she turned the corner.

All she wanted was to stand under a cold shower until the heat of the day left her. Her t-shirt clung like a second skin. It felt as if every gram of moisture had left her body in the gardens and soaked into the cotton fabric.

She neared the gift shop and stopped. All the blinds were down and the sign showed 'Closed'. Wilf had gone to soccer practice. He'd regret that decision. By the time she was through with him, a shredded soccer ball and kit would be the least of his problems. She rattled the locked shop door in frustration.

Her keys jangled as she took them out of her pocket and unlocked the door.

"Wilf!" Her brother stood against the counter. "Why have you closed up the…"

"Hello, Myra." Ermentrude released her broom, and it hovered next to her. "I'm Ermentrude Wakefield. I'm sure you've heard of me."

"The Witch Council sent you?" she asked, closing the door.

"That's right." Ermentrude stepped in front of Wilf. "Your stepbrother and I were about to leave."

"Wilf won't leave Hong Kong." She moved to make eye contact with Wilf. "Tell her."

"Eh…" Wilf said.

"Look, Dear, I'd love to stay and explain his change of heart, but it's time we departed." Ermentrude moved to her left.

"He's not going," Myra said. "Has she used magic on you?"

"I agreed," Wilf said.

"Your stepbrother is a very important wizard." Ermentrude pushed him towards the door.

Myra put down her backpack. All the times he'd defied Reginald and the punishments he'd suffered for refusing to perform magic. Why would he agree now?

"What have you done?" Myra dug her nails into her palms, trying to resist the growing urge to use her magic.

"I found the workshop," Wilf said.

"And the journal?" she asked. Reginald's book held details of any new spells and potions he worked on. The formula had to be in it. She'd already struck a deal with the Wizard Council and they expected her to deliver the journal to them. The old crone couldn't be allowed to leave with it.

Ermentrude edged forward.

"Why do you need Wilf?"

"It's my civic duty to take an untrained wizard of his age back with me." Ermentrude wriggled her fingers and the door opened.

"Oh, please! You need Wilf to… decipher it?" She didn't take her eyes off of Ermentrude. "If Wilf wants to go to the Magical Realm, then I'll take him." She took a step towards Wilf and tried to grab his hand.

Ermentrude blocked her. "But that would be to Kureyamage, and I need him in Mathowytch."

"Myra, did you know my magic will destroy me if I'm not trained?" Wilf asked.

"Is that what she told you? Did she explain that if the Witch Council had surrendered Mathowytch, the virus wouldn't have been necessary? They brought it on themselves."

"You can't be naive enough to believe that propaganda," Ermentrude said.

"I asked if you knew I was dangerous." His ring flashed.

"She's the problem. Not me. Why are you listening to her?" Myra asked, raising her hand.

"Put your hand down." Ermentrude's voice was icy cold.

Myra spread her fingers.

After all, she'd suffered living in this inferior realm, she wasn't about to let this wart-faced crone claim Wilf like a piece of lost luggage. She had her own plans for that book, and her stepbrother.

"You did know. Didn't you?" Wilf said. The ring's ruby flared and the shelf next to him exploded, sending pottery crashing to the floor.

"Let us through, Myra." Ermentrude's voice sounded like a stern school principal's. "Wilf, take a deep breath and calm down."

"You're not taking him," Myra said.

"Don't do anything you might regret." Ermentrude's broom floated to the door.

"Wilf stays here." Darts of white magic flew from the ends of Myra's fingers. They formed into a cluster that whistled through the air towards Ermentrude. Sparks trailed behind them, and a smell of hot iron filled the air.

"You think you can stop me?" Ermentrude zapped the darts. All that remained were five small, deep holes, seared into the store's wall. She advanced on Myra.

"Why are you fighting? I told you I want to leave with Ermentrude," Wilf said, gawking from one witch to the other.

Myra edged along the aisle.

A glowing ball of blue magic erupted from Ermentrude's palm and spun through the air, towards Myra. The ball fizzed as it whirled across the store, leaving a wake of sparks.

Myra ducked behind a rack and the ball exploded, sending fragments of charred postcards fluttering down to the floor. The aroma of singed paper was added to the smell of hot metal and brimstone. A cloud of smoke rose to the ceiling, and with a warning hiss, the sprinkler system gushed into life.

Ermentrude spun to face her target.

Wilf edged through the door as magic crackled in the air.

Dodging around the shelving, Myra approached Ermentrude from behind. She peered around the end of the aisle. It was empty. A hiss made her twist around.

"Bat's blood!" Another bolt of blue magic came hurtling towards her. She dove behind the counter and sent a set of darts at Ermentrude. That had been close.

A loud crack, like the sound of a whip, sent the counter flying into the air. Searing pain ran up Myra's arm. She'd narrowly missed being engulfed by that last spell. A long splinter of wood stuck out of her left bicep and blood dripped from her fingers.

"We don't need to do this," Ermentrude said. The sprinkler system shut off. "I don't want to hurt you. So be a good girl and let us leave, before you're injured again."

"You're not taking Wilf," Myra shouted. She took a deep breath and charged up a large bolt of white magic. It fizzed in her hand. Then, she hurled it with a dose of pure desperation to where Ermentrude's voice had come from.

A yelp, followed by a loud clatter, sounded as Ermentrude dived out of the bolt's path. Every corner of the store was lit with a blinding white light as the missile exploded against shelving and sent shards of obliterated porcelain Happy Cats around the store.

Myra edged around the racks of souvenir mugs and magnets. It had been reckless to use that much power on one shot, but she wasn't sure how many more chances she'd have.

"You've acquired some skill, and I would have enjoyed a longer spat, but I really don't have the time or the inclination to play this cat-and-mouse game any longer," Ermentrude said.

The racks Myra hid behind parted, and a wall of power knocked her into a shelf of Laughing Buddhas. She tried to move but couldn't. Her limbs were unresponsive under the paralyzing spell.

"With some training, you could be quite a formidable witch," Ermentrude said, peering down at her. "It's a pity you've chosen the wrong side."

Myra screamed mutely at the clanking sound in her head. The image of chains holding her magic captive developed in her mind, preventing her from breaking the spell.

"I'll let your mother know I saw you," Ermentrude said, summoning her broom and climbing on.

"Myra!" Wilf took a few steps into the store towards his stepsister.

"She'll be fine in a couple of minutes," Ermentrude said.

"I can't leave her like this."

"If you go to aid her, she will attempt to stop you from leaving." Ermentrude gestured around the store. "Look at the damage she's already caused. I can't guarantee her safety if we have to continue discussing the matter." She floated closer to him. "It takes a lot of energy to negotiate the Thermals between the realities, and I don't want to waste any more on your stepsister. So, climb on and we'll be on our way, before that spell wears off."

"I'm sorry, Myra," he said, straddling the broom.

Ermentrude glided into the street with Wilf clinging onto the broom's shaft.

Myra's legs and arms twitched as the chains loosened in her mind. She stumbled towards the door. The throbbing pains in her side and arm slowing her down. A green flash greeted her as she floundered through the doorway. A fissure expanded in the sky and a channel of magic pulsed down to cover Ermentrude and Wilf.

"Say goodbye to your old life," Ermentrude said as the broom floated higher on ribbons of magic that flowed from the rift. The broom picked up speed at the entrance and shot forward, into the Magical Thermals, the pathway between the realms. Then, the fissure snapped shut.

Myra slumped against the doorframe, perusing the store's wreckage of mangled racks, broken shelves, and smashed, wet merchandize. Her left side hurt from a long gash and blood oozed through her t-shirt and jeans. Using a tie, she made a tourniquet around her left arm and pulled out the wooden splinter. She sucked in air as the pain seared through her. Bandaging her arm, she glanced around the store, trying to locate her backpack. Its strap jutted out from under a pile of t-shirts. She shuffled through puddles to reach it.

She had to follow Wilf and, somehow, save him from the Witch Council, but entering Mathowytch wasn't going to be easy. First, she had to explain how she'd lost control of Wilf and the journal to the Wizard Council. She shuddered. Hywel wouldn't like this, especially when she told him Ermentrude was involved.

Pulling out a small, red make-up bag, she unzipped it and took out three vials. She drank their contents. The elixir warmed her as it spread throughout her body. The magical enhancement would take several minutes to kick in. It was addictive in large quantities, but she hoped she had enough to stop the bleeding and minimize the pain.

Flicking open her compact mirror, she took a deep breath. There was no point in stalling any longer.

Grabbing shelving for support, she wove her way to the wall with the concealed alcove. It sprang open to her touch, and she placed the compact into a larger relay mirror. Contact runes scrolled over the mirror's surface. She took a breath before placing the call to the Magical Realm. The mirror darkened for several seconds, and then an image flickered into view.

"Myra," Hywel said. "I hope you're imaging to tell me you've found Reginald's journal." His likeness wasn't current; it showed a much younger wizard's portrait.

"Wilf has it." She winced with the effort of speaking through her pain.

"Then, I presume you will be relieving him of it very soon."

"There's... been a complication." Her pulse raced, and her vision clouded. Perhaps she shouldn't have taken all three vials at once. She would need a magical healer soon. "We had a visit from Ermentrude."

"She was there?" The image changed to show a middle-aged wizard with a salt-and-pepper, neatly trimmed, short beard. His round cheeks were ruddy. If he hadn't been a wizard, you'd have thought he suffered from high blood pressure. "That's not good."

"No, it isn't," Myra said. "She attacked me, then took Wilf and the journal. They're probably in Mathowytch by now."

"That's incredible." He sounded shocked. "It's worse than I thought. The witch community is becoming lawless. I always said it would be wrong to give them too much power. And look what happens when they seize it. She attacked you. Terrible. Terrible."

"I'm going to need help entering the Magical Realm. I used a lot of energy trying to secure Wilf for you."

"Of course," he said. "Though, if you can't get into Reginald's workshop, then the nearest wizard portal is in Tsim Sha Tsui."

She couldn't take a trip across the harbor. There was no way she could use the MTR or the Star Ferry in her condition. "Where's the next one?"

"Adjacent to the mid-level escalator in Soho. There's a place called *The 1841 Bar*. It's in the back room, last booth."

A crowded bar in Soho! With the amount of magical energy it must take to maintain a connection to Kureyamage, the place must shimmer.

"A wizard used to own the place," Hywel continued. "It hasn't been used in decades, but the portal's still active for emergencies."

It would take magic to close up the store and get a taxi. The traffic would already be at a standstill on Hennessy Road and Queen's Road Central. Would she have enough magic left to make the crossing through the Thermals? She couldn't flex the white, numb fingers of her left hand. Magic might be the least of her problems. She could be in danger of blacking out from blood loss on the way.

"You're sure there's nothing closer?"

"We only keep four in the Hong Kong area. Reginald controlled the one there in Wan Chai. The other two small emergency portals

I've already mentioned, and there's a large one up in the New Territories for imports."

"I'll leave now."

"Very well," he chuckled. "I'm going to give someone quite a fright suddenly appearing in that booth if the shielding isn't working."

His image disappeared, and the mirror went blank.

Stepping unsteadily over to a pile of t-shirts, she removed her own, tied two around her middle, and then put on a clean, larger one that covered the blood on her jeans. She picked up her backpack and stumbled out into the empty street.

Outside, she raised her hand at the store, preparing to change its facade. Wriggling her fingers, nothing happened. She tried again. All her magic couldn't have been depleted, but she'd used so much conjuring that last energy ball. Tears of desperation blurred her vision. There had to be some left. She focused on the facade again. A rush of energy spread through her veins as the magical enhancer kicked in.

The store's neon sign slowly disappeared, to be replaced by a burned-out one with missing letters. She took a deep breath, wincing from a sharp pain in her side. Boards, decorated in printed advertising bills, flickered into place and covered the windows. The building appeared abandoned and neglected.

The pain in her side throbbed and sweat beaded on her forehead from the effort. Her hand shook as she took a sip of water from her canister. She limped slowly along the road. The sweet smell from burning joss stick at the Hang Sing Temple added to her dizziness. She stopped and bent over, trying to clear her vision. The grinning face of the porcelain deities, along the Temple's tiled roof, seemed to mock her. A red taxi, waiting at the corner, switched its light on and moved closer. She shuffled along the backseat.

"The 1841 Bar, Stauton Street, Soho," she said, leaning back and supporting her left arm.

She glanced out the windshield, past a plastic yellow daisy that danced out of time with the radio's Cantonese music. The talismans dangling from the mirror caught her eye as they swayed and collided together, causing a wave of nausea to sweep over her.

The taxi weaved through the traffic. It would be so easy to slip into the darkness floating at the edges of her vision, but she had to hold on. Her body trembled with the effort. She'd soon be back in the Magical Realm, with her real brother, Thiemus. She wondered if he still hated her.

# Chapter Seven
# Breaking Curfew in Mathowytch

Wilf sat bolt upright on the broomstick and bit down on his tongue to prevent the building scream from escaping. Magic surrounded him as they entered the Thermals. His legs and arms tingled. He wobbled and clung on to the broom's shaft with a death grip. Ribbons of neon-colored lights dashed past his eyes.

Ermentrude hunched lower over the broomstick and their speed increased. He tried to stay upright but was forced to bend low, his face only centimeters from Ermentrude's back.

She tilted the broom, dodging objects invisible to Wilf until his eyes became accustomed to the strange light of the Thermals. His vision switched focus, and he could see shapes materializing into spectral figures that tried to seize the broom. A hand touched his leg and it burned with an icy coldness. Ermentrude veered to the left, raised her hand, and blasted two specters that darted into their flight path.

He yelped as the broom took a nosedive, careening through a downwards branch of light. Wind rushed past him and his cheeks rippled. He whooped. Ermentrude glanced around and smiled at him. It was amazing that at one moment he feared his life was about to end, and then the next he was experiencing the biggest adrenaline rush he'd ever felt.

A fissure opened and Ermentrude steered the broom through it. They floated slowly down into a clearing in the center of a small wood. The broom hovered until Ermentrude's feet touched the ground.

Wilf stumbled off the broomstick. His legs buckled and he collapsed. The spongy plant covering ground engulfed his hands and a pungent smell of rotting fish hit him. He retched several times before he could stand.

"It's always strange, your first flight. Also, this realm's air is thinner than you're used to. Here, take a sip." Ermentrude handed him a water bottle. "Riding the Thermals is quite the experience, isn't it?"

Wilf nodded, not trusting his voice. He peered up at the sky. A dim, crescent-shaped moon hovered above. It was surrounded by red, green, and blue stars that littered the sky in no discernible pattern he recognized. Tree limbs groaned as they swayed in a cold breeze. He shivered, wishing he wore more than shorts and t-shirt. A loud crash reverberated through the wood.

"Time to move," Ermentrude said, producing a small globe.

Tall trees surrounded them like stoic sentries, standing shoulder to shoulder, their branches entwined, blocking any exit. Tight buds of new spring growth decorated the bare limbs.

Ermentrude glanced towards the crashing sound and then marched towards the trees in the opposite direction.

"Why did you fight with Myra?" Wilf asked through chattering teeth. "She could be badly hurt."

"I very much doubt that," Ermentrude said, coming back for him. "And, if you remember correctly, she attacked me first. We can discuss this later, but right now I suggest you pick up the pace."

"She was trying to stop me from leaving?" Wilf asked. "We should have stayed to listen to what she had to say."

"Nonsense. Myra wasn't going to listen to anything we had to say," Ermentrude said. "We need to leave here. It's not the place to linger for a chat. Do you want me to supply you with a little persuasion?" She pointed her outstretched fingers at him.

Wilf stared at the witch.

This would be his life, always under her threats. He might be vulnerable in this strange land, but he wasn't about to let her give him a dose of a compulsion spell. He needed to be able to make his own decisions.

Wilf stepped forward and a branch snapped under his foot.

"Quiet," Ermentrude said, glancing around. "No need to wake folk up. It's a little past the usual time allowed for flying."

"There's a night curfew on flying?" Wilf asked.

"More a noisy-neighbor warning. A witch out this late flying around is usually up to no good. If you know what I mean…"

"Yes," Wilf said, "I've read the stories, and now I know firsthand."

"You can't always believe what the tabloids say," she said, puffing up a little. "And stop being so theatrical."

An image of Ermentrude with her picture plastered all over the witches' daily newspapers as a known serial con-witch flickered through his mind.

A crashing noise sounded closer, and branches on the trees along the left side knotted together, tighter. Birds, the size of hawks, took flight and angrily swooped down on them. Ermentrude waved the birds away with a wriggle of her fingers.

"What is that?" he asked.

"Nothing to worry about." Ermentrude allowed the globe to shine a little brighter.

"If that's true, then why do you keep glancing over there?"

She quickened her step towards a gap appearing in the wall of trees. "Try to follow me without rousing the whole city."

Wilf ran after her. This was all countryside. He couldn't see any signs of a city as he chased behind her, down a winding mud trail. Branches creaked overhead and swayed in the wind. He hugged his arms around his middle for warmth and kept his head down to maneuver around the objects littering the ground. Ermentrude's pace quickend as she marched ahead. He tried to keep up with her, but his breathing became noisier with each step.

"I have to stop for a moment," he said, wheezing. He bent over, hands on his knees, drawing in large gulps of the thin air.

"Not yet. Remember, you're an athlete. Think of this as training; push through," she said, returning to grab his arm. "Once we're through the gate, you can take a breather."

"How far is that?" Wilf asked.

"About half a mile. That's why I chose this clearing. Close to my house. Not too many watchers." She pulled him upright. A deep bellow sounded on the trail behind them, followed by a low growl that sounded closer.

"Watchers?"

"We don't want just anyone landing near the city," Ermentrude said, dragging him along behind her. "We really must keep moving."

Wilf stumbled along until Ermentrude stopped at the tree-line and glided over a wooden stile. He climbed over and landed with a splash in a muddy puddle.

"Make sure you take those sneakers off before you enter my home," Ermentrude said, hurrying on.

The mud-trail gave way to a paved lane that ran between high hedges. He lagged behind in silence, except for the squelching noise his sneakers made.

Ermentrude stopped at a large wooden door with iron bars and studs, blocking the way. She placed her hand on a panel that swished open. A coded plastic card appeared in her hand that she fed into the reader inside the panel. A sound of well-oiled bolts being drawn preceded the door swinging open.

Wilf could hear panting and jumped inside after Ermentrude. He gasped. A cat the size of a horse bounded down the trail towards them. It roared, showing two pairs of large fangs and sprang towards them. Wilf stepped back. The door swing shut, but he heard claws ripping at the other side.

"Come along," Ermentrude said, gesturing towards a cobbled path that stretched along the underground tunnel.

"What was that?"

"A watcher. They're very diligent in their duties, but sometimes a little too much." She fanned the air and smiled.

"It tried to kill us," Wilf said.

"There you go exaggerating again."

Wilf's vision blurred, and he reached out for support on the damp stone walls. In the time it took him to catch his breath, Ermentrude was nearly out of sight. He sighed, and sprinted along the tunnel to catch her.

"Nearly there," Ermentrude said, adjusting her grip on the broom as they approached a flight of stairs, leading up. "I'm gasping for a brew."

Wilf counted a hundred steps as he climbed up and then emerged onto a city street. Glass skyscrapers, dark, except for a few brightly lit windows, towered above them. Tram wires ran down both sides of the road, with regular stops along the way. At the intersections, traffic lights ran through their usual color sequence of red, amber, and green. Stores displayed their wares in dim internal security lighting. Except for Ermentrude and himself, the landscape seemed devoid of people or animals.

"Curfew," Ermentrude said, waiting for him. "We cross here, then walk two blocks, and my street is off to the left."

The lights changed from a stationary black witch with a red-lit background to a walking black witch on a green one.

Wilf shook his head.

This could be any new city in his realm. He'd thought it would be different. Soho seemed more magical than this place. Perhaps it was a bad dream. He would welcome reality if that were true. He sniffed. This city smelled different, more of an acrid and plant smell filled the air.

He followed Ermentrude into a dead-end street that held about 20 houses, all with neat, spring-tidied gardens. Small patches of closed crocuses and snowdrops, and the green tips of daffodil leaves, could be glimpsed through the railings. A low crackle and fizz sounded from each gate they walked past.

Ermentrude led the way down to the penultimate townhouse on the left. She pulled open a heavy, wrought-iron gate and then continued along the short path. Her rambling garden needed some work. Last season's dead plants lay molding in the flowerbeds. A small square patch of lawn was barely visible through rotting leaves.

Wilf's feet moved on automatic as he trudged behind Ermentrude, up the garden path, too tired to offer any resistance. His fingers and toes were so cold he couldn't feel them.

At the front door, she placed her hand on a plaque bearing her name. The door swung open, and the globe floated inside to sit on a bracket above a small, polished table.

A petite ginger cat slinked out of a room on the left and wrapped itself around Ermentrude's legs.

"It's good to see you too, Catcus," Ermentrude said, hanging her broom on a rack next to the front door. She pointed at Wilf's sneakers.

Large clumps of mud came off as he untied and stepped out of them.

"Come in, and close the door. No need to let everyone know I'm home and not alone."

Her bag jumped out of her coat pocket and floated into the back room. The door of a small closet opened, and Ermentrude threw her jacket towards it. It landed on a hook and the door closed. She disentangled from the cat. "That will do, Catcus. I haven't been gone that long."

"In here," Ermentrude said, entering the living room. A fire sprang to life, and a wing-backed leather chair plumped up its cushions. She sighed as she sank into its welcoming depth. "Where are you?" Ermentrude glanced around the room. "There you are. Come here." A footstool appeared from behind a sofa. It crossed the room on short, stumpy legs and positioned itself for the witch's feet. "Charms these days aren't what they used to be."

Wilf tripped over the tasseled edge of the rug.

Ermentrude smiled. "Sit down before you fall down." She waved towards the chair at the other side of the hearth.

"So, what happens now?" He settled down into the chair's soft floral cushions.

"Sleep, I think," Ermentrude said. "You can meet my daughter, Katryna, in the morning." She leaned forward. "Just one thing I need to mention. Probably should have told you before, but with all the excitement... Wizards aren't allowed in this city. So I think, for all our sakes, it would be best if you remain indoors for the present."

"What?" Wilf sat up straight. "You mean I'm a prisoner here?"

"No, not a prisoner. It's a silly rule, really, but better if you obey it, for your own safety."

"Rule?"

"Well, actually it's a law, but don't let that worry you. No one will know you're here." The drapes drew themselves with a snap. Ermentrude tutted and shook her head. "So there's no need to worry. Now, why don't I show you to your room?"

"What's the punishment if I'm caught?" Wilf asked.

"There's no need to even think about that, as you won't be leaving this house. It'll just worry you for no reason." She stood and held open the door. "Shall we?"

Wilf remained and crossed his arms. "Tell me."

Ermentrude sighed. "Death."

"For me, or you, or both of us?" Wilf asked.

"Death for you, banishment for me. So, you see, I have more to lose than you."

"How'd you figure that one?"

"I would have to give up my life here, all my friends and my position. That's a lot more than you'd be giving up. You haven't really had time to make a life yet. So you don't have much to regret leaving."

The chair pushed him to his feet.

"Now, let's not even contemplate troubles we don't yet have." She left the room. "You're at the top of the stairs. Room at the back of the house."

He stood in the living room for a few minutes, watching the dying light from the fire's embers until they puffed out. He stumbled in the small amount of light from the hall globe.

"You might need this," Ermentrude said, producing his backpack from her bag.

He hadn't noticed her taking it from him; nor had he missed it.

The globe floated up the stairs in front of him and bobbed into a bedroom. He threw his backpack at the foot of the bed. Blue cotton sheets turned themselves down as he entered. A door to a small shower room stood ajar. The bedroom door clanged shut behind him. It sounded twice as strong and heavy than it should have.

Sighing, he readied himself for bed and climbed in. He reached into his backpack, took out the deflated soccer ball, and hugged it. The globe extinguished with a pop.

He touched the ring on his finger. The ruby glowed. He was a wizard. He should never have trusted Ermentrude. No one in his or her right mind trusted a witch; not even another witch. All that time he'd told Myra he would never use magic. Then, at the first sight of a true witch, he abandons all his principles. Suddenly, he's a wizard and in the Magical Realm.

He hoped Myra was all right. Perhaps she would follow them and rescue him. But he wasn't in Kureyamage. This was Mathowytch. A city filled with magic-wielding witches who hated wizards. Magic; nothing good ever came from being involved with it.

He rolled onto his side, pulled up his knees, and hugged the ball tighter. A wizard. He shivered. He'd never wanted to be a wizard. What he wanted was to be back in his own bed, thinking of tomorrow's soccer match. His body trembled.

Ermentrude had called him powerful. He should have known. It was the reason he refused to use magic. The only time he used it, he hadn't been able to control it, and look at the damage he'd caused.

He clenched his jaw. He wouldn't think about that now.

A shadowy image, whose features he could no longer remember, but whose love he had known for only a few brief years, filled his thoughts. *Oh, Mother, I'm so sorry.*

He wept silently until exhaustion allowed him to sleep.

# Chapter Eight
## Myra in Kureyamage

Myra's eyes fluttered open. A blonde-haired wizard in a long, brown robe leaned over her. His large hand rested on her arm, its brown shooting star glowed and heat pulsed from his short, stubby fingers over her wound. The skin closed layer by layer; a thin, white scar the only sign of the injury.

"She's awake," the healer said.

"Thank you, Thiemus," Hywel said.

"Thiemus?" Myra hated the longing in her voice.

The total lack of emotion in her brother's green eyes, when he met her gaze, chilled her. He'd been seven the last time she'd seen him, and he'd been fighting back tears then.

Their mother, Griselda, had displayed little sympathy with his pleading not to be left behind.

"Why must I stay?" Thiemus tugged on Griselda's arm.

"I have an important assignment from the Wizard Council. I can't have an untrained wizard with me," Griselda prized her arm free. "You need to stay here. I'll return for you when I can."

"But you're taking Myra." Thiemus threw her a look of loathing.

Griselda wriggled her fingers, and their luggage shrunk. "Put that in your pocket, Myra."

"Mother," Thiemus pleaded. "Don't leave me here, please."

An expression of sadness briefly touched her mother's face.

"I have no choice," she said.

Thiemus' eyes searched his mother's face, and then he stepped back. He stood erect.

"I'm sure you don't." His voice and eyes lost all of the earlier emotion.

It seemed he'd managed to keep it that way since they'd parted.

"Thiemus, it's me, Myra," she said.

"I know who you are." Her brother lifted his hand from her arm. "She shouldn't move for a few days. The wound in her abdomen needs more time to knit." Thiemus limped to a small washstand.

He'd grown only a few inches taller than her, but his 17-year-old body created the impression of strength. A strong, thick neck suggested henchman rather than healer. Her eyes settled on his withered left arm. She tried to sit up. "Thiemus, what happened to your arm and leg?"

"They were an indirect gift from Mother," Thiemus said, drying his hands. "I've spent the last few hours healing you. The least you could do is lie still and try not to undo all my work."

"I'm sorry." Myra eased back down, guilt washing over her. She hadn't known, at first, the true nature of Thiemus' apprenticeship with Hywel. She'd only been 11. Griselda had never spoken to Myra about leaving her brother. But in the first month, she'd frequently stumbled across her mother weeping over his image. As time passed, she'd learned not to upset her mother by asking about him.

"You can return to your duties in the workshop." Hywel rested his hand on Thiemus' shoulder. "You and your sister can have your little reunion later."

Thiemus's face took on a puppy's devotional expression. He bowed his head and left the room.

She stared at the black shooting star on the back of Hywel's hand as he stroked his short beard. His black eyes bore into her's.

"What haven't you told me?"

She stammered, "I've told you everything…"

He twisted his wizard's ring around his finger and held her gaze. The ebony stone at its center flashed.

"That's not true."

She opened her mouth, but he held up his hand.

"Don't deny it again. I don't want to hurt you. Especially after Thiemus has taken such good care of you. He becomes a little sulky if I ask him to heal the same person twice in one day."

Hywel pulled up a chair next to the bed. "Shall I help you? You were found by Reginald in his workshop…"

Somehow, he knew. She hadn't thought he would find out so soon.

He took hold of her hand. "You're trembling."

She tried to pull away, but he crushed her fingers together.

"It was an accident. I didn't mean to," she blurted.

"Why don't you start at the beginning?" He released the pressure but continued to hold her hand, his ringed finger rested on her pulse.

"Reginald surprised me. I had the journal in my hand. I panicked."

"You attacked?"

"He cast a spell. I thought he was attacking me, but he placed an enchantment on the journal."

"And…?"

"I told you, I panicked. He evaporated. The journal and workshop disappeared."

Hywel released her hand. "Ermentrude has the journal now and the boy?"

"Yes." Myra rubbed life back into her fingers.

He studied her for several long minutes. "Rest for now," he said, returning the chair. "You leave in the morning for Mathowytch. I'll make sure Wilf is brought here. You're there purely as backup, if I need you. Do not make contact." He opened the door. "And Myra…"

She stared up at him.

"No more accidents."

Collapsing into the pillows, she pulled the covers up to her chin. Her body trembled with shock, and it wasn't only from her injuries.

She didn't see Hywel or Thiemus for the rest of the night. A servant brought her breakfast and clean clothes, and she'd left soon after. Going through the gate, she glanced back at the tower. Thiemus stood in the upstairs window. Her brother hadn't checked on his patient since the healing.

Hywel led the way through the twisting streets of Kureyamage. She still felt weak from the healing of her side, but she struggled on. The wizard floated along the narrow streets at a pace that made her breath come in increasingly louder bursts.

"Can you slow down a little?" she asked to his cloaked back. "I won't make it through the tunnels if you keep up this pace."

"We have to keep moving," he said. "You don't have a pass to be in the city, and the guards are patrolling with more frequency after the last attack. The witches are becoming more desperate."

"The witches are attacking openly?"

Hywel shook his head. "They're too cowardly for that. It's small ambushes to disrupt order and transportation. A number of portals have been compromised. They keep buzzing around like stingflies you can't swat, but their time is running out."

The witches would be entering through the tunnels. So that was why Hywel needed her. Any wizard entering those tunnels would raise an alarm in Mathowytch.

"We've begun giving our witches charmed bracelets to identify them, but it's not ideal."

"Do you have one for me?"

"They're all serial numbered for residents only." He stopped and stared at her. "You need to earn it."

She'd thought that was what she'd been doing for the last two years, but every time she'd asked to return, Hywel had told her to remain in Hong Kong with Reginald a little longer. Telling her the reports she kept sending were invaluable.

"You think you've been mistreated?" Hywel grabbed her and pushed her against the wall. "Considering what your little accident has cost me, I think I've been very lenient." Hywel's face was inches away from her's. His hot breath wafted over her, a mixture of garlic, peppermint, and brimstone. "Try not to evaporate anyone else without my express permission."

"I…"

He slammed her against the wall again, knocking the breath out of her. She felt the stones imprinting on her back. She nodded vigorously.

He let her go and stepped back. Her legs buckled, and she placed her hands on the wall for support. She glanced around the alley Hywel had pushed her into. The walls appeared to meet at a point as she tried to see through the darkness to its end. Ivy peeked over the top of the opposite wall, but no vines had invaded this side. Small mounds of litter were trapped against the wall, and greasy-looking puddles lay in the cracked pavement.

She kicked an empty bottle that spun away from her. The sound of tinkling glass, as it rolled away, seemed to fill the space between herself and Hywel. A pile of trash moved, and a cat struggled out. It tilted its head, regarding her.

The large cat appeared completely black, except for a white patch near the base of its three-quarter-length tail. A scar ran across its face, marking his eye, nose, and chin. It strolled towards Myra with a slow, swaggering gait, placing each paw deliberately as it inched forward. It arched its back and hissed at Hywel. The wizard turned his nose up in disgust as it spat at him. Reaching Myra's side, it purred and wound through her shaking legs.

"Nipits?"

The last time she'd seen this cat was before Griselda had left. Ermentrude had said her mother was in Mathowytch. She hadn't believed the crone, thinking it had been a ruse to lure Wilf. "How can my mother's cat be in Kureyamage?" Griselda wouldn't willingly be separated from her familiar.

"What does it matter?" Hywel asked. "Take the thing with you, if you want. But you'd better not fail me this time." He reached into his pocket and handed her three vials of enhancer. "I need the answers contained in that journal."

She'd thought the Wizard Council wanted it destroyed. Now, it seemed they were interested in its contents, and that meant the formula. Or perhaps there were other secrets contained within its bindings that they needed.

Myra took the vials, then pushed off the wall and held Hywel's gaze. "Why do you want the journal?"

He raised an eyebrow at her question but then turned towards the alley's entrance. He placed a finger over his lips.

Nipits stood in front of her, facing the entrance. His fur stood on end and his back arched.

There had to be something Hywel wanted or hoped to gain from the Council. He'd lost a lot of standing when Ermentrude escaped with her daughter; especially after it had been discovered she'd been one of the leading rebels. Could it be possible that the journal would repair some of that damage or... did he hope for a seat on the Council? It had been years since any of the members had been rotated off. Becoming a councilman would make Hywel very powerful.

The sound of boots marching on the cobblestone street brought her back. She moved into the shadows with Hywel and Nipits as the four-guard patrol made their rounds. The men were so close she could hear the clank of metal on their uniforms. Instinctively, Myra raised her hands, drawing on her magic, preparing to strike first.

Hywel pushed them back down. "You can't use magic," he whispered. "They will detect it before you can generate enough power." His mouth was inches from her ear as he spoke, his pungent breath causing her to grimace.

She pushed her body farther into the shadows, edging away from the alley's entrance and the approaching patrol. The smell of rotting garbage, mildew, and animal waste made her gag. A clang sounded as her shoe's heel collided with a metal post.

"Who's there?" a guard shouted into the alley. "Show yourself."

Nipits meowed and scampered past the patrol.

"A damned cat," the guard said. "How I hate them. It's a pity the virus isn't wiping them out as well as witch magic."

Myra heard agreeing laughter from the rest of the patrol. They started to move away, and then stopped.

"Wait. Don't you think that was a rather loud noise for a cat?"

"You had better make a dash for it," Hywel said. "I will stay here until the patrol has gone. It's only three blocks to the entrance of the tunnels. You will be safe once you enter them."

"You're leaving me?" Myra asked.

"No," Hywel said. "You are leaving me."

They had been using hushed voices, but Myra felt they'd been shouting, as the guards closed in on the alley.

"They'll catch me," she said. "I can't avoid four guards without using magic."

"Use your cat to distract them." He handed her an etched stone talisman on a long chain. "Here, take this. You will need it to pass through the Veil."

She placed the chain over her head and tucked the talisman under her shirt. Hywel pivoted away.

"How will I locate the entrance?" A blue flash temporarily blinded her. Hywel disappeared.

"You bastard," she muttered. He'd lied about using magic and letting her leave first. That flash charm was bound to have alerted the guards. He might as well have sent up a flare and a blinking locator arrow showing where she was.

"Over here," a guard shouted. The sound of running feet came closer.

She raised her fingers as the first guard appeared and sent a blast of white magic spinning into the man. He yelled and collapsed to the ground.

*Nipits.* She sent her thought to the cat. *Let me see.*

Using her internal sight, she peered out from the cat's eyes at the three guards surrounding the alley's entrance.

When would she learn never to trust wizards? She edged her way along the wall, into the darkness. Praying that it wasn't a blind alley, or that at least the walls were scalable.

It hadn't been an illusion of darkness; the alley actually came to a point at its end, like an ice-cream cone. She whirled around but couldn't see the entrance anymore. The bricks of the wall were rough under her fingers as she began to climb. Dirt and crumbling cement collected under her fingernails, and the skin around the wound in her side pulled. She sucked in air against the pain.

Reaching the top, she paused. Nipits jumped up, trotted back along the top of the wall for a few feet, and then jumped down. He called to her. Peering again through the cat's eyes, she saw the thick stems of a wisteria clinging to the wall. She tested a branch with her foot, and then began to lower herself. The branch moved, and she inched quickly along to the main stem. Her left arm burned from her recent injury. Her hands stripped bark and buds as she climbed down. Crouching against the wall, she let her heartbeat return to normal while trying to get her bearings. She swallowed the contents of one of the vials Hywel had given her.

A paved path meandered, in and out of the shrubbery, along the perimeter of the garden. She followed it to a tall wooden gate and eased open the bolt at the top. Placing a hand over the latch, to muffle any noise, she lifted it and then peered out into the street. Nipits placed his paw on her right leg and then started off down the street, glancing over his shoulder at her.

The cat seemed to know where the tunnels entered Kureyamage. Keeping to the shadows, Myra set off after Nipits. They crept down the narrow, twisting street. Alleys branched off along the way. Their names blinked on and off in red neon lights as she crossed their entrances. She kept glancing over her shoulder to see if the guards were following, but she'd given them the slip.

She and Nipits crossed over two more streets, keeping to the main road. The Veil, a gray, shimmering barrier that separated Mathowytch from Kureyamage, became visible as they drew closer.

Nipits hissed.

Myra spun around to see two guards approaching from behind. Her pace had slowed, and the light from a sign had stayed on too long, alerting them. Holding her side, she ran after Nipits as he bounded towards the Veil.

She'd be in trouble if the cat hadn't come through the tunnels but had negotiated the Veil. Was it even possible to go through it? Rumor had it that anyone entering the Veil would wander for years within its depths, never to be seen again and would only be found when the Veil was finally taken down.

Nipits sprung down a pathway along the edge and gray wisps seemed to reach out to stroke the cat's fur.

She followed. Tendrils left icy burns on the skin of her neck and arms. The guards behind her hesitated. Then, one came along the path. A long strand from the Veil struck the guard, sending him screaming backward against a building. His companion ran in the opposite direction.

Myra surveyed the buildings as she struggled down the street. All the windows had been bricked in. The only light was an eerie gray haze coming from the Veil.

Nipits stopped and waited for her to catch up. She put her hands on her knees and took several gulps of air. Pain coursed from her wounded side. "Now where?"

The cat placed a paw on the building in front of them.

She scanned the building.

"It looks the same as all the rest."

The cat meowed at her and then leaped at the bricked-in lower window. He disappeared. Placing a hand on the bricks, she pressed. Nothing happened. She studied the building.

*Nipits.* She tried mentally to reach him but couldn't. The cat's head appeared, and he meowed annoyance.

"Is there a tunnel under the street?"

Nipits disappeared again.

Myra took a deep breath and put her foot against the bricks. The talisman around her neck grew hot, and she held it off her skin. It glowed yellow, then blue, and finally purple. The window's surface changed from hard brick to gel. It seemed alive as she pushed through. It yielded slowly, and at the same time she had the impression it read her mind.

She stood in a small room with a flight of stone steps leading down. The street entrance vanished. The buzz from the enhancer finally kicked in and her pain subsided.

"I hope you know the way," she said, producing a globe out of her pocket.

Nipits placed his paw on her leg.

"Lead on," she commanded. "Let's find Wilf."

# Chapter Nine
# The Morning After

"It's about time you were up."

Wilf opened his eyes and peered over the covers. Ermentrude's image materialized in the mirror facing the bed.

"Ahhh…"

"Thank you," Ermentrude said. "And the same to you."

He flipped the mirror.

"Shy, are you?" she chuckled. "Make yourself presentable and get down here. Katryna's made a lovely breakfast."

His inspection of the room revealed no other communication mirrors, but he dove under the sheets to tug on his pants and a clean t-shirt, in case he'd missed one. Opening his backpack, the journal peeked out from under his soccer kit. Last time he'd seen it, Ermentrude had placed it in her bag. He shrugged. Ermentrude had probably decided he should hold on to it.

"I'd like you to meet my daughter, Katryna." Ermentrude's eyes shone with pride when he stepped into the kitchen.

A teenager stood next to the stove. She wore a short, black skirt, striped stockings, and a purple peasant top that slipped off one bony shoulder. She smiled, and he took a step backward, bumping into the table and making the crockery rattle.

"I do believe she's the ugliest witch ever," Ermentrude said, standing straighter and puffing out her large chest.

"I don't disagree." Wilf struggled for breath. He'd thought Ermentrude ugly, but Katryna was in a class all by herself. He felt sure her face could oxidize fruit in seconds. The wart on her right cheek disappeared, and then reappeared on her pointed chin. Her eyes were small, deep-set, and hazel.

"Thanks," Katryna said and smiled.

Ermentrude scowled. "Ugly is not a compliment in his realm."

The spoon stopped stirring the contents of the bright-blue cauldron.

"That's extremely rude," Katryna said.

That hadn't been a smart move, but he'd been caught off-guard. It was like passing a ball straight to the opposition, in front of an open goal, and then being surprised when they scored. "I'm sorry," he muttered. "There seem to be a lot of rules I don't understand." He glared at Ermentrude. "Like wizards dying if they're found in Mathowytch."

"We'll let it go this once," Ermentrude said. "Katryna, you'd better stop making that face or you'll curdle the milk again."

"Very funny," Katryna said, ladeling a gray mush into a bowl and offering it to Wilf.

Light reflecting off the stainless-steel hood made him squint. "What's this?"

"Porridge, oatmeal... Whichever you'd prefer to call it," Katryna said. "There're honey and berries on the table."

Ermentrude accepted a bowl and sat down at the small, yellow kitchen table. "Did you manage to visit everyone on the list?" Ermentrude glanced briefly at him. "She helped visit virus sufferers for me."

"Yes," Katryna said, picking up the jar of honey and adding a spoonful to her bowl.

"Everything all right?" Ermentrude's brow furrowed.

"It's been giving me nightmares, this virus business. I'm checking my face every five minutes to make sure I've still the same number of warts," Katryna said.

"Every five minutes?"

"You know what I mean."

Ermentrude took another mouthful of porridge. "This is very good."

"What's the council going to say about him?" Katryna inclined her head towards Wilf. "You've brought a wizard into the city."

"Don't worry, he's not a real wizard." Ermentrude smiled at him. "He might be Reginald Gilvary's son, but he has no magical instruction. He can't make a globe flicker, let alone light one."

"No magic." Katryna blushed, and Ermentrude laughed. "He has magic, just refuses to use it."

Wilf let his spoon clatter into the bowl. "Now who's being rude? I'm right here."

"Well, you're the first wizard I've seen," Katryna said. "We've been told they're dangerous and scheming. You look more like a toad hoping it's not going to be a part of the next spell."

"I..."

"Children, play nice." Ermentrude waved the empty bowls into the sink.

A cricket chirped ten times.

"Is that the time? I'd best make my report to the Council." Ermentrude's jacket floated into the room and waited. She put her arms into the sleeves. "Make sure he doesn't start a panic amongst the neighbors."

"You're going to tell the Council that there's a wizard in the city?" Wilf asked.

Katryna and Ermentrude looked at him.

"He has lots of backbone, I'm sure. It's just well hidden," Ermentrude said. "Don't worry. That's the least of our problems."

"Doesn't feel like it to me."

"I shouldn't be too long." Ermentrude's bag jumped into her pocket.

"But…"

"Wait here until I return." Ermentrude left the room and the front door banged shut behind her.

Katryna wriggled her fingers and a sponge leaped onto the stovetop and began to clean it. The cauldron jumped into the sink and the dish liquid squirted into it. Water and bubbles filled the vessel and a brush began to scrub it.

His stomach had a sinking feeling, and it wasn't the oatmeal. "Do you use magic for everything?"

"What?" She glanced over at the stove. "Almost. To be honest, I don't even think about it."

"But this Pulch Virus is attacking magic?"

"It's really terrible. I went to visit this witch yesterday and she had no magic left. Can you believe that?" She picked up her compact mirror. "Mom tells me you're here to help, but you're under some delusion about not liking magic."

Wilf leaned back, crossed his arms, and met her gaze. "What do you know about me or my life?"

"Nothing, but you can't survive if you don't learn to control your magic. Everyone knows that," she said. "The Council's very strict about passing the magic exams to prove you have control. But you haven't been attending school."

"Of course I go to school, but in my realm people don't have magic."

She pointed at the bowls being washed in the sink. "Then how do you do household chores?"

"With machines or your hands," he said.

"I'm never leaving this realm," she shuddered. "How primitive your life sounds."

*Myra would agree with her*, he thought. "Tell me about this place. Where's Kureyamage?"

"It surrounds us. Mathowytch is actually in the center of Kureyamage. It wasn't meant to be its own city. More an elite borough for the Wizard Council members, their families, and the Red Wizards." She glanced at his hand. "You would have lived here."

He pulled down his sleeve to cover the wizard marking. "Why don't they take it back?"

"The Veil protects us," she said. "It's the most amazing piece of witch magic. No wizard can cross through it. So, we're perfectly safe here."

"Except for the Virus."

Katryna snapped shut her mirror. "Yes, there's that."

"But if you're only a witch population... I mean... How can you survive?"

"It's not supposed to remain this way forever," she said, blushing. "We're holding the city until the Wizard Council gives in to our demands. The Veil will then be taken down and we'll be one community again."

"I see," he said. "So how long has this been going on?"

"14 years. I was two when we arrived here."

"That's a long time. I take it talks haven't been going well?"

"Now that you've brought the formula, negotiations can restart," she smiled. The dishes and cauldron floated through the air, cupboard doors opened and closed. A teakettle filled with water and plugged itself in.

"Would you like some brew?"

Wilf shook his head.

A cup appeared on the counter next to the kettle.

"What do you do around here for fun?" he asked. "Do you play games, like soccer?"

"I've never heard of soccer. What is it?"

He stood up. The room tilted as he looked out the window. He placed a hand on the table to brace himself. "Ermentrude said the air was thin here."

"She added a spell to your porridge."

He groaned. *Not again.*

"Just something to keep you inside."

"What gives her the right to place a spell on me?" He backed away from the table.

"It's for your own good. You don't want anyone else to know you're here," she said.

"My own good." He bit his lip, but the anger boiled up.

"It's added security."

"And what about me and how I might feel about having magic used on me? Is that what you always do? Cast spells over everyone and hope they don't notice?" He pointed his ringed finger at her. The ruby in the center glowed.

She raised her hand. "Put the finger down and don't make any sudden movements."

"What are you talking about? Are you deranged?"

"Do as I say. I don't want to harm you."

"This is totally beyond belief. You place a spell on me to keep me in this house, and now you're threatening me?"

"Lower your ring and we'll talk," she said, spreading her fingers.

"Is that better?" He shook his fist at her. "Would you rather this than pointing?"

"Yes." She lowered her fingers. "Why don't we sit back down?"

"So you can poison me with more magic?"

"For someone with a wizard for a father, you seem to know very little about magic and how it works."

He glared at the young witch as she plucked the teacup out of the air. Every fiber in his body told him to run. He glanced at the window again, and the room spun.

"What spell did she put on me?"

"Agoraphobia. Fear of open spaces."

"I know what it is," he snapped. "How long does it last?"

"A couple of hours." She paused. "Look, I'm sorry if you find it upsetting, but you're a wizard."

His legs trembled, and he collapsed into the chair. "You really must hate wizards a lot."

"I've never met one before," she said. "All I know is that they don't want to give away any power to witches and they treated us badly in the past."

"What do you mean?"

"When witches demanded seats on the ruling council, the wizards rounded up the ring leaders and imprisoned and tortured them. They had this cat-and-mouse policy where they would release

74

the witches, then recapture them once they'd healed and sling them back into prison."

"I can't see that working," he said.

"No, it didn't. Instead of making them give up their struggle for power, it 'galvanized their spirit'. That's how it's written on the statue outside the new Witch Council building." She took a sip of brew before continuing, "Why don't you want to use magic?"

"That's none of your business." He stood up and made sure to avoid the window as he looked at the clock. If time worked the same way in this realm, then he should be at practice now. Coach would probably recruit another striker for the team when Wilf didn't show up for weeks on end. He needed to kick a ball around and clear his head.

"You don't have a ball pump, do you?" he asked.

"A what?"

"Wait here." He stumbled out of the kitchen and retrieved his soccer ball. "Something to inflate this."

"That's easy." She wriggled her fingers and the ball filled with air.

He shook his head. Of course she'd use magic. He half-expected the air to shimmer and fizz with the amount of magic she'd already used today.

Bouncing the ball on the floor a few times, he then caught it on his foot and flicked it over his shoulder, onto his back. He let the ball bounce on the floor again, and then passed it from one knee to the other.

"That's amazing." Her tone changed. "You need to stop. Now."

"Why?"

She caught the ball and held it.

"Hey, give it back."

"No. Look." She pointed at a flickering red light on the wall. "That's an alert of unsanctioned magic being used. It came on when you started playing with this ball."

He watched the light fade. "It's not true." He snatched the ball back and held it close to his chest.

"You use magic, but Mom said you couldn't light a globe."

"It's a trick," he said, pointing at the alarm.

Her compact began to chime.

"Hello," she said. "Alarm Central. Yes, everything is fine, thanks... I was trying an advanced charm for my exams and must have said the wrong spell... My name...? It's Katryna Wakefield. My password...? Yes, of course. It's tarantula... Thank you."

She closed the compact.

"What's going to happen to me?"

"Who knows? The Council isn't going to be happy there's a wizard in the city. Mom's going to have to do some quick thinking on this one." She pointed at the soccer ball. "It's about time you started using your magic for more than ball tricks."

"Forget it," he said, storming out of the room.

# Chapter Ten
# Call to Hywel

Wilf rolled the ball under his foot and stared at the journal. It was still so much to take in. His ring flashed and the locks sprung open. The pages fluted as they turned.

*Be on your guard. My role is to help you through your training, and by hiding information you don't understand, protect you from those who would harm you. I'm trying to keep you safe.*

*Ermentrude will help you, but only as long as you are of value to her. You need her protection—for now. As long as I'm by your side, I can help you. Keep our journal safe.*

A sizel sign floated above the page.

His ring flashed again, and the words disappeared.

Sighing, he ran his fingers through his hair. The journal snapped shut and locked. He reached for it, but it flopped away from him.

"Great deal of help you are," he said.

The front door slammed. He slunk down the stairs and into the kitchen.

"What did the council say?"

Katryna glanced at her mother, filled the kettle, and put it on to boil.

"They're still debating the matter." Ermentrude collapsed onto a chair.

"You've been gone a long time," Katryna said.

"I needed a walk."

The front door buzzer sounded. "I'll get it," Katryna said.

She came back carrying an official-looking envelope and gave it to her mother.

Ermentrude ripped open the wax seal.

Wilf peered over her shoulder, but the pages were blank.

"Oh, no," she said. "How could they?"

"What can you see? There's nothing there," he said.

"Mother's the only one who can read the document. It's addressed to her." Katryna shook her head at him.

"It's fine." Ermentrude's hand shook as she placed the letter on the table. "We're to leave in two nights. But first, Wilf's been summoned to appear before the Council."

"Leave?" Wilf and Katryna said together.

"Everyone is worried you will set off the alarms here and cause panic in the city." Ermentrude took a deep breath. "You're to be trained in Kureyamage."

Katryna handed her mother a steaming cup of brew.

Ermentrude took another document out of the envelope and gripped it tightly.

"Do you know who will train him?" Katryna asked.

Ermentrude sighed. "I've some arrangements to make. I'll use the inter-regional mirror upstairs." She snatched up the remaining documents in one hand and her teacup in the other.

"Which wizard?" Katryna asked, louder.

"It really doesn't concern you," Ermentrude said.

"I've been told my father is alive. I could come with you. I'd like to meet him."

"You shouldn't believe the sick ramblings of some poor witch," Ermentrude said, leaving the kitchen.

"But, she insisted that he's alive and living in Kureyamage," Katryna said, following her mother out into the hall.

Ermentrude turned to face her daughter.

"Did she? And how would this witch have any information about who lives in Kureyamage? She sounds like a second-rate witch who would never be in a position to have dealings with wizards," Ermentrude said.

"Then, you can't object to my coming with you and finding out for myself," Katryna said.

"I don't think that's a good idea, not with the current situation between the two Councils."

Wilf observed both witches, expecting to see sparks flying at any minute. He was ready to duck for cover, should he need to, but he wanted answers.

"You've never expressed an interest in Hywel before. Not in all your 16 years," Ermentrude said.

"What… I didn't know he might be alive, did I?" Katryna stared down at her mother.

"This isn't an opportunity for you to explore the family history. It's extremely dangerous traveling through the Veil, especially accompanying an untrained wizard." She motioned for her daughter to sit.

"When you left Kureyamage, had my Father evaporated?" Katryna remained standing but never took her eyes off her mother.

"No." Ermentrude took another sip of brew, regarding her daughter over the rim of her teacup.

"So he might be alive?"

"He is quite dead to us," Ermentrude said.

It seemed to Wilf that neither witch had blinked for a very long time. Then, Ermentrude looked away.

"That's not quite the same, and you know it. Is my father alive?"

"Nothing good would come out of you meeting him. You have your life here."

"I'm coming to see my dad, and there is nothing you can say that will change my mind." Katryna folded her arms.

"Don't call Hywel that." Ermentrude banged down the teacup. "I'll have enough to do looking after this helpless boy without having to worry about you in a city full of wizards." Ermentrude reached forward to place a hand on her daughter's arm but Katryna pulled away.

"I can look after myself," Katryna said.

"You don't have the right travel documents." Ermentrude stood and nearly collided into Wilf as she left the room.

"Ermentrude…" he said.

"I'll get some," Katryna shouted after her mother.

They heard Ermentrude's bedroom door slam shut.

He reached the top of the stairs and stopped. A male voice sounded from Ermentrude's room.

"Wizard Hywel Wakefield here. Who's calling? Show yourself." There was a brief pause. "Ermentrude."

"Good afternoon, Hywel," Ermentrude's voice sounded detached of emotion.

"By the moon, is that really you?" Hywel sounded glad.

"Of course it's me," Ermentrude said. "The Council has asked me to contact you."

"The Council? Of witches?"

"This will take a long time if you keep interrupting."

"Then by all means speak." All pleasure had vanished from his voice.

"I don't know how you did it, but the Council has requested that I bring a young, untrained wizard I found to you. We need you to help him acquire the rudiments of magic," Ermentrude said.

Wilf crept closer to the closed door. She spoke about him like he was a rookie that no team particularly wanted and the coach was giving them no choice but to accept him as a player.

"I see," said Hywel. "And where did you acquire this wizard? On your doorstep, or did you steal off in the night with him?"

"Very funny," Ermentrude said. "Will you help or not?"

"Not… unless you bring my daughter with you."

There was a long pause.

"She's my daughter," Ermentrude said. "And she's too busy with exams to take a trip."

"Then no deal. I'd say it's been nice talking to you after all this time, but…"

"Wait," Ermentrude said. "What if I tell you who the young wizard is?"

"If you bring Katryna with you, I don't really care who he is or how you… acquired him."

"It's Reginald Gilvary's son," Ermentrude said, an undertone of panic in her voice.

"I'm intrigued," Hywel said. "I'd love to know how you came to have young Wilf. Last I heard, he'd given magic the brush-off and lived in some kind of novelty shop, pretending to be a Normal."

"Then you'll help?" Ermentrude asked.

"Same condition… daughter's visit for help."

"You always did have a stubborn streak," Ermentrude said.

"Yes. I think you've told me that on several occasions," Hywel said. "Do we have a deal?"

There was a long silence.

"Ermentrude, I can't wait here all day for you to acquiesce," Hywel said. "You need me to help with Wilf. Stop procrastinating."

"Bat's blood," Ermentrude said. "My daughter's safety better not be compromised in any way, or I'll hold you personally responsible."

"Threats. I see you haven't changed at all. However, you can tell Katryna I'm looking forward to meeting her. When should I expect you?"

"We have clearance for a night crossing in two days," Ermentrude's voice had lost some of its fight.

"Of course. See you around dawn in two days. Hywel out."

There was a loud crash from inside Ermentrude's room and then silence.

Wilf turned but heard another voice.

"Ermentrude, is that you?"

"Yes. Hywel has managed to convince the Council..." Ermentrude's voice stopped.

"What is it?"

"I can't believe he's managed to manufacture this." Ermentrude's voice trembled. "I'm to deliver Wilf to him."

"You? But that isn't safe. Ermentrude, you can't go. How can you trust Hywel?"

"I can't, but this might be the opportunity to find evidence about who the spy on our Council is."

Wilf took a step closer.

"It sounds too risky. Can't they send someone else?"

"No. That was one of his demands for helping—Katryna and me."

"It's a trap. Once he has Katryna..."

"Alert the Resistance not to come near me," Ermentrude said. "I don't want to risk Hywel infiltrating the whole network. If I find a way to pass on any useful information, I'll contact them."

"If you're sure, then I'll pass the word along, but be careful."

"Aren't I always?" Ermentrude said.

A snort sounded from the other speaker.

Wilf heard footsteps coming towards the door and he hurried into his room.

He was to be delivered to this Wizard Hywel for training. Everyone was trying to control him. He'd never agreed to being passed around from player to player. And Ermentrude still hadn't told him about Griselda. She'd said his stepmother wasn't well and he could visit her. He'd remind her of her promise, but first he had to go before the Witch Council...

A blood-curdling scream came from the kitchen. He ran towards the stairs, almost bumping into Ermentrude. The witch pushed past him.

Katryna stood with a mirror in her right hand.

"Look," she said, trembling all over. "My gorgeous, large wart is shrinking. Isn't it?"

Ermentrude hugged her daughter. "I think you're right."

Katryna turned to Wilf. "This is your fault."

"How's that?"

"If you'd learned to perform magic, like a proper wizard, you'd be able to read your father's journal. We'd be making a cure by now." She stepped forward and grabbed his arm.

He winced and tried to pry her fingers open.

"And I wouldn't be losing my warts and power." She pointed her fingers at him.

"It's not his fault, and harming him won't help." Ermentrude said, stepping over and grabbing Katryna's hand.

She glared at her mother but released Wilf.

"How did you get that?" Ermentrude asked, pointing at the deep puncture wound on her daughter's arm.

"Griselda grabbed me, and her nails…"

Ermentrude's face paled. "She infected you. But how could she? Her name wasn't on the list."

"I'd visited other witches with the Virus… I thought you'd forgotten to write her name on the list… Why should I think she'd want to harm me?" Katryna collapsed into a chair.

"I'll ask the Council to send another witch with Wilf," Ermentrude said. "They can't refuse under the circumstances."

"No. You can't tell them I'm sick. I imaged about Griselda, and they took her away."

"But…"

"You'll have to take me with you." Katryna's voice quivered.

"I don't…"

"Please, Mom. You can't let them take me into quarantine."

"Perhaps it might be best if you came."

"Thank you." Katryna hugged Ermentrude, before running from the room.

"I know you listened to my call to Hywel," Ermentrude said, turning to Wilf. "But you breathe a word to Katryna, and I'll make you wish we'd never met."

"Wouldn't dream of it." He already wished he'd never met her. Further persuasion wasn't necessary.

She walked past him and out of the kitchen.

He thumped into a chair. Griselda was in quarantine, and she'd infected Katryna. This was bad. And soon, he'd have to step outside into a city full of witches who hated wizards. This was his father's fault. Placing that spell on his journal had put Wilf's life in danger. His father would find the situation amusing. If only he could have lived to see it. He'd finally found a way to force his son to learn magic.

# Chapter Eleven
## Surveillance by Myra

Myra approached the counter of the brew shop. The majority of the tables were filled with teenage witches hunched over their compact mirrors.

"What kind of brew would you like?" the witch behind the counter asked.

"Green with honey," Myra said. She slid a Moon card through the reader and headed for the pick-up side of the counter.

It had taken hours of hanging outside the school, listening to the endless prattle of teenage witches, until she'd managed to find out which one was Katryna Wakefield. Now, she saw the young witch sitting alone in the back and weaved her way through the tables and chairs. Customers turned to look and whisper as Myra passed.

Katryna reached into her bag and brought out a small, black compact mirror. On the front was a large $K$ in tiny sparkling stars. She flipped it open and drew her finger over the surface. The mirror flickered, and a rolling list of symbols appeared on it.

"Do you mind if I join you?" Myra asked. Hywel might have told her to keep her distance, but she had some questions of her own she wanted answered.

Katryna looked up and hesitated. Myra watched the witch react to her face, trying to work out if she had the virus. The problem with spending most of her life not in the magical realm meant she wasn't ugly. However, it did have the advantage that no one would be able to tell how much power she possessed. If she needed to stay in Mathowytch for a long time, she'd have to change her looks, growing her hair from its short bob would be the first step.

"Please sit down. You're new here, aren't you?"

"Yes." Myra placed her brew on the table. She took her arms out of her backpack and let it fall to the floor. "I've only recently arrived in Mathowytch."

"You escaped from Kureyamage?" Katryna picked up her cup and took a sip.

"My mother came here first," Myra said. "It took me longer to find a way through." She pulled out her own compact. It was blue, with a white half-moon decorating it. "I've been trying to reach her, but there's been no answer."

"What's her name?"

"Griselda Picton."

"Oh," Katryna said.

"Do you know her?"

"I've met her." Katryna rubbed her arm and wouldn't meet Myra's eyes.

"I know she has the virus."

"No, it's not that." Katryna put her compact away and gathered up her bag.

"Has something happened to her?"

"She's very sick, and…" Katryna leaned back and shot a fierce look at Myra. "My mother could explain better. We don't live far from here."

Katryna was inviting her home. Myra hadn't expected that and wasn't ready for another run-in with Ermentrude. It wouldn't be a good idea while she was still feeling the effects from the last one.

"I've to meet someone soon," Myra said. "But if you give me your address, I'll come later today."

Hostility oozed from the young witch. Griselda had done something. That would be just like her mother. Katryna would discuss their meeting with Ermentrude, giving the witch advanced notice that Myra was in Mathowytch, but she needed to know what had happened to Griselda. It could jeopardize her mission. Hywel couldn't know that Griselda had met Katryna. He wasn't going to be too happy if he found out she'd also talked to his daughter, but it was worth the risk to stay ahead in this game.

"18 High Flyer Mews." The young witch stood and pushed her chair under the table.

"Hello, Katryna."

"Hello, Witch Mitchell," Katryna said, acknowledging the elderly witch sitting down at the next table.

"You sick?" Witch Mitchell asked Myra.

"No." Myra watched the young witch weave through the crowded brew shop.

"Haven't seen anyone with that little power unless they were sick," Witch Mitchell said to the other older witches at her table but addressed the entire brew shop.

Myra drained her cup, glared at the table of old crones, and left the shop. She followed Katryna into the park and along the pink gravel path leading to the central fountain, its statue of a group of witches looking skyward. The plaque under the statue said it was dedicated to 'The raising of the Veil'.

The heads of the tulips in the ornate display were tightly closed, and a damp, earthy smell invaded the air. Small ripples spread across the water in the fountain as the first few drops of rain landed on its surface. Katryna glanced up at the gray clouds covering the sky and veered to the left.

Myra stopped to watch the ducks splashing noisily in a small pond when the young witch met with a friend. She clenched her jaw as the enhancer began to wear off and pain from her injuries filtered through.

Small umbrella-shaped enchantments kept the rain off the teenage witches as they chatted in the formal gardens. Boxwoods and small grassy areas glistened in the shower. When the friends parted, Myra continued to follow. She needed to make sure the address was correct. The young witch had seemed so anxious to escape that she could have given Myra a false address.

The rain fell in a steady downpour as Katryna exited the park and strolled unhurriedly down a street of townhouses with iron railings and gates.

Mathowytch wasn't the same as the map in Hywel's study. In fact, it had been a real challenge trying to navigate the city. It was all Wilf's fault that she'd had to sneak into this city. She was still amazed that he'd been tricked so easily into finding the workshop and accompanying Ermentrude. The hours she'd spent searching the store from floor to ceiling and hadn't found a clue to its entrance.

Katryna headed down a dead-end street. At the second-from-last townhouse, the girl opened the gate, strolled down the short walkway, and ran up three steps. She placed her hand on the door panel, and the door swung open.

Myra stood on the corner, looking at the house. It had been the correct address. Pain from her injured side flared. She'd need to find a place to rest soon. If only she knew where her mother lived. Opening her backpack, she took another vial of elixir out and drained it. She'd used the three Hywel had given her, but she still had another three she'd stolen from his office.

Ermentrude emerged from the house. Myra hurried back to the main street and into a store doorway. She leaned against the frame, waiting for the enhancer to kick in.

Ermentrude hurried past her without a sideways glance. Myra let out a sigh of relief and stepped back out into the street. Her head buzzed, but the pain was receding to a dull ache. With Ermentrude out of the way, she could risk checking on Wilf and finding out where her mother lived.

She rang the doorbell.

"I'm sorry, my mother isn't here." There was nothing welcoming in the young witch's expression.

"Do you mind if I wait?" She stepped over the threshold, forcing Katryna back.

"No… not at all." Katryna led the way into the kitchen. "I won't be a minute, I've left a spell running in the other room. I'll be right back." She almost ran from the room.

Myra smiled and edged to the kitchen entrance. She wriggled her fingers and could hear Katryna's voice in the living room.

"There's a witch here, so don't come out for any reason," Katryna said. "Even if the house is burning down."

Wilf made a huffing noise Myra recognized. She moved back to the kitchen table as Katryna entered.

"If you could tell me where Griselda lives, I'll be on my way," Myra said. "I don't really have the time to wait for Ermentrude."

Katryna looked at her long, gray fingernails. The kettle whistled, made brew, and two mugs floated over to them.

"She's no longer there," Katryna said. "The virus had robbed her of her magic. I'm afraid she was taken into quarantine three days ago."

"Quarantine?"

"I'm as shocked as you." Katryna said, shaking her head.

"Hardly," Myra said. "She wasn't your mother."

Katryna went to place a hand over Myra's but then hesitated and withdrew it.

"Did she mention me at all?" Myra asked. Her hands clasped so tightly that the knuckles showed white.

"Yes… She thought I was you. She asked you to promise… that you wouldn't leave your brother with Hywel."

Myra stood slowly. "I appreciate you being with her." She stared down at Katryna. "There's only one more thing—I'd like to speak to my stepbrother."

Katryna stood, knocking over the chair.

"Myra," Wilf said, entering the kitchen. "I thought I heard your voice. I've been worried about you. Are you okay? When did you get here?"

Myra raised her fingers, pointing them at Katryna.

"I'm fine now." Myra said. "I arrived a day ago. I've come to make sure you're not being mistreated."

"No. I'm fine," Wilf said. "How did you find me?"

"Through a friend of mine in Kureyamage," Myra said.

"I'll soon be there for you to introduce me." There was an edge to his voice.

Myra backed up to stand next to her stepbrother. "What do you mean?"

Wilf pointed at Katryna and then dropped his hand,

"The Witch Council wants me in Kureyamage. They're giving us travel permits," he said.

"Is that true?"

Hywel had told Myra that he could arrange for Wilf to be brought to him. It seemed he'd pulled it off.

"Yes," Katryna said, folding her arms

"You're going to leave me here, aren't you?" Wilf grabbed her arm.

"I know it's not perfect." Myra kept her eyes focused on Katryna, watching for any sudden movement. "But it's better if you travel with them through the Veil. I'll find you once you're in Kureyamage. My friend is longing to meet you."

"I'm to be bought by the highest bidder?" He stood in front of her.

She tried to move so he wasn't blocking her line of sight, but he kept moving with her.

"You can't threaten Katryna if you then want me to stay here. Just leave, Myra."

"Wilf…"

"I said, leave. Do it now, before Ermentrude returns."

"It's for the best." Myra lowered her hand and fled down the hall and out the front door. She glanced over her shoulder several times before she entered the main street.

"What are you doing here?" a police witch, of medium power, asked.

Myra spun round, but the police witch was addressing a young, pretty witch she'd stopped.

"Nothing," the young witch said.

"You a Virus sufferer?" The police witch reached for her compact.

"No," the young witch said.

"Officer," a witch with a very impressive number of warts said. "What is this person doing here?" She wore an old-fashioned witch's hat, black cloak, red and black striped socks, and sensible black shoes. A grand dame of witchery, and there was no mistake about it. Her companion was of equal strength but didn't possess an overbearing presence.

The police witch pushed the young witch off the sidewalk and into the gutter.

"That's what I'm trying to ascertain, Madam," the police witch said, bowing slightly.

"I remember when the subclass knew its place," the grand dame said to her companion. "Now look, two of them actually making eye contact. I blame this virus and the lack of leadership from the Council."

The two witches swept down the boulevard.

"I'll be back this way in ten minutes," the police witch said. "And I don't want to see either of you here."

Myra helped the young witch up. She was a few inches taller than Myra, with short black hair and only a very small wart on her stubby nose. She seemed wiry, but when Myra took hold of her arm, she felt strong muscles beneath the beige jacket sleeve.

"Do you have the virus?" the young witch asked, a malicious look in her brown eyes.

"This doesn't seem the best place for a non-powerful witch."

"Who asked you?" the young witch said, looking Myra up and down.

Myra smiled, knowing it wasn't a friendly, reassuring smile. More a 'Really, do you want to push that button?' type of a smile.

She raised her hand and pointed her fingers at the young witch.

"Very scary," the young witch said. "What are you going to do? Show me you can turn me into a frog, or a cat, or something? Don't embarrass yourself. With your looks, you'll probably strain something trying," the young witch sneered at her.

"You're absolutely right." Myra lowered her hand, and turning as if to walk away, she spun back around, raised her hand, and blasted the young witch off her feet, back into the gutter.

"Was that really necessary?" The young witch sat on the curbstone and folded her arms.

"Respect is everything, and you definitely need some lessons in how to show it." She held out her hand to help the young witch up. "What's your name?"

"Seldan."

"Well, consider that a lesson not to trust what your eyes tell you. Any witch might be powerful and able to hide it." Myra moved away, but Seldan followed her. She stopped. "Look, if you think I'm going to feel sorry for you or something, forget it."

"Me?" Seldan said, stepping in front of Myra. "I don't need help from no one. You're the one who looks out of place here, doesn't know the laws, and might need somewhere to hide out."

A flash of lightening lit the sky, and a rumble of thunder followed it. No one moved on the street. They all stood looking up at the sky. The ground seemed to ripple.

"What's that?" Myra asked. Seldan grabbed hold of her arm and she winced with pain. The young witch looked shocked.

"It's another of those quakes."

"Quakes?" She prized Seldan's fingers open and pushed the hand off her sleeve. So it was true. The realm was becoming unbalanced. There was too much wizard magic and not enough from the witches. The Pulch Virus's consequences were far greater than Hywel had told her.

"It's the wizards causing the earthquakes. Some witches believe we might have to evacuate the realm altogether," Seldan said.

"What's the Council doing?"

"The Council. Don't make me laugh. What do they know? I tell you. It's the wizards trying to frighten us into running back to them for protection. Well, they don't scare me. There's no way I'm ever going to leave Mathowytch. We all know we're better off without the wizards controlling us."

The sky cleared again.

"Time we moved."

Myra caught hold of Seldan. "You mentioned somewhere to hide out?"

Seldan smiled, "I know the perfect place." She guided the way to a tram stop.

Myra observed the witches and their children and breathed a little easier realizing that no one appeared particularly powerful. She hung back until the tram arrived, and then she scrunched herself into a corner seat beside Seldan.

"The windows are made of a special glass that's non-reflective. So you don't have to crouch down in the seat so much. Witches in this city are very careful about who can see their reflection. You won't believe the uses that can be made of them."

"Even with the communication mirrors?"

"They've been treated. Although, I still know several older witches who refuse to use them. The old crones are a suspicious bunch, hate new technology," Seldan said, her voice soft so only Myra could hear her.

Myra counted the stops as the tram made its way down the increasingly narrowing streets. The wide avenues and parks had given way to rundown, older buildings. No glass and steel apartment buildings here, only concrete monoliths from a time when this city had been whole instead of divided. Carts selling spell ingredients appeared and disappeared as the tram continued its journey.

"Here we are." Seldan stepped off into the terminus. "This is as close as the trams run to the border." She waited for Myra to join her. "Most of the buildings around here are warehouses that hold supplies transported from the other realm."

"By portal, I take it?"

"We use them to ship a warehouse full of supplies at a time. I used to be part of one of the circles. Didn't like the hours or the exhaustion."

Myra stared at the end of the road. A guard's hut stood in front of the opaque Veil. It appeared as if the world ended at the hut. Nothing could be seen or heard of Kureyamage, even though it was only meters away.

She couldn't believe Hywel was going to have Wilf enter that level of witch magic. He must have no idea of Wilf's phobia or his lack of control. Myra shuddered; glad it wasn't her responsibility.

# Chapter Twelve
# Council Chamber

The tram picked up speed. Wilf peeked around the cloak's hood at the passing landscape. The streets were sparsely populated with witches of all shapes and sizes. Knots formed and reformed in his stomach. A tingling sensation grew in his palm.

"A lot of the buildings are unoccupied," Ermentrude said as the tram clattered along the wide, tree-lined street. "We mainly live in the central district. There are too few of us to be able to power a city this size."

"Power?"

"It all takes magic," Ermentrude said. "The utilities, maintenance, transportation, and supplies don't happen by themselves. We need witches using their magic to run the city."

"I'd never given it any thought."

"Neither did we when we captured the city. In the early years, it was a struggle. A number of witches returned to Kureyamage, and that was quite a blow." She sighed, and shook her head. "The system was working well, and we were able to portal additional supplies from your realm, until the Virus struck."

"Because it reduced the amount of witch magic available?"

"The Wizard Council's trump card." Ermentrude's voice sounded bitter. "It's exhausting working the portals, and so we rotate duties. Witches don't like having to spend days without magic while they recover from a shift. The virus has cost us dearly. That's why Reginald's formula is so important. We're not sure how much longer we can hold out."

The tram jerked to a stop.

"Here we are." Ermentrude made her way along the tram and alighted.

Wilf cringed from the cramping pain in his stomach as he stepped down behind her. A bell sounded, and the tram moved off. He strained his neck trying to see the top of the glass and steel skyscraper ahead. The Council Hall was the largest building by far. It took up one side of the plaza. Ground-level shops lined the other three sides, with office buildings towering about them. He hurried across the wide concrete plaza, dodging pedestrians, and circled the central fountain. Ermentrude was already climbing the wide bluestone steps when he caught up to her. A large steel canopy protected the glass-etched door of the Hall. Once inside, they joined the line inching forward at the bank of elevators. He tugged at his hood and kept his head down.

Ermentrude had wanted to place an illusion on him for disguise, but he'd protested very strongly about any spell being placed on him. Once inside the Council Hall, the spell would have been stripped away by the security enchantments anyway.

He glanced around the edge of the hood. A high glass-domed atrium let in light. Witches walked purposefully across the marble floor to the various branching corridors. The hum of conversation surrounded him like the spectators at a home match.

A narrow-faced witch sat behind a green granite reception desk. The wall behind her displayed a digital directory. The room numbers of the various occupants were constantly being updated. It reminded him of the departure board at Hong Kong Airport.

"Ermentrude Wakefield."

He jumped and spun round, surprised to see two guards standing next to them.

"Yes?" Ermentrude said.

"Come with us," the taller guard said.

"Come where?" Ermentrude asked.

"Head Witch Akuna asked that you and your companion be escorted to her," the guard said, placing her hand on Wilf's shoulder.

"Lead on then," Ermentrude said. "Although, I know perfectly well where Akuna's office is."

The other guard hung back as they went through a set of double doors. Wilf's footsteps were the only sound echoing on the marble floor of the long, narrow corridor. The guards and Ermentrude moved silently. The two guards stopped at a pair of very impressive wooden doors with images of witches with swirling cloaks carved into it. He followed Ermentrude inside.

The room's soft lighting, dark wooden panels, and deep-piled carpet gave the room an inner-sanctum feel. The only furniture in the reception area were a brown leather sofa, two chairs, and a coffee table with magazines spread across it. A witch with blonde hair and red eyes sat behind a small desk. Her left hand rested on a large crystal ball filled with swirling mist. The door opened behind the reception witch.

"There you are," Akuna said, holding the door open. "Come along in. I was beginning to think you'd run into trouble getting here."

"No. Everything went smoothly. Although, being met by those guards won't do my reputation any good," Ermentrude said, following Akuna into the inner room.

"So this is Wilf?" Akuna asked, once the door closed securely. She sat down behind an oak desk and indicated that he and Ermentrude should take the chairs facing her.

"Yes," Ermentrude said, sitting down.

"On behalf of the Witch Council, I want to express our thanks to you for agreeing to cooperate in our current dilemma." Akuna stared directly at him.

"Eh… When did I…?" Wilf massaged his hand. His tattoo had become a dull ache since entering the building.

"What else would you expect, under the circumstances?" Ermentrude asked.

He glared at Ermentrude. Her plan must be to have him speak as little as possible. He hadn't agreed to that either.

The thin Head Witch's angular features were covered in a skin stretched so tight it gave her a cadaverous look. He resisted the urge to shudder when she peered at him with her beady, dark eyes. Large gemstone rings adorned her claw-like fingers. With a jangle of bangles, she pushed back an escaping strand of wiry, gray hair into the jeweled clasp at the back of her head.

"I see what you mean," Akuna said. "But he must stay hidden until you leave. The rumor of a wizard in Mathowytch would cause panic. Even I'm not convinced this was a wise decision on your part."

"She tricked me," Wilf said.

"I did no such thing," Ermentrude said. "You might be right, Akuna. I will admit it was more a reaction than a decision. After all, I was under attack."

"Griselda's daughter. Do you think she will follow you here?"

"Yes, she did." He wasn't going to sit there like a benched substitute hoping the coach would let him play if he behaved.

"She arrived at my home yesterday, enquiring about Griselda." Ermentrude glared at him.

"She…" Wilf said.

Ermentrude raised her hand at him. "I apologize, Akuna. Wilf hasn't been trained in magic, or, it would seem, manners. He doesn't know that he should only speak when directly addressed."

Akuna brushed the apology aside.

He slumped back into his chair. They were discussing what was going to happen to him and he was supposed to sit dumb. Ermentrude really thought she could parade him around like a well-trained mascot. The knots in his stomach eased. He wasn't going to let her harness him.

"Where are you keeping Griselda?" Ermentrude leaned forward.

"You know I can't tell you. It's to remain strictly Council business at this time." Akuna nodded towards Wilf. "And I don't think we should discuss this in front of…"

"You're talking about my stepmother." Wilf turned to Ermentrude. "You said I could see her, help her, if I opened my father's workshop. Does that ring any bells with you? And now you won't even discuss her in front of me?"

"The situation has changed," Ermentrude said. "Stop interrupting."

"I wasn't sure about him going to Kureyamage," Akuna said. "But, Degula thinks it's our only option. We don't want him setting off alarms and causing mass panic."

"Oh, no," he said. "We can't have that."

"Wilf, be quiet," Ermentrude said. "Are we sure the Veil Guardians will let him through?

"It's been agreed that could be a serious problem," Akuna said.

"What do you mean, a serious problem?" Wilf asked.

"Wilf, for the last time," Ermentrude said. "Shut it."

"He can't stay here. I've been advised he already caused a breach yesterday at your house," Akuna said.

"I didn't…"

"That's it." Ermentrude wriggled her fingers at him.

"You…" His throat contracted, and he grunted. He tried to send her looks of pure hatred, but she refused to look at him.

"I did warn you." She turned back to Akuna. "Wilf performs some magic without knowing he's doing it. The breach was nothing serious."

"You didn't tell us he was volatile." Akuna's hand pressed to her chest and her eyes glistened. It took Wilf a lot of effort not to give them a few choice hand gestures.

"It's only been the one small incident," Ermentrude said. "But the situation does need to be addressed."

"The Council has agreed to grant him a talisman for safe passage, but there was strong opposition." The color drained from

Akuna's face. "Especially as we've lost so many witches protecting those tokens."

"But they know Wilf must go to Kureyamage to be trained?"

"There was a suggestion that perhaps Wizard Reginald Gilvary had an ulterior motive in not teaching his son magic, and then placing this restriction on his journal? That maybe he'd planned it so Mathowytch would be at the mercy of the wizards again," Akuna said.

"I've known Reginald for decades, and he wasn't like that," Ermentrude said, moving forward in her seat.

He gripped the chair arms and fumed at the injustice of being silenced. He could have told them that his father's motives probably had more to do with his son than any power struggles of this realm. And in that, Reginald was succeeding: Wilf was drowning in magic. He glanced at his tattoo. It looked as angry as he felt.

"Are you sure? Wizard Gilvary did live in the other realm for years." Akuna leaned back and folded her arms.

"He had a disagreement with the Wizard Council. They wanted him to create the virus, and he refused. It's that simple," Ermentrude said. "That's why he worked on the vaccine for us."

Akuna stared from Ermentrude to Wilf. She sighed, and then opened the top desk drawer, taking out a large, buff envelope.

"Here are your travel permits. Are you sure you want to take your daughter with you? Wouldn't you be better with a more experienced witch to accompany you?"

"Katryna is more than capable." Ermentrude scooped up the documents and placed them in her bag. "And she already knows Wilf."

"Very well." Akuna waved her hand at the door and it opened. "I wish you every success."

Wilf's throat eased as the spell released him.

"Why did I need to come?" Wilf stood and looked down on the Head Witch. He took several deep breaths. An uncontrolled display of magic here was the last thing he wanted.

Akuna shuffled some papers on her desk before glancing up at Ermentrude. "Degula wants to meet him. She has the authorizations for Veil talismans."

"Who is Degula?"

"She's the Head of Witch Security." Ermentrude gave him a warning glance.

"I'm sure it's routine," Akuna said.

"Wilf, put your hood back up." Ermentrude headed for the door. "We don't want you scaring anyone."

Another meet and greet session. This morning was turning into a take-your-freak-to-work day with him as the main attraction. His tattoo went back to being an annoying, dull ache.

The two guards were waiting for them in the hall.

"We'll escort you to Security." One of the guards took up the lead position. Her companion fell into step at the rear.

They were led back down the corridor, but at the end they turned right. The Council chamber's doors were twice the height of normal doors and about three times the weight. They opened with a soft swish and the effortlessness of a tongue over a plastic mouth guard. The room's vaulted glass dome let Wilf see the dark clouds gathering across the sky. His footsteps echoed around the round room as he walked over the mosaic-tiled floor towards the dais. A lone witch sat on a high-backed, wooden chair.

"So good of you to stop by and bring this young wizard with you." The large, powerful witch pushed back her hat to reveal a forehead covered in an astonishing amount of warts. "I heard you'd been back for several days, which makes it curious that you've failed to file a report or contact your head of department. But see, I've managed to afford you the opportunity after all."

Ermentrude bowed her head. "That was very thoughtful of you."

"How's your daughter?" Degula asked. "It must have been such an unpleasant experience for her, attending a Virus victim. Not many witches would run the risk of becoming infected. Or be brave enough to want to visit Kureyamage. She must be a remarkable young witch. I would enjoy meeting her."

"Katryna is indeed remarkable." Ermentrude's face turned red. "But not enough to warrant the attention of anyone of your standing."

"Come now, you know how much I value your devotion to this city and the Council." Degula gestured at the empty council bench before she continued, "However, it came as quite a surprise when I learned that you'd brought a wizard into Mathowytch. Some council members are questioning your judgment. It's to be hoped this information isn't leaked to the general public. I'd hate to think what the repercussions of that would be."

"As you can see." Ermentrude pointed at him. "There isn't any danger to Mathowytch or its occupants from Wilf." She folded her arms. "I find it rather insulting, after all my years of service, that you and the Council would think I'd risk the city. Wilf doesn't have any magic yet, so he's quite harmless."

"Is he?" Degula stood up, placed her hat on the table, and stepped off the dais.

Wilf couldn't take his eyes off the hat. It reminded him of... His skin crawled as the witch approached, but his eyes kept returning to the hat. An image of his mother wearing a similar hat, in their garden out in the New Territories, came to him. His mother had loved her small garden. He furrowed his brow—had he always known that about her?

Degula stood beside him. He drew in a sharp breath. Embroidered on the black brocade of Degula's dress was his mother's favorite plant. Its long leaves and stems twisted up the front of the garment. Tiny clusters of bell-shaped buds and deep purple flowers appeared so real he almost reached out to touch them.

"Will you please stop using Wilf's memories in this way? You're frightening him." Ermentrude stepped closer.

Degula's appearance changed to be that of a witch of athletic build in a black suit and white shirt. The hat remained on the table. A bead of sweat trickled down Wilf's back as Degula held his gaze. The ache disappeared from his hand.

"He'll face worse than that in the Veil." She grinned and then marched back to the dais. "You say this young wizard doesn't have enough magic to trigger the alarm. But what you've done is a breach of our first rule."

"I've always regarded the rules more as guidelines, especially under our current predicament."

"I know." Degula leaned forward. "It's been brought to my attention on numerous occasions."

"I don't see why you're upset. Doesn't anyone realize I made a split-second decision whilst under attack?" Ermentrude said.

Degula spread her fingers and cleaned under her nails. "He does understand what the punishment is for a wizard smuggled into Mathowytch, doesn't he?"

Wilf's heart raced. Degula could have him arrested. It had been a bad idea to come and meet this witch.

"For him to be a wizard, he must be able to consciously perform magic. He can't," Ermentrude said.

"If he can't," Degula said. "He won't be able to survive in this realm."

"I didn't say he doesn't possess magic." A note of irritation entered Ermentrude's voice. "I said he couldn't perform magic. Therefore, he's no threat."

"Unless he's a spy. Sent here to report back to the Wizard Council on how the virus is progressing. Perhaps we should burn him."

"What?" He took several steps backward.

"Stop trying to frighten the boy," Ermentrude said. "That went out with the last century. What are you trying to achieve here, Degula? We need to convince Wilf to help us if we hope to survive, and you're playing games."

"I have misgivings about his ability to be of any use, especially having met him."

"This isn't helping." Ermentrude took a deep breath. "Why don't you and I discuss your misgiving while Wilf waits in the antechamber?"

"I'd rather stay here." His voice trembled.

Degula turned to look at Ermentrude, and then nodded to the two guards. Each took one of Wilf's arms and dragged him out of the chamber through a side door. They threw him into a chair and left.

He sprung out of the chair and rattled the locked door. Great, he was locked in a small one-windowed room. He threw himself onto one of the five chairs arranged in a cluster at the back of the room. A painting of a witch riding the Magical Thermals hung from a picture rail against the light-yellow walls.

Ermentrude had used magic on him again. In the last few days, he'd had more spells cast on him than in his entire life.

A shout came from the courtyard, and he glanced out the window at the witches standing in small groups.

Perhaps, he should stand at the window and let them know a wizard had entered. That would freak them out and cause mass panic in the square. He'd like to see the look on Degula's face then… Or maybe not.

He needed to get out of this city. If he agreed to help, then he'd be guaranteed safe passage into Kureyamage. A city filled with wizards. He slumped down further in the chair. What was wrong with him? At least that would improve his situation. He'd be able to move around in Kureyamage without scaring everyone. And that would give him a greater opportunity of finding a way of escaping the realm. If the wizards also used supply portals…

His tattoo flared and the ruby at the center of his ring flashed. The other chairs moved away from him and huddled together in a corner.

The door flew open. Ermentrude entered, followed by the guards with their fingers raised at him.

Sirens sounded throughout the building.

"What did I tell you?" Ermentrude addressed the guards. "Nothing serious." She grabbed hold of Wilf and pulled his hood up over his head.

"Do try a little self-control." Her mouth was close to his ear. "I know Degula can be a little over-enthusiastic in her duties, sometimes, and likes to flex her authority, but you're not helping." She propelled him through the door. "Luckily, I'd already secured her permission and the authorization we need." Ermentrude patted her bag and continued down the corridor with him. Witches ran in all directions. "We're to leave tonight."

# Chapter Thirteen
## Into the Veil

Wilf expected a barrier across the road, similar to war movie scenes. But no barbed-wire fencing, searchlights, or machinegun turrets could be seen. A single guard stood next to a small brick hut. Her silver-gray uniform made her outline merge with the Veil. She watched them approach with her arms folded across her chest, legs together at attention.

Standing between Ermentrude and Katryna, Wilf stared beyond the guard at the Veil. It was a pale, gray wall of witch magic that he was expected to walk straight into. The thought of it made his palms sweaty and his mouth dry. He felt very cold inside. He shoved his hands in his pockets to hide how much they shook. All he wanted was to turn and run.

Ermentrude passed their permit to the border guard.

"A wizard in Mathowytch," the guard said after reading the document. "No wonder you're here at this time."

Ermentrude nodded.

"Permit seems in order," the guard said.

"Good. Then, I suggest you perform the incantation as quickly as possible and allow us to pass," Ermentrude said, tightening her grip on his arm. "The sooner this renegade is back in wizard lands, the better we'll all feel."

The guard studied Wilf and the two witches. "Alright," she said. "Glad I'm not the one having to handle him."

"You're a credit to your post," Ermentrude said.

Three talismans on long chains, in the shape of clear, glass triangles, appeared with a wave of the guard's hand over the permit.

"You'll need to wear these," Katryna said to Wilf.

He shook his head.

"You must," Katryna said. "No one can pass safely through the veil without it."

No way. He didn't trust them. Once he put that thing on, they'd probably be able to control him. This might all be a trick. They'd never intended to take him to Kureyamage. They'd throw him in some prison cell and then...

The guard handed a talisman to Katryna and one to Ermentrude. She then stepped in front of Wilf and hit him hard in the stomach. He doubled over.

"Be a good little wizard," she said. "Put on the talisman and get out of Mathowytch."

"That wasn't necessary," Ermentrude said.

"Looked like it was to me." The guard placed the chain in Wilf's outstretched hand.

Katryna and Ermentrude looped the chains over their necks. The talisman changed from yellow, to blue, and then purple. They all looked at him.

"Would you like me to help you?" The guard smiled, showing the one central tooth left in her mouth.

"No, he doesn't," Katryna said.

"You hoping he'll become your mate, do you?" the guard asked. "Is that why he's here? Did you sneak him into Mathowytch?"

"That's enough," Ermentrude said. "Put it on and let's get moving."

Wilf's hands shook, but he took a deep breath and placed the chain over his head. The talisman lay over his heart and turned from yellow to blue, and then back to yellow.

"That's not good," the guard said. "It must be purple for him to enter."

Ermentrude reached into her pocket and produced a vial. "I'm sorry about this," she said, pouring its contents over his head.

A fine dust floated over him, and on his next inhale, up his nose. "What are you doing to me?" he spluttered. The talisman flickered, and then turned blue and, finally, purple.

The guard turned to Ermentrude. "Have you traveled through the Veil before?"

"Only the tunnels."

"As you approach, it will reach out for you and draw you in. Don't resist at all. You must pass willingly. Once inside, it will open a pathway for you to follow. Don't stray from the route under any circumstances."

"Thank you," Ermentrude said.

The guard extended an arm towards the Veil. She closed her eyes and wriggled her fingers. A shadowy doorframe appeared.

"Have a nice trip," she said, lowering her arm.

They walked towards the Veil with Ermentrude and Katryna each holding one of Wilf's arms.

"What was in that dust?"

"A little masking power," Ermentrude said. "Hopefully, it's enough to see you through."

"Do you trust the guard?" He glanced back over his shoulder.

"You have to stop being suspicious of everyone who performs magic," Katryna said.

"Easy for you to say." He let his gaze drop to the blacktop and concentrated on placing one foot in front of the other, trying, with difficulty, to block all thoughts of being consumed by the Veil. It didn't help that he could hear whispering coming from it as they drew nearer. The indistinct voices chattered excitedly with each footstep he took.

Ermentrude stopped.

"Wilf, remember that you have to enter willingly. It will be able to feel any reluctance," Ermentrude said.

"And if it does…?"

"I'm not sure," she said. "Its purpose is to protect witches, and Mathowytch, from wizards. You can't appear to be a threat, and then you should be able to pass unharmed through it."

"You think that's going to make me relax and enter cheerfully?" Wilf took a few backward steps. His ring flashed, which only added to his panic.

"Keep moving," the guard said. "You only have minutes to get inside once the talismans have been activated."

"Wow," Wilf muttered. "More really useful information that would have been nice to know."

"Stop being so negative," Ermentrude said. "We'll be with you the whole time. What could possibly go wrong?"

"Don't answer that," Katryna said, before Wilf could take a breath. "Please, Wilf. You can do this. I know you can. We're relying on you. I'm relying on you."

He glanced from Katryna, to Ermentrude, and then at the Veil. He was sure it would feel his loathing and fear.

Katryna laid a hand on his arm. She had a clear complexion with not a wart in sight. Her eyes seemed larger, and when she smiled, the golden flecks shone in her hazel eyes. Even her hair had lost its lank appearance. It must be frightening how quickly the virus was reducing her magic and making her pretty. He'd hate it if he lost all his soccer skills and couldn't play. The choice was simple. He'd already made the decision to help. Part of him screamed to run, but he locked the thought down, took a deep breath, and stepped closer to the Veil.

A gray strand unfurled and floated towards them. It wove around Ermentrude, then Wilf, and finally Katryna. It felt like a damp early morning mist as it grew to cover them completely.

His heart beat loudly as the Veil seemed to invade his body. He could feel a tickle in his nose and ears. He swallowed, and his throat's movement felt restricted. He fought the raising panic threatening to overrun his mind.

Katryna squeezed his arm, and he turned, but all he could see was her shadow. The Veil drew him forward and his feet obeyed.

"We're inside." Ermentrude's voice was muffled.

He could feel her hand on his arm as they moved. The mist started to lift to reveal a red stone pathway. It pulled back further, forming a tunnel, making Ermentrude and Katryna visible again.

"So far so good," Ermentrude said. "That is not an experience I would want to go through on a regular basis. How are you feeling?" She faced Wilf.

"Panicked and invaded," he said. "All I want is to get out of here as soon as possible, if not sooner."

"I'll second that," Katryna said. "Although, you have to admire the creation of something as complex as this magic. It's astonishing."

"I'll leave that to you. I'd rather not think about it at all," he said.

Ermentrude set off in front to lead the way.

A hand shot out, trying to grab him. "What the...?" He jerked back and collided into Katryna.

"I was afraid that the masking powder wouldn't work once we were inside," Ermentrude said. "This is powerful witch magic, and it won't be pleased that a wizard, even one with as little usable magic as you, is inside its spell."

"What does that mean?" Wilf's voice was a little higher than usual.

"It's probably going to try to destroy you," Ermentrude said. "I suggest we pick up the pace."

"Fantastic."

"Stop talking, and run," Katryna said as a second arm appeared through the tunnel wall.

Ermentrude's speed matched his as they dashed along the red path. Groans and thuds grew louder. He tripped over a foot but caught himself before he fell. A face appeared, but only its long nose made it through the wall. It drew back and thudded at it again. This time, a chin, nose, and leg appeared. He yelped and swerved around the apparition. Katryna was behind him, but he didn't dare to turn around to look. Screams, cackles, and thwacks filled the tunnel as the walls grew thinner and the tunnel narrower.

"How much longer?"

"No idea," Ermentrude said, between pants.

They turned the corner to find the tunnel filled with a faint mist.

"That's not good," Katryna said.

"Don't stop." Ermentrude plunged into the mist.

"But…" Wilf slowed down.

Katryna pushed him on, and he stumbled. A hand locked around his arm, pulling.

"Mom," Katryna yelled. "Wilf's in trouble."

Katryna grabbed hold of him and yanked.

He tried to pry the fingers open, but they felt like hooks piercing his skin.

"No." Ermentrude said, but Katryna had already sent a blast of magic.

He fell back as the arm withdrew.

"That wasn't a good idea," Ermentrude said. "You're not supposed to use magic inside this spell. Keep moving." She pushed Katryna into the lead, and then followed Wilf.

The tunnel began to dissolve, making it difficult to see the red path. A sharp, stabbing pain pierced Wilf's back. He staggered two faulting steps before he regained his stride and pushed on.

The mist covered the route, making Katryna and the path disappear. He plunged on regardless. It was the only option open to him. The pain in his back pulsed, sending new waves of searing agony through him with every step.

He stumbled forward. His fuzzy vision made the path tilt and sway. Holding out his arms, he tried to feel his way through the mist. Tendrils touched his face and he swatted at them. Ghostly figures reached for him, and pinpricks of pain caused him to flinch with each new touch.

Glowing in the distance, a bright red light shone like a beacon. He surged towards it, stumbling as he went. A high-pitched scream came from behind him. He turned, but the mist was too dense to see through. The red light pulsed and he glanced around, desperate to find an escape. Tendrils of mist wove together along the sides of the path, forming a tightly-knit fence. The outline of a woman in a long, floating gown of purple mist swept down towards him. Her eyes glowed amber.

"Give me the journal," the specter shouted. "Wizard magic will corrupt the Veil."

His pocket banged against his leg. He reached inside. The journal vibrated and he stoked its cover. The book quieted with a shudder.

He moved to meet the mist head on. His only option was to dash through as quickly as he could. Dodging along the path, he imagined dribbling a soccer ball while looking for a gap in mist figure's defense as she bore down on him. Her arms extended, and from her fingertips flashes of blue energy crackled and fizzed. Then, he saw his chance. The apparition hovered slightly above the ground. He sprung forward and then slid along the ground in a slide tackle that would have gained him a red card in any match.

He pushed on his legs and sprang up into a full charge for the red light as fast as his adrenaline-enhanced legs would carry him. Screams of outrage filled the void as the woman spun around to chase him. The maneuver had given him the edge he needed, and he sprinted for the goal: the red light and the doorway out of the Veil.

"Never return," the woman's voice filled his head as he broke free from the last clinging tendrils of mist.

"Welcome to Kureyamage," Ermentrude said as Wilf skidded to a halt on the wet cobblestone street.

He stood with his hands on his knees, sucking in air.

A flash lit up the street from Ermentrude's fingers.

His back throbbed, but the pain had disappeared.

Ermentrude held a wriggling hand with long, red fingernails. "I don't think you need an extra hand." She tossed it over her shoulder, and the Veil reached out to catch it.

"Really, Mom?" Katryna sighed.

"I'm glad you both think it's funny. I very nearly didn't make it out of there."

"But you did." Katryna spoke to Ermentrude, "Which way do we go?"

"This way." She led them down the road to the right. "We have to avoid the patrols. Witches have to wear a bracelet to show they're citizens of Kureyamage." She moved off, and then stopped. "Don't let Hywel put one on you, Katryna. He will probably try, but you wouldn't be able to return to Mathowytch if you're wearing one."

Katryna nodded, and Ermentrude set off again.

Wilf moved the muscles in his back. They felt sore but were no longer painful. Kureyamage reminded him of the narrow streets and alleys of Kowloon. It was in vast contrast to the glass and steel structures of Mathowytch. A dark, secretive atmosphere lingered in this city. The buildings leaned against each other, trying to catch glimpses through their neighbor's shuttered windows.

Ermentrude wove her way through back alleys, avoiding the main streets, like a city native. They climbed up a long, winding hill, edged on both sides by high stone walls. Large wooden doors with metal studs and hinges appeared at irregular intervals. Signs threatening bodily harm flickered on and off above each entrance. At the top of the hill, dominating the street, stood a lone tower.

"Here we are." Ermentrude paused to take a few deep breaths. "I'd forgotten what a climb that was." She placed her hand on the panel next to an impressive twin-lintel double door.

"Seems I'm not forgotten." She stepped over the raised threshold of a small entrance that materialized inside the larger right door. Wilf had to duck as he went through the door and into a small courtyard. Ermentrude tutted as she went past a neglected fountain that stood in the center.

The door opened and light spread out. A man only a few inches shorter than Wilf stepped out. He wore dark pants, shirt, and a sweater. His white hair was cut short. A globe of light floated over to them.

"I see you remembered your way," Hywel said.

"Indeed." Ermentrude stopped in front of the wizard.

In the light of the globe, he could see faint red veins on Hywel's wide nose and ruddy cheeks, above a neatly-trimmed beard. The smile on his full, fleshy lips didn't reach his black eyes.

"Come inside." Hywel moved to allow his guests to enter.

Ermentrude, Katryna, and Wilf stepped into the large marble-floored entrance. The door closed with a bang.

Hywel beckoned them to follow him up the stairs to the main floor.

"Your stepsister should be joining us soon," Hywel said to Wilf.

Hywel was Myra's friend in Kureyamage. Wilf wasn't sure if her arrival would be good news or not, but he doubted this family reunion would go as Katryna hoped.

# Chapter Fourteen
## Katryna's Bedroom

Katryna stopped in the doorway of the living room.

Hywel sat in a wing-backed chair next to a large fireplace. Ermentrude perched on the edge of an overstuffed, flower-upholstered armchair opposite the wizard. A footstool bounded across the room and positioned in front of her.

"I'll never forgive you for taking my daughter." Hywel moved over to the fireplace. He glared down at Ermentrude.

Katryna edged back into the hall, where she could listen without being seen.

"You didn't even know she was alive most of the time, unless it was to be annoyed by her." Ermentrude folded her arms into her lap.

"That's a lie, and you know it. I was around as much as you. The way I remember it, you were always rushing off to your little meetings. She spent most of her time with the housekeeper, if the truth were told."

"My little meetings. Isn't that typically condescending of you?" Ermentrude said.

"If I'd known what you were involved in, I would have banned you from ever leaving the house." Hywel spat the words at Ermentrude.

"And that's another reason why I left with Katryna." All pretense of civility was being stripped away with each comment. "So she wouldn't have to put up with your draconian ways."

"You could have destroyed everything I'd worked for if your treason had been discovered."

"So, what you're saying is that it was a good thing I left," Ermentrude sat back in her chair, a smug look on her face. "That way you couldn't be tarnished by association."

"Trust you to twist every word I say." Hywel balled his fists at his sides. His whole body seemed rigid with rage. "You probably cast a love spell over me when we met."

"You're delusional." Ermentrude leaned forward. "You think I would have chosen to be linked to you? It was arranged. I had no say in the matter."

Hywel took a deep breath. "Someone was able to manage you. I find that really hard to believe. Isn't it time you grew up and stopped looking for the next adventure? In a witch of your age, that's not an attractive characteristic."

"How did you manage to arrange for Wilf and I to be delivered to you?"

Hywel's face turned red. "I've no idea what you're talking about."

Ermentrude tapped the footstool with her foot, and it backed away. She stood to face her ex-husband.

"Who are you talking to at the Witch Council? It's a very simple question to answer."

Hywel stuttered.

"Oh, come now." Ermentrude advanced on him. "Did you think I came all this way to discuss the old days with you?"

"You came because you needed my help with young Wilf." Hywel took several steps back and bumped into the chair. He sat down with a thud.

Ermentrude raised her hand. "Perhaps I can help you to be a little more co-operative."

Hywel clapped his hands and Katryna turned around as she heard running feet. Guards burst into the room and surrounded Ermentrude.

"This witch threatened me in my own house. Take her to the basement cells," Hywel said. "She is to stand trial for treason and sedition by order of the Wizard Council."

A guard secured Ermentrude's arms.

"No," Katryna ran into the room. "Leave my mother alone."

Another guard grabbed hold of Katryna.

"Katryna, you heard her. How can I let her wander around the city? She's a terrorist." Hywel stepped over to Katryna. "I know this is upsetting, but it's for your own good. You don't want to be associated with her kind."

Katryna raised her hand and spread her fingers.

"That is insulting," Hywel said. His ring flashed and Katryna collapsed to the floor. "Take my daughter."

The guards escorted Ermentrude.

"You're a tyrant," Katryna screamed as the guards carried her to her room.

Katryna was placed on her bed. A tingling spread over her body as the spell dissipated. She ran to the door and tugged on the handle, but it wouldn't move. She beat on it, tears of frustration running down her cheeks. Finally, she sent fire bolts at it, but they puffed out as soon as they touched the wooden surface.

Exhausted, she collapsed onto the bed. Her knuckles were red and swollen, and her throat hurt from all the useless shouting she'd done. The door didn't even have a scorch mark on it. There should have been a large hole.

She rolled over onto her side and faced the wall. A white bear in a black top and skirt sat in the corner. She reached over, picked it up, and hurled it over her shoulder onto the floor. She needed to sleep, but she didn't trust Hywel not to be waiting for her to do that. He could be watching her now.

She sat up and glanced at the dark communication mirror on the dresser. It didn't seem to be active, but you could never be too sure. She moved off the bed, opened a drawer, took out a child's sweater, and placed it over the glass. Then, she continued opening drawers. They were all full of a small child's clothes. Hywel had kept all her outfits.

It took her several attempts before she could light the globes around the room. At least she hadn't completely depleted her magic, but it was very low.

She studied the room in the dim light. The windows were shuttered. A small, pink chest stood at the foot of the bed and a child's moon and stars quilt was draped down on it. The silk rug covering the floor had a picture of a witch flying on a broomstick. Along its border were cats of various colors, shapes, and breeds. The bookcase took over an entire wall. Its shelves held ornaments, dolls, and books. She ran her finger down some of the spines and read the titles: a witch's first spell book, an alphabet book, a book of witch tales, stories of wizards throughout history.

Someone knocked at the door.

"Is it safe to come in?" Hywel asked. "I've brought you something to eat."

"Do what you want." She retreated to sit on the bed, facing the door.

He came in, and a tray floated over to the nightstand.

"Do you remember me at all?"

"No."

"I've missed you," he said. "It was a cruel and selfish act on Ermentrude's part to take you away."

"Don't you dare talk about my mother that way. She's a brave and noble witch."

"Shhh." He picked up the witch bear. "You mustn't talk that way. Ermentrude is a traitor to the wizard state. She's led raids against the Council and endangered lives."

"I'm pleased there are witches that stand up to your Council," she said.

"Have you ever given a thought as to how the selfish actions of a few degenerate witches have altered life here in Kureyamage? We've had to create new rules and restrictions almost on a daily basis. The citizens of Kureyamage live in constant fear of where your mother and her kind might strike next."

Katryna shook her head.

"No, I didn't think so." Hywel sat on the end of the bed. "The witches of Kureyamage are the real victims here. For self-preservation, we've had to curtail their freedoms one by one. Do you know they all have to wear bracelets showing which wizard they belong to?"

"Mom told me." Katryna edged along the bed, away from him.

"Did she indeed?" Red blotches appeared on his face and neck. "Did she also tell you that no witch is allowed out on her own after dark? A witch. Not allowed out after dark."

She didn't know what to believe. Hywel seemed to have sympathy for the witches of Kureyamage. He didn't seem at all the wizard her mother had described. It was confusing knowing whom to trust.

"It's outrageous the measures we've had to take. And it's all the fault of those unthinking, self-serving witches of Mathowytch." He took a deep breath and reached out to pat her arm.

"I had no idea," Katryna said in a hushed voice. "I've never thought of it that way."

"There is no such thing as a victimless crime." He shook his head. They sat in silence. "But, I think that's enough of politics for one night."

"I didn't know you were a supporter of witches' rights," she said.

Hywel smiled. "There's probably a lot you don't know about me. But, I didn't mean to get into all the injustice that's felt here." He straightened the bed cover. "I've looked forward to seeing you back in this room. You really don't remember living here at all?"

"When can I see my mother?"

"You can visit her tomorrow, if you want." Hywel gave a long sigh.

"You'll let me out?"

"Of course." He took a tight grip of her arm.

"What are you doing?"

"As I said, all witches in Kureyamage need to wear a family bracelet." He produced a black metal bracelet and snapped it around her right wrist.

She pulled, but he held her in a vice-like grip.

He pointed at the bracelet. The black stone at the center of his ring glowed and the clasp fused. 'Hywel Wakefield' had been etched into the band in white lettering.

He released her, and she fell back onto the bed.

"Now, you are free to travel around the city," he said.

"How could you?" Her whole body trembled, and tears blinded her.

"It's for your own safety," he said. "I'll leave you to your supper, but I look forward to seeing you in the morning." He walked to the door. "Oh, I should also tell you, the bracelet limits the amount of magic you are allowed to use. Although, looking at you, I don't think that should be a problem. It is very disappointing to see how pretty you are. You seemed such a promising child. I would have expected a daughter of mine to possess a lot more warts." He walked out of the room, and the door slammed shut behind him.

It opened again slowly, and Katryna backed into the corner of the bed. Wilf peered around it.

"How did you open that?"

"It wasn't locked."

"I don't suppose Hywel feels the need now." She held up her wrist. "Look what he's done."

"Ermentrude told you not to let him put a bracelet on you."

"Yes, I know. But I just couldn't resist such a beautiful piece of jewelry." Katryna burst into tears. He sat down beside her.

"Look at me. I used to be such an ugly witch," she said, through sobs.

"I think you're ugly." He took her hand.

"You're just saying that to make me feel better."

"No. I mean it."

"You realize I can't go back to Mathowytch now? And I can't do magic. I can't even walk in the street when it's dark."

"That's bad."

She buried her head in the pillow. "I wish I'd never come here."

"It sounds like your father and mine would have been great friends," Wilf said.

# Chapter Fifteen
## Hywel's Workshop

Wilf followed Hywel down the dark, twisting stone steps. He tripped several times on the uneven floor. A globe floated along, giving a dim light.

In front of him stretched a long passage. Its dank walls emitted a musty smell of earth and damp. Small rivulets of water trickled along the mud floor. He splashed through a couple of small puddles trying to keep up with the wizard.

"Your workshop is down here?"

"This passage connects my tower to the Central Palace." Hywel's cloak trailed along the ground, picking up its hem over the puddles. "It's quicker than walking down the hill and up the next street. My grandfather, when he was Chief Wizard, excavated this passage to connect the tower and Palace."

Wilf followed Hywel, but his thoughts wandered.

He should be grateful Hywel had rescued him from Ermentrude, but he wasn't sure he hadn't merely changed captors. Katryna hadn't replied when he'd knocked this morning, and her door was locked again. Hopefully, nothing else had happened to the young witch.

"Can't we stay in your study?" Being trapped underground with Hywel wasn't adding to his comfort level.

"No. I want to show you what your father and I were working on."

"But I thought he collaborated with the Mathowytch witches." His father had been working for both sides. It would be like him to try to manipulate every situation.

"It's true we didn't agree over this Pulch Virus business, but previously we'd been trying to create magical biomes in your realm together." A large door appeared on their right, and a key rose out of Hywel's pocket and into the materializing lock. It turned with a clank, followed by the sound of bolts sliding. The door swung open on creaking hinges.

"It's a bit medieval looking. You sure there aren't any irons and racks to torture people in there?"

Hywel laughed. "It amazes me, the imagination of teenagers. Although, in this case you are half-right. The dungeons, during my grandfather's time, were rather busy. I believe he put enemies, and a few rivals, down here."

Wilf shuddered.

"But of course, that was centuries ago." Hywel stepped into the room and beckoned Wilf to follow.

Wilf wrinkled his nose at the room's mixture of smells. The walls were painted with magical symbols and signs in bright blue, red, and gold. The large, scrubbed, rectangular wooden table occupying the center of the room reminded him of his father's. Benches stood on each side.

One wall had floor-to-ceiling shelves containing jars, vials, and canisters, all labeled with signs. On the opposite wall, similar shelvings held books and scrolls. A slowly-rotating mobile of multiple colored spheres hung from the ceiling in one corner. A round communication mirror dominated the remaining wall.

Hywel turned towards the mirror. "You remember that from your father's workshop?"

"I didn't visit it very often."

The wizard went over to the scrolls on the bookcase. "Sit over there." He nodded towards two comfortable wing-backed chairs that stood on either side of a table with a chessboard carved into its surface.

He watched as Hywel touched several scrolls and a large leather-bound book. They floated over and settled down on the chess table.

"What is a biome?"

"An entire ecosystem under a protective dome that maintains magical energy. Here, look at this." Hywel said.

He studied the symbols running in columns down the page and glanced back up at Hywel.

"Don't you read symbolic language?"

Wilf shook his head.

"Oh," Hywel said. "I would have thought…" He unrolled another scroll. Number formulae covered this one. "Numeric code?"

He looked up at the wizard.

"Impossible. You really don't have even the smallest amount of wizard training." Hywel let the parchment snap shut.

"Sorry," Wilf said, although he wasn't sure why he should be apologizing.

Hywel sat in the chair facing him, leaned back, and steepled his fingers.

Wilf fidgeted under the wizard's scrutiny.

A younger man entered.

"Let me see the journal." Hywel held out his hand.

The young wizard shuffled over to Wilf and took the journal out of Wilf's pocket.

"Hey!" Wilf made a grab to reclaim the book.

"I don't believe you know Thiemus, Myra's brother," Hywel said.

Thiemus handed the journal to Hywel.

"She never mentioned a brother." Wilf tried not to look at Thiemus' shriveled left arm. The young wizard's features were similar to Myra's. He had the same blond hair, and he was also short, but his body looked powerful. Their eyes met, and Wilf saw pure hatred in them.

"Thiemus, how old were you when you had your little accident?" Hywel asked.

"16."

"It could have been a lot worse. He only lost the ability to use his arm and acquired a limp," Hywel said. "But, at least it wasn't his dominant hand. He's been taught how to use magic safely now. It's such a pity his mother didn't have him trained at a young age by a wizard."

"Why didn't Griselda bring you with her? My father would have loved to have a wizard to train," Wilf said.

"That witch wasn't allowed to take a wizard out of the Realm," Thiemus said. "Wizard Hywel rescued me from her."

"Ah, yes," Hywel said. "If only I'd known sooner. Then, your roommate and your arm could both have been spared." He shook his head. "You see, Wilf, Thiemus didn't know he'd been tapping into his magic in his sleep. He simply dreamed of all the liquid leaving the other boy's body, and it actually did. Such a pity." Hywel leaned forward. "What about you, Wilf? Had any bad dreams come true?"

Wilf could feel the heat rising in his face.

"Been dabbling, I'll bet." Hywel held Wilf's gaze.

"It's dangerous doing that." Thiemus stroked his damaged hand.

"The problem is that you're almost 16 and haven't been taught the disciplines of magic." Hywel relaxed back into the chair and crossed his legs. "That makes you a danger to the societies of both realms. Using magic, and not being aware of it, means no control," he said in a hushed tone.

Wilf found breathing difficult, and his heart raced.

"What if you, like Thiemus, are angry at someone and wished them harm? You wouldn't mean to actually cause injury or death, but your magic would enable you to do so."

"And then, there are the dreams," Thiemus said, shaking his head.

"Dreams?"

"They can become very real, and with the aid of your magic, you could enter one. You might never find your way out of it. You'd be trapped inside your own nightmare."

A shiver ran down Wilf's spine, and his hands trembled.

"Wizards are taught to partition magic in a locked part of their minds while they sleep, to prevent such accidents," Hywel said.

"I would hate this to happen to anyone else." Thiemus raised his withered arm.

"My father would have told me if there was such a risk."

Hywel regarded him over his fingertips for a few moments.

"Would he? Perhaps he'd decided to keep a close eye on you," Hywel said. "Once you turned 16, he would then have to take steps to train you. The Wizard Council wouldn't have allowed you to remain unrestricted."

"Oh!" Wilf said.

"I can teach you to partition your mind once you have a rudimentary grasp of your magic." Hywel opened the journal and flicked through its blank pages. "An enchantment to prevent anyone but you from viewing it pages?"

"Maybe," Wilf said.

"Do I risk tampering with it?" Hywel asked. "That could destroy the journal."

"Then we can't risk that," Wilf said and reached for the journal, but Hywel sent it floating well out of reach.

"Why do you care if the Mathowytch hags catch the Pulch Virus?"

"Infecting witches to dominate them isn't right. Besides, I would have thought you'd want to find a cure for your own daughter."

Hywel sat up straight. His face drained of all color. "Katryna's been infected?"

"Didn't she tell you? That's why her looks have changed."

Hywel got up, and the journal floated down to the table. He paced up and down the workshop. He stopped in front of Wilf.

"This puts a different complexion on the problem. You are going to commence studying magic immediately."

"I'm willing to learn to control my magic, so I can't harm anyone with it," he said, glaring at the wizard. "But as soon as I have enough power to reveal the contents of the journal, I'm returning to Hong Kong and my life there."

"Are you sure?" Hywel took a step back. "Magic has a lot to offer."

"I am," he said without hesitation.

"Then we'd better get started." Hywel went over to one of the shelves. "These are all the first spells you will need to perform." He took down a large book. "They are the basis for everything else that will come later." The tome landed on the table with a thud. "Since you are about ten years behind in your education, I suggest you study this book cover to cover. You can take it back to your room with you."

He went to speak, but Hywel held up his hand.

"I have shielded your room. It's what we always do when wizards are first discovering their ability. You can practice without fear of injury to any of us. Permanent injury, that is." Hywel opened the book and flicked through the introductory pages to the first lesson, which was about how to light a globe. He summoned a globe off its wall stand, and it floated over to Wilf.

"The secret with magic is being able to see what you want to achieve. For instance, I want the globe to extinguish, so in my mind I see an unlit globe," Hywel said. The light went out. "Now you visualize it lit."

He looked at the dark globe and concentrated, trying to visualize a lit globe. It remained dark. Not even a flicker.

"Are you trying?" Hywel said.

"Yes." He closed his eyes and held his breath. Light, he pleaded silently, opening his eyes. The globe wouldn't cooperate. It remained stubbornly extinguished.

The furrows on Hywel's brow deepened, and the black stone in his ring flared.

"Perhaps it would be better if he practices on his own," Thiemus said. "Without an audience."

"What?" Hywel glared at his assistant. "Perhaps you are right. Leave us."

Thiemus held the door open.

Wilf put the journal in his pocket, lifted the heavy book, and wandered into the corridor.

"At dinner tonight, you can demonstrate your progress," Hywel said.

"I'm sure you can find your own way back to the tower." Thiemus closed the door, leaving Wilf standing in the cold, dank corridor.

The light globes in the corridor began to fade.

"Seriously?"

Pop! All the globes went dark.

He took out his cell phone and started the flashlight app. The battery life was less than 20%.

"Bloody wizards." He started running down the passage, towards Hywel's tower.

# Chapter Sixteen
## Myra Arrives at Hywel's Tower

Myra entered the tower as her stepbrother came crashing up the stairs from the basement, panting and holding a large, heavy book.

"Wilf?"

"You work for Hywel?" he asked, through gulps of air.

"I do errands for him—sometimes." She adjusted the strap of her backpack.

"Is that why you were looking for the journal? To give it to Hywel?"

"It was my ticket back to Kureyamage, since you were so insistent on staying in Hong Kong." She met his gaze.

"You were going to bail on me after Father evaporated?" He shifted the weight of the book.

"I would have made sure you were safe."

"Wow! You've been my sister for nine years, but I don't know you at all." He stepped around her and headed for the stairs.

"I know you're pissed I left you at Ermentrude's, but honestly she had the best plan for getting you here."

"Forget it. The trip through the Veil, with permission, was frightening enough." He climbed the stairs. "I'm getting used to being abandoned by you."

"That's unfair." Myra followed him. She motioned towards the book. "A little light reading?"

"Hywel and your brother gave it to me."

"So you've met Thiemus. How is he?"

"He's seems very... serious, but that's probably a result of his injuries." He'd reached the first floor and stopped.

"Do you know what happened?"

"Hywel said it was because he couldn't control his magic." He put the book down on a small hall table and shook his arms. "Why didn't Father warn me?"

"You wouldn't have listened. I know he worried about the leaks of magic that had started to happen. I think when you broke the

Mage's Crystal… Well, after you left that morning, he was very concerned."

"You think I caused him to evaporate?" His ring flared.

"Of course not." She reached out to put a hand on his arm. "I meant he was terribly worried, that's all. If he hadn't evaporated, I think he would have explained why you needed to study magic."

"This is all too much to take in." He put one foot on the stairs leading to the upper levels.

"So, how did Hywel entice you to start your studies?"

"He didn't." He wouldn't meet her eyes.

"Then why?"

Wilf tucked the book under his arm, and continuing up the stairs, said, "It's my decision to learn enough magic to help Katryna."

She followed him to his room.

"Years of resistance washed away because of some teenage witch you've just met?" She gave a bark of laughter.

"No. I'm going to know enough magic to read the formula, and then I'm returning to Hong Kong."

"Hywel agreed?" Myra entered the room.

"Yes. I'll give him the journal and leave."

The wizard had convinced Wilf to turn over the journal to him. She didn't know what game Hywel was playing or how it involved Thiemus, but her brother's injuries were not a result of him being untrained. That much she did know.

"Are you sure that's wise? Did it cross your mind to wonder why Reginald put a non-reveal spell on the journal?" She took a deep breath, trying to control her temper. "Probably, and this is just a guess, it was to protect you from wizards like Hywel and my brother."

"I know why he put that spell on it: to force me to use magic. And it's worked. He finally found a way." His voice rose. "Once I hand over his journal, I no longer have to use my magic unless I want to."

"Still trying to outsmart your father?"

"And finally succeeding." His eyes shone brightly.

"I wouldn't bet on it," she said.

He threw the book of spells on his bed.

"What do you care?" He clenched his fists, and his lips thinned.

"I'm not the bad guy. If you remember, I was injured trying to save you from Ermentrude."

"Only because she was taking me to the wrong city." He pointed at her and the ruby at the center of his ring ignited.

She ducked, covering her head with her arms. A globe exploded on the wall behind her.

"What the?" His eyes were wide as he stared at the shattered glass. "Hywel said this room was shielded. I'm so sorry. I didn't mean to do that." He shoved his hand into his pocket.

"The shielding doesn't work on small accidents inside the room." Myra wriggled her fingers and the broken fragments came together. The repaired globe floated back to its stand. "They're to encourage you to work harder."

He collapsed onto the bed.

"There's more magic in this realm. That's why control is so important." She sat beside him.

"My father's managed to make me a target in this power struggle. The only way for me to escape is to give them what they want. Then, I'm out of here, and they can leave me alone. I don't see another way to survive."

She shook her head. He was so naive if he thought he could take on both Councils and win.

"Are you going to help me? Or now that I've been delivered to Hywel, is your mission completed?"

"My mission, as you call it, had to do with the journal, not you." Taking hold of his chin, she turned his face towards her. "I'm sorry if you no longer trust me. I can understand it, but I am on your side. I will always try to protect and help you." She dropped her hand to the book and flipped over to a page on lighting globes. "Let's start with something simple."

She wriggled her fingers at a globe, and it floated from its wall bracket into Wilf's outstretched left hand.

"I already tried to light one of those and failed."

"Relax. Can you feel the place inside of you where the energy is stored?"

He shook his head.

"Close your eyes. Take some deep breaths. Focus on them to clear your mind. Push any thoughts away before they're fully formed. Breath in for five counts, hold for five, and then release for five." She spoke in a soft voice with no intonation.

Wilf followed the breathing pattern.

"Keep your eyes closed, and place your ringed finger on the globe."

He did as she asked, and the globe flickered weakly into light, and then instantly extinguished.

The globe slid from his fingers and rolled under the bed.

"What is it?" she asked.

His face had lost all its color and he trembled.

"I remember what it feels like to use magic." He stood up and stumbled over to the window.

"This is different." She stood next to him and placed her hand on his shoulder. "What happened with your mother was a freak accident of misdirected magic. Here, you'll learn control. Nothing like that can ever happen again."

"It felt the same. A part of me seemed to meld with this outside energy source." He looked like a cornered rabbit. "There's so much trying to force its way through me."

"You have to learn to allow only a small amount to enter at a time, otherwise it will consume you. It can become addictive to be connected to that much power."

Wilf glanced over to the bed. Myra wriggled her fingers. The globe rolled back into view, and then floated to its wall bracket.

"Perhaps you should read the first few chapters of that book. It will explain wizard magic better than I can."

"Thanks." He hugged her.

"I'd better find the housekeeper and let her know I've arrived." She picked up the book, put it on the bedside table and left the room.

She wriggled her fingers to light and extinguish globes as she strolled down the corridors.

*Poor Wilf.* She couldn't image being that scared of something so wonderful. She felt the prickles of pleasure connecting with that power.

Hywel's housekeeper stood directing the kitchen.

"You're like the conductor of a philharmonic orchestra," Myra said.

"A what, Dear?"

Pots bubbled on the stove. Dishes washed themselves in the sink. A broom swept the floor, and the garbage pail returned from a trip outside.

"Never mind," she said. "Is there a room ready for me?"

"Third floor at the back. Hywel said you'd need access to the back stairs."

"Very thoughtful of him." She helped herself to a muffin from the cooling rack. "Where did he put Ermentrude and Katryna?"

"The traitor he sent to the cells almost as soon as she stepped over the threshold," the housekeeper said, wiping her hands down her apron. "His daughter is refusing to leave her old bedroom on the second floor. I'm getting sick of sending trays up that are never touched."

"He had Ermentrude locked up? The Witch Council isn't going to like that," Myra said.

"Who cares what a bunch of renegade witches think?" the housekeeper said. "It would be better for everyone if they stopped all this nonsense and gave themselves up. If you ask my opinion, they should be begging for mercy from the Wizard Council, not attacking innocent wizards and witches."

"That's not going to happen." She licked the tips of her fingers.

"He's put a bracelet on his daughter," the housekeeper said.

"Hywel's made sure she can't leave. Well, that was only to be expected," Myra said, shrugging her shoulders. "One less witch to worry about in Mathowytch."

"He's feeling pretty pleased with himself at the moment," the housekeeper said. She nodded at Myra. "You should ask him for a bracelet of your own."

"Perhaps," she said, leaving the kitchen and heading for her room.

A month ago, she would have done any task he'd asked to secure a bracelet. Now, she wasn't in such a hurry. There were parts to this puzzle she hadn't solved yet. No need to rush into making a decision that would curtail her freedom. She was much better off playing a wait-and-watch game. Later, she could make a more informed decision, if he offered. That would definitely be the smartest option. The one resolution she would keep was to stay close to Wilf and that journal. Nothing was going to make her break that promise.

# Chapter Seventeen
# Ermentrude's Trial

Wilf dined alone in his room, relieved not to have to answer questions about his progress. The journal sat on the nightstand. He placed his ringed hand on the cover and the locks sprung open.

Pages fluttered and turned to the dedication page. He reached to close the book, but his ring flared as he touched the corner and ripples ran across the page. He lifted his hand quickly as the journal snapped shut and then opened at the *Wilf Gilvary* section.

*To access his magic, Wilf needed to forget the past and embrace his future.*

"Really good advice," he said. "Not at all helpful."

*But he would be wiser to learn from the past and trust in his future.*

"That's it." He touched the page. The ruby glowed and the words disappeared.

"Great. I have a journal full of life-affirming anecdotes. Can't you give me the formula without all this cryptic shit?"

The journal snapped shut and locked.

He shoved the book in a drawer and wandered downstairs for breakfast.

"Did you spend the night in the dark, or were you finally able to perform a kindergarten level of magic and succeed in lighting a globe?" Thiemus asked, before bursting into laughter.

He'd been glad when Hywel and Katryna appeared.

Soon, they'd all left for the courthouse, but Thiemus' comment still rankled him.

The oppressive courtroom had a strange half-light to it from the dimmed globes. A loud buzz of gossip permeated the room from the witches and wizards jostling each other for a better viewing position in the gallery.

Distinguished-looking wizards in long, flowing cloaks nodded at Hywel as he headed for the front row.

Once they were seated, Wilf glanced over his shoulder, trying to locate Myra in the crowded gallery. Thiemus' blond hair made him easily visible.

Silence fell as Ermentrude entered from a side door, escorted by two guards. Her hands, handcuffed and covered, were secured behind. She stood erect in the dock and stared ahead at the unoccupied judges' bench. The gallery erupted into noisy chatter.

The 11 members of the jury filed into the room and sat down.

"Not one witch," Katryna whispered.

The clerk, usher, and lawyers entered the room and sat in their appropriate places. Files and papers appeared in front of them, and they proceeded to shuffle through the documents. One lawyer went over to talk to Ermentrude, but she turned away from him. He returned to his table when the usher stepped up on the dais and opened the door behind the judges' bench.

"All rise," the usher said.

Chairs scraped across the tiled floor as everyone stood. Loud shushing noises came from the gallery.

Five white-haired wizards, all wearing long, flowing robes of different colors, entered the courtroom. The first wizard wore a blue robe with three gold bands on his shoulder. He was thin and of average height, with an angular nose and large ears.

The next wizard also wore a blue robe, but he had four gold bands on his shoulder. He made his colleague look overweight. He sat taking up only a third of the chair, and slouched forward. He took a ragged breath through lips almost the same shade as his robe. Wilf wasn't sure the wizard would survive the trail, he appeared that frail.

The third wizard was a stout figure dressed in a burgundy robe with white fur trimming. Five gold bands decorated his shoulder. He nodded to several of the wizards in the courtroom like royalty acknowledging his subjects. His white hair was thin on top, except for several wispy strands combed strategically across his scalp. He had a doughy face with sunken, beady eyes. He sat in the central ornate chair of the Head Judge.

The last two wizards wore emerald robes with two gold bands on their shoulders. One was a large wizard. His chair creaked ominously when he sat. The final wizard's small neck and head poked out from the oversized collar of his robe. He sat and faded into the cushioned backrest, becoming almost invisible.

With the parade of judges completed, everyone sat, except Ermentrude.

The black-robed clerk handed several documents to the Head Judge.

"The case before the court today is that Ermentrude Wakefield, a witch currently residing in Mathowytch, did willfully participate in the Witches' Rebellion. That she did cause damage to buildings belonging to the people of Kureyamage. Also, that she performed acts of terror against the witches and wizards of Kureyamage. The accused also kidnapped a young wizard and abducted Wizard Hywel Wakefield's only daughter, Katryna." The clerk took a breath. "Ermentrude Wakefield, these are the charges laid against you. Do you understand them?"

"Yes," Ermentrude said.

"How do you plead? Guilty or not guilty?" the clerk asked.

"Not guilty."

"You may be seated," the Head Judge said. "Wizard Forsyth, please make your opening statement."

The short black-robed wizard in front of Wilf stood up and cleared his throat.

"Thank you, Your Honor," Wizard Forsyth said. "I will prove that this witch has, on numerous occasions, entered this city illegally with the sole intention of undermining the Rule of Wizard law." He pointed at Ermentrude as he spoke. "She was responsible, with others of her coven, in creating the monstrous Veil that has robbed this city of its newest borough, Mathowytch. A borough built at tremendous expense to this city, and stolen in a manner that caused several wizards to evaporate prematurely. This witch, members of the jury, is a cold, calculating terrorist with no loyalty to the society she grew up in. Not only is she accused of abducting her daughter and robbing the child of the love and protection of her father, but she has now kidnapped a young wizard from outside the Magical Realm. For what purpose, I shudder to think."

There were cries of 'shame on her' and 'burn the witch'.

The Head Judge banged his gravel. "Silence from the gallery."

"Your Honor, I now call Hywel Wakefield to the stand," Wizard Forsyth said.

The usher led Hywel to the witness box.

"Place your dominant hand on the Book of Oaths," the usher said. "Please repeat after me. I promise to tell the truth, the whole truth, and nothing but the truth."

Hywel repeated the oath and then handed the book back to the usher.

"Please, tell us your full name for the record," Wizard Forsyth said.

"Wizard Hywel Wakefield."

"Your occupation?" Wizard Forsyth asked.

"I'm the lead scientist in biomes for the Wizard Council."

"And tell us your relationship to the defendant," Wizard Forsyth said.

"She is my wife and the mother of my child, Katryna." He stared directly at Ermentrude.

"Please, tell the court briefly what you know of the activities of Witch Wakefield," Wizard Forsyth said.

"14 years ago, I arrived back at my tower to discover that Ermentrude had left me a note."

"See Exhibit A." Wizard Forsyth handed an evidence bag to the usher. The usher took it to the judges. They examined the contents, and then handed it back to the usher.

"Please hand the note to Wizard Hywel," Wizard Forsyth said. "Can you read it for the court, please?"

Hywel took out a pair of half-moon glasses and perched them on his nose.

"Don't look for me, because I'm never coming back. I'm taking Katryna. She will grow up in a society that appreciates witches and doesn't try to suppress them at every turn. Goodbye."

Murmuring came from the gallery. The Head Judge banged his gravel again for silence.

The usher took the note and returned it to Wizard Forsyth.

"Did you have any idea that your wife had been involved with treason?"

"Not until I read that note," Hywel said.

"And what happened next?" Wizard Forsyth prompted his witness.

"I went looking for them but discovered that Ermentrude was part of the coven of witches who had stolen the borough of Mathowytch and performed the most outrageous incantation to produce the Veil."

"Isn't that hearsay?" Katryna whispered to Wilf. "Why isn't the defense lawyer objecting?"

"I think the outcome has already been decided."

Her face lost all its color, and she slumped back into her chair.

He placed his hand over hers and squeezed it.

Hywel adjusted the cuffs of his shirtsleeves. "I was worried what would happen to Katryna under the influence of a witch with such rebellious attitudes."

"And in your opinion, what do you think prompted Witch Wakefield to return, given that she had stated in her note that she was never coming back?" Wizard Forsyth glanced at Ermentrude.

"Mother's never going to get a fair hearing, is she?" Katryna asked.

Wilf shook his head. This was a hatchet job.

"She had recently kidnapped a young wizard, the son of Reginald Gilvary, and the Witch Council requested my help with the boy," Hywel said.

"She had kidnapped an orphaned young wizard." Wizard Forsyth added emphasis to each word. "But why would the Witch Council contact you?"

"I had heard, from one of my sources, that Ermentrude had taken the boy, and so I made contact with the Council. They wanted Wilf deported as soon as it could be arranged, and I offered to take him, as long as my daughter was returned."

"Young Wilf here must be very indebted to you for his rescue," Wizard Forsyth said.

"I'm glad I could be of service," Hywel said.

"Thank you," Wizard Forsyth said. "I have nothing further to ask, but please stay there, as my learned friend may have some questions for you."

Ermentrude's defense lawyer stood up and cleared his throat. The Head Judge gave him a withering stare.

"I have no questions for this witness, Uncle. Sorry, I mean Your Honor." He sat back down.

The Head Judge nodded at the usher, who then led Hywel back to his seat.

Wizard Forsyth stood again. "Your Honor, I now call upon Wilf Gilvary."

"What?" Wilf said.

"Nothing to worry about," Hywel said, waiting to let him out of the row.

He was ushered to the witness stand and sworn in.

"Is it true," Wizard Forsyth said, "that Witch Ermentrude Wakefield brought you from Hong Kong and has performed incantations on you without your permission?"

There was an intake of breath from the gallery.

"Yes, but…" Wilf said.

"Please, restrict yourself to answering only the questions I ask you," Wizard Forsyth said. "Is it further true that she brought you into Kureyamage through the Veil?"

"Yes."

"While you were in Mathowytch, did she perform witch magic on you to keep you a prisoner in her home?"

Wilf stared first at Ermentrude, then at Katryna. He wished he could help.

"Yes."

"Could you speak a little louder?" Wizard Forsyth said.

"Yes."

"And tell the court why you were brought here," Wizard Forsyth said.

Wilf struggled to keep his mouth closed. He could feel the beads of sweat on his forehead. It was no use. The oath compelled him to speak.

"My father, Reginald Gilvary, left a journal that only I can read, but I must perform magic for it to reveal its contents. The Witch Council wants Wizard Hywel to help advance my abilities, so they can…" Wilf paused. He didn't want to give damaging evidence against Ermentrude. He had no desire to see her locked away in a wizard prison, but he couldn't stop talking.

"Continue," Wizard Forsyth said.

"They wanted to be able to read my father's journal because…"

"Yes." Wizard Forsyth leaned forward and smiled, showing small, pointed teeth.

"Because…" Wilf struggled not to speak. He looked over at the defense lawyer, wanting him to object. They seemed to do that a lot in the movies, but not in this court. "It contains a vaccine formula that will prevent the spread of the Virus."

"I see," Wizard Forsyth said. "No further questions, Your Honor." He sat down, leaned back in his chair, and crossed his legs at the ankle.

"I've no questions for the witness." The defense lawyer said, bobbing up and down from his chair.

"That's outrageous," Katryna said.

"Silence. If I hear another word, you will be removed from the court," the Head Judge said.

Hywel laid a hand on her arm as the usher brought Wilf back to sit with them.

"Why did you tell them all that information?" Katryna asked.

"I couldn't stop myself." Wilf folded his arms across his chest. "The oath makes you tell the truth, and that's why the defense isn't asking any questions."

The Head Judge turned to Wizard Forsyth. "Do you have any other witnesses?"

"Not at this time, Your Honor. Unless I need more?"

"I don't think that will be necessary," the Head Judge said. "Wizard Wilson, do you have any witnesses for the defense?"

"No, Your Honor. There is no one willing to testify on behalf of this witch."

"Very well," the Head Judge said. "Closing speeches."

Wizard Forsyth strutted over to the jury.

"Thank you, Your Honor." He cleared his throat. "Members of the jury, as you have seen, this witch is guilty of kidnapping and repeated spell attacks on a minor wizard. Her character was already known to the authorities when she abducted Katryna Wakefield from her loving father, 14 years ago." He paused. "This witch is also known for sedition and for her participation in the occupation of Mathowytch, a borough rightfully belonging to the wizards of this great city." He spun on his heel and walked over to stand in front of Ermentrude.

"This witch is dangerous and holds our society in contempt. I shudder to think what would have happened to poor, defenseless, fatherless Wilf Gilvary if Wizard Hywel hadn't rescued him. As you have heard from my learned friend, no one is willing to stand as a character witness for this... witch. Not one single person. That is telling in itself." He gestured towards Ermentrude.

"This witch is guilty. There can be no question." He sat down with a flourish, and a smile.

"Wizard Wilson, would you like to give a closing argument?" the Head Judge asked.

Wizard Wilson stood up and walked over to the jury. "Members of the jury," he said. "It has been difficult for me to perform my role when there is no defense I could find. All I can do is reiterate that Ermentrude says she isn't guilty."

He turned and walked back to his seat with his head lowered.

"You call this a proper trial?" Katryna shouted.

"I warned you," said the Head Judge. "Usher, have that young witch removed from the court. If this is an example of the way witches are being educated in Mathowytch, I shudder to think of the lawlessness there must be in that city."

The usher spoke to two guards, who came over, grabbed Katryna's arm, and dragged her from the court.

Wilf went to follow, but Hywel placed a restraining hand on his arm. "She'll be fine. They know she's my daughter."

The Head Judge now addressed the jury.

"I think this case is a simple one. Witch Ermentrude has been unable to offer a defense and, therefore, must be found guilty. I don't expect it to take you long.

"Just one minute," Ermentrude said.

There was a moment of stunned silence in the courtroom.

"I object to this ridiculous sham of a trial," she said. "It seems there is no justice in Kureyamage for intelligent, independent witches. A gag spell, really. It's insulting that you thought that would hold me."

"Guards," the Head Judge shouted. "Remove that... that... witch from my courtroom."

"Look at you, sitting there like dressed-up toads, croaking your heads off," she said as the guards dragged her from the dock. "Your days of suppressing the rights of witches are numbered. Soon, we will sit on the ruling council, and you..." she nodded towards the Head Judge, "will receive justice for all the outrageous sentencing you've handed down over the years."

"Why is she speaking?" The fragile emerald-robed judge asked, clutching at his chest.

"Quiet," the Head Judge shouted.

"You're destroying this realm. One day, you'll have to answer for your actions," she shouted as the guards bundled her from the courtroom.

The Head Judge mopped his forehead, took a deep breath, and turned to the jury. "You may retire and consider your verdict."

The jury filed out of the court. The judges didn't leave, but they stood and talked in hushed voices.

"That wasn't a trial," Wilf said. "It was a show. The verdict's going to be guilty, isn't it?"

"How can it be anything else?" Hywel asked. "She is guilty."

The usher came over, bent, and spoke to Hywel.

"Thank you," Hywel said, and the usher withdrew. "They are holding Katryna in an anteroom. We can collect her when we leave." Hywel sat back in his chair with a smug look on his face.

The jury filed back in.

"Have you considered your verdict?" the clerk asked.

"Yes," the jury spokeswizard said.

"Do you find the defendant guilty or not guilty?" asked the clerk.

"Guilty."

"Thank you, members of the jury. The court will now sentence," said the Head Judge. He consulted with the other wizards sitting on the bench. They all nodded in agreement.

"Since the Witch Ermentrude Wakefield has willfully misused her abilities, it has been determined that she can no longer be trusted with their use. She is to receive treatments that will suppress her magic permanently." The Head Judge banged his gravel. "Inform the prisoner."

"Can he do that?" Wilf asked.

"It's what I expected." Hywel began to stand. "Ermentrude won't be surprised. She did bring it on herself. They'll probably give her a dose of the Virus." He patted Wilf's back. "You're safe now, and so is my daughter." He turned to speak to a wizard behind him.

"That's outrageous," Wilf said, watching the last of the officials leave the courtroom. The trial had been a total farce. The only reason for holding it appeared to be to send a warning to the witches of Mathowytch. The penalty for sedition was the Virus. He was caught in the middle of a vicious power struggle, like a ball between two rival teams. The Manchester United and Liverpool of the Magic Realm. Instead of a trophy, the victor of this game would receive the formula and control.

His ring flared, and he thrust his hand deep in his pocket before Hywel noticed. He took several deep breaths. This would be the wrong place to show his lack of control.

"Come along, let's collect my daughter."

Wilf struggled with the rage building within him as he shuffled out of the courtroom, behind Hywel.

# Chapter Eighteen
## A Solution

Katryna pushed past Hywel, ran up the stairs, and slammed her bedroom door. She threw herself face down on the bed. Racking sobs shook it as she wept.

There had been no justice for her mother. The whole trial had been a farce, and not one person had spoken on her mother's behalf.

She sat up. The defense council hadn't asked her. If Hywel could speak against Ermentrude, then Katryna should have been allowed to be a character witness. And now, her mother was to be injected with the Virus. She couldn't imagine her mother without her warts.

A knock at the door interrupted her thoughts.

"Leave me alone," she screamed, and hurtled a figurine at the door. It smashed into tiny fragments. Crockery jangled in the corridor. A tray must have been sent up. She sat back on the bed and shuffled into the corner, hugging her knees.

If only she could help her mother.

The words 'Hywel Wakefield' shimmered on the bracelet, and she pulled violently at the fused clasp.

She hated him for what he'd done to Ermentrude, and for trapping her here in Kureyamage.

If only she hadn't insisted on coming. She should have listened to her mother, but then again, Ermentrude hadn't been honest about Hywel. It was only natural that, having learned about her father, she would want to meet him. After all, he'd been described as a great wizard. If her mother were here, she'd tell her how angry she was with all this deception.

She rested her chin on her knees.

Perhaps she was blaming the wrong person. The real villain had to be Hywel. He'd betrayed them both from the moment they'd stepped foot in his tower.

She let out a sob. Her life was about to change, and not for the better. Tears flowed down her face, but she dashed them away.

Crying wasn't going to solve anything. *Think, Katryna.* Her mother had spies everywhere. They must have watched the trial from the galley. The Witch Council would order Ermentrude rescued. Wouldn't they?

She sighed. If her mother did manage to escape, she would have to return to Mathowytch without her. The bracelet would keep her here. She buried her face in her hands. She was going to be in Kureyamage until all her magical power were gone and the Virus took her.

"Katryna," Wilf said, through the door. "You okay?"

"Of course not."

"Sorry," he said. "I just thought you might like some company."

"Not unless you have a cure for the Virus or a way of removing this bracelet."

"I was thinking more about having someone to talk to," he said.

She wriggled her fingers at the door. It unbolted and swung open. Wilf stepped over the tray of cold brew and curled sandwiches. The door slammed shut behind him.

"You should have heard Ermentrude condemning the judges." He sat next to her. "Hywel and Thiemus said the whole court was shocked she'd managed to revoke the gag spell. No one has ever been able to do that."

"I'm glad she gave them a nasty surprise. They deserved it."

"It might have worked against her, though," he said. "It could be the reason they're taking away her magic."

"I think they'd already made that decision. We'll both soon have to adjust to life without magic."

"I'm trying my best to help," he said.

"Don't be so defensive. It's not your fault."

"Really? I thought you'd decided it was." He twisted the ring around his finger.

"Well. I don't anymore." She gave him a weak smile. "I was wondering if the Witch Council would try to rescue Mom."

"Do you think that's possible?" His eyes glittering with hope.

"You like my mother, don't you? After everything she's done to you."

"I'm coming around to the notion that she might have helped me." His face flushed. "I'd started having strange dreams. So, I guess I should be grateful."

"Don't let Hywel hear you say that, but thank you."

He smiled and his eyes searched her face.

Katryna's stomach fluttered and her face heated. She smiled back at him, and then glanced down at the bracelet on her wrist and shuddered.

"What's wrong?"

"This bracelet. Even if Mom's rescued, I won't be able to go with her. As long as I have this thing on, I'll have to stay with Hywel."

"Is there no way to magic it off?"

Katryna's laugh was hollow, even to her own ears. "Not until I perform a joining bond with a wizard."

"A what?"

"When a wizard is chosen to be my mate, then the etching will change to show I'm no longer Hywel's property but belong to that wizard," she said. "It's so degrading."

"Does your father arrange it all?"

"I suspect so."

"But he wouldn't do it for… How old are witches when…?"

"I'm of age, if that's what you're trying to ask. It's another way he could keep me from returning to Mathowytch." She twisted the bracelet. "And he'll want to do it soon, before I lose all my power and no one wants me."

"And how old does the wizard have to be?" He inspected his hands.

"He can be any age, really. As long as he accepts the arrangement."

"So, we could…?" He grabbed hold of her hand.

"What?" She tried to pull free, but he held on to her.

"If you and I performed the ritual, then when I leave Kureyamage, you'll be able to go with me."

She wrestled her hand free. "Now, wait just a minute. This is very kind of you to want to help, but the ritual…"

"Would keep you safe until we have the formula."

She stared at him.

He was offering her a way out, but he didn't understand magic. She should tell him that it would be binding, but then he might refuse to perform it. This could be her only means of escape, and staying with Wilf would give her an opportunity to restore her magic. She couldn't live without it."

"I'm not even sure I have enough magic left to participate in the ritual." She could hear the panic in her own voice.

The ritual had been covered in class once, about three months ago. She and Mazzy had giggled through it.

"It's ridiculous," Mazzy had said. "There aren't any wizards in Mathowytch. Why are we learning about a bonding ritual?"

"Maybe there's a secret supply being grown somewhere?" Katryna laughed, and they had both sniggered.

But now… this could save her and frustrate Hywel's plans, if the bonding was successful.

"Though, I'm not even sure I can go back to Mathowytch." Wilf had moved over to the window and stared out.

"What do you mean? How can you abandon all those witches, especially now you've seen the Wizard Council in action?" She advanced towards him. He couldn't be trying to back out now.

Wilf retreated, his hand up, until he was trapped in a corner.

"Calm down. I meant the Veil probably wouldn't let me."

"Oh!" She slumped against the wall.

"Perhaps you're right," he said. "I mean, we hardly know each other… I'm not sure I could…" His face had become magenta-colored as he tripped over the words. He gave her a wide-eyed appeal.

"It's not complicated magic."

"Oh."

"It's just a spell… Or an oath. You thought we have to…? No." She laughed and took his hand. "Come, sit down and I'll explain."

He left some distance between them, and looked nervous.

She smiled at him. "The ritual binds a witch and wizard together…"

He backed up a little farther from her.

"Bad choice of words," she said. "It's a promise to mate in the future. We are committing to each other only."

"Like an engagement?"

"A what?"

"When a guy asks a girl if she'll marry him, and he gives her a ring. Sometime later, they get married before the authorities and become husband and wife."

"Yes. It's like that. After the ritual, the etching on this thing…" she held up her arm, "will change to 'Wilf Gilvary', in the color of your wizard class."

He stroked the red shooting star on his hand and paced the room in front of her. His brow creased. "Let's do it," he said, stopping in front of her.

"No. I can't let you do this. You're only 15." It might be her only hope, but she couldn't ask him to make the oath.

"You said age didn't matter, and I'll be 16 in less than 2 weeks."

"What if it's not reversible?" Katryna watched him begin to pace again. It was amazing that he'd consider helping her this way, especially as they hardly knew each other. She wasn't sure it was right to place her future freedom on this young wizard.

"I can't think of any other way." He ran his fingers through his hair. "They wouldn't be able to separate us if we're bonded, and when I finally decode the journal, you'll receive the vaccine."

"If you're sure, then thank you." She threw her arms around his neck and kissed him on the cheek.

"How…" He coughed, and started again. "How do we perform this ritual?"

"I have to bind our hand together, and then we both say the incantation. It's not very difficult, but you must say it correctly." She scoured the room, picked up a black silk scarf, and came back to stand in front of him. "We have to speak at the same time," she said. "You're absolutely sure?"

He nodded and smiled.

"The words are, 'Together we stand. Together we bond. No other shall we seek. No other shall we want. Proclaim to all our choice is made. We two are as one'."

"That's it?"

"The magic is strong," she said. "The words are filled with power when said in this order."

She lifted her hands, and the scarf rose into the air. She held her left hand palm-up. "Put your dominant hand so our palms are facing and your finger is on my pulse."

He did as she said. She placed her right hand on top, with the palm over the back of his hand. "Place your other hand, palm covering the bracelet."

The scarf wrapped itself around their joined hands and wrists.

She nodded at him, and they both spoke the words of the ritual together.

Light spun around them from the ground up, encasing them in a warm flow of magic until it covered them. It gathered in a ball above their heads, and then dived between them and spun rapidly around their bound hands.

Katryna couldn't see either of their hands. A burning sensation started in her abdomen and spread across her chest.

In the distance, she could hear a pounding sound. Her heart beat so loudly she expected it to burst.

The light spun off their hands, shot up into the ceiling, and was gone. The scarf fell to the floor.

The pounding continued. Wilf screamed and bent over, holding his ringed hand. His face contorted with agony.

The door to her room burst open. Wilf took a step towards her, leaned forward, and pressed his lips on hers.

"Stop," Hywel shouted.

Hands pulled at her shoulders, parting them. She put her fingers on her lips. They tingled in a pleasant way, and the fluttering in her stomach increased.

"You two fools! What have you done?"

She glanced at Wilf's hand. He had an extra knuckle on his ringed finger. She turned to look at the angry face of her father and lifted her arm to reveal the red lettering of Wilf's name on the bracelet's surface.

# Chapter Nineteen
## Myra's Future Plans

Hywel pointed his ringed finger at Wilf.

"That wouldn't be a good idea," Myra said, walking into the room and standing in front of Wilf. "You need him."

Hywel bellowed in rage, glared at her, and stormed out of the room.

"That was close," she said, staring at Wilf. "Would you like to fill me in on what possessed you two children to perform this particular ritual?"

"What's it to you?" he asked.

"Do you understand what you've done?"

"Of course," he said. "Katryna can now go back to Mathowytch. I'll give them the formula before I leave for Hong Kong, and they can cure her."

"And everyone lived happily ever after." She turned to Katryna. "Do you want to tell him, or should I?"

"What?"

"Your fiancée seems to have forgotten to explain that, at some stage within the next ten years, you must fulfill the promise. In your language, my simple stepbrother, you must marry her," she said.

"The Witch Council might be able to undo the ritual once we're back in Mathowytch," Katryna said.

"Have you ever heard of anyone, anyone at all, being released from the ritual?" Myra folded her arms across her chest.

"No, but that doesn't mean it isn't possible."

She couldn't leave Wilf alone for one minute without him walking from one minefield into another. Perhaps, she should tether him like a goat, although, at the moment, he was behaving more like a sacrificial lamb. On second thoughts, she was more likely to be the one wanting to slaughter him if he continued like this.

She did have sympathy for Katryna. The Virus was certainly ravaging the poor witch. She was now as attractive as a magazine cover girl in Wilf's realm. Her dirty, straw-colored hair was golden blonde, and it was so shiny it almost hurt Myra's eyes to look at it.

Even her complexion had cleared and now had the most unnaturally healthy glow to it. In Hong Kong, she would have been stunning, but here, she was an outcast.

Myra stroked the wart on her chin that had been growing over the last few hours. The longer she was exposed to the magical energy of this realm, the more her outward appearance was changing.

She took a step away from the young witch.

"Do you know how you caught the Virus?"

"Worried I might infect you?" Katryna said, and laughed. Her voice sounded like the tinkle of bells, rather than its usual nails on a chalkboard. "You should have visited your mother. She would have been more than happy to oblige."

"Griselda did this to you?" Myra shuddered.

"I don't believe it," Wilf said.

"She was working for the Wizard Council, just like her daughter is," Katryna said. Wilf groaned and sat on the bed.

"I had my own reasons for working for Hywel, but after seeing what happened to Ermentrude, I'm not convinced I want to spend the rest of my life here under wizard rule."

"Why should we believe you?" Katryna asked.

"What do I have to gain from lying?" she asked. "You're already here with your father. Wilf has agreed to learn magic in order to decipher the journal. My importance to Hywel is at an end. It's time I made my own decisions regarding what happens in my life."

"Just like that you'll change sides?" Katryna stepped so close Myra had to look up at her.

"No. I'm weighing my options, and while I do that, I will still be on the side of my stepbrother, as I promised him," she said, in a slow, deliberate voice.

Katryna huffed and sat down next to Wilf.

"What do you think?"

"I think you're both as bad as each other," he said. "I'm not sure I can trust or believe either one of you." He stood and left the room.

"See what you've done?" Katryna said.

"Do you even like Wilf?"

Katryna's face reddened, and she couldn't meet Myra's eyes.

Myra laughed and raised her eyebrows. "I see." She picked up Katryna's hand, looking at the red etching on the bracelet. "A red wizard. When Mathowytch comes back under wizard rule, you'll still be able to live there."

"That never crossed my mind. I like Wilf," Katryna said.

"I hope so. When he comes into his powers, he isn't going to be easy to control. You might have landed yourself in more trouble than you know."

"Or, I might not survive the Virus."

Myra nodded, and then stopped. "Sorry, about Ermentrude."

"Nice wart," Katryna said.

Wilf appeared at the door carrying a tray of food and a jug of water.

"It would have been more impressive if you'd used magic," Myra said. "You have to stop fetching and carrying." She reached for a sandwich, and he moved the tray.

"Magic yourself some then."

"Okay." She wriggled her fingers. A sandwich flew over Wilf's head and into her outstretched hand. "No problem."

"It's strange that his natural reaction isn't to use magic," Katryna took a bite of the sandwich that had gravitated towards her.

"That's why he isn't progressing. He doesn't feel magic," Myra said. "Now, put him on a piece of grass, give him a ball, and tell him to put it in the back of a goal, then you'll see some magic."

"The name's Wilf, and I'm standing right here," he said.

Both girls giggled.

"Now that you've bonded, what's your next step?" Myra asked.

Katryna and Wilf looked at each other. He put down the tray on the dresser top.

"Please tell me you've thought at least that far ahead." She took another bite of her sandwich.

"Not exactly," Katryna said.

Myra rolled her eyes. It was absurd. Wilf always felt the need to help everyone. He was always befriending the kid at school no one else would and helping out lost causes. But ask him to do something he didn't want to, or agree with, and his stubborn streak kicked in.

"I was wondering if the Witch Council would plan to rescue Mom."

"They might try to make contact with you, but since Hywel isn't going to let either of you out of the house in the near future, that would be difficult. I could try to make contact, if you want?" Myra said.

"That makes sense," Wilf said.

"Glad something does around here." She brushed the crumbs off her fingers. "I'll also make a few enquiries, see what I can learn about when sentencing is due to be carried out on Ermentrude." She moved towards the door. "Don't stay too long on your own." She laughed and shook her finger at them.

Wilf huffed, but they stepped a little farther apart.

Myra went down the stairs to the front door.

"Leaving so soon?" Thiemus asked, coming out of Hywel's study.

"Thought I might take a look around." She edged towards the door, but he barred the way and grabbed her by the shoulders.

"I hope you aren't thinking of changing sides, Sister." His fingers dug into the flesh at the top of her arms. "You're so like our mother in that respect."

"Of course not," she said, wincing. "I thought, since Wilf and Katryna managed to pull the ritual on Hywel, it might be an idea to gain their confidence."

Thiemus pulled her into the study. He dug his fingers into her side and she sucked in air with the pain.

"You've healed nicely." He twisted his fingers. She screamed.

"But I remember how you're stitched together, so remember where you're loyalties lie." He let her go and limped over to the fireplace. "I have daily reminders of what you and my mother have already cost me when you displeased Hywel." He rubbed his withered arm and glared at her.

"You could leave. You're a fully trained healer." She grabbed the back of a chair for support.

"I've learned to like this work," he said, grinning.

She glanced away. He'd always had a sadistic nature, and working for Hywel hadn't brought out his better side.

"Hywel is furious, but he can't deal with Wilf for that little trick… yet," he said.

"I'm sure it's upset one of your plans too. Were you hoping to be the lucky wizard?" She massaged her side, trying to ease the burning sensation. Her stomach knotted.

"That is none of your business," he said. "And it's a moot point, since the girl contracted the Virus. There isn't a wizard who would want to be associated with her."

"Unless Wilf comes up with the formula from his father's journal," she said. "I'm sure you would be willing to take the risk to be bonded with Hywel's only daughter." This wasn't smart. She shouldn't stay in this room with him. She had to escape and find Seldan.

"With the lack of progress that boy is making, I'm not holding out much hope." He massaged his arm again. "He doesn't seem to think magic, and that's a fundamental problem."

"You could try using the bond between him and Katryna." She had her own reasons for wanting to know what Reginald had written in that journal. He'd come across her one morning on an inter-realm communication to Hywel.

"I don't know what that wizard has been telling you, but I've had no communication with the Witch Council. Perhaps he's been confusing me with my mother," Myra had said.

"Myra, you sneaky little witch, he described you down to your pointy toes. So, let me make this clear, as I did to Griselda. The reason I took in your miserable, low-talented brother is to make sure you follow my instructions. If you don't, he will suffer, and he will know why he is paying for your misbehavior. Do I make myself clear?"

"Perfectly." She hadn't met Hywel's malicious gaze.

"Good. Now find me that journal and stop all your communication with the Witch Council."

"Yes, Hywel."

The mirror went blank. She heard a swish and turned in time to see the edge of Reginald's cloak disappearing down the stairs to the workshop.

Myra mentally shook herself. She needed to stay fully focused when she was alone with Thiemus.

"It might be possible to use the bond." Thiemus crossed the room to the shelves. He ran his finger along the books and then lifted one down.

"Katryna had the potential to be a very powerful witch, before the Virus struck. She might be able to use his power through the link."

"I see what you're suggesting." Thiemus put the book on the desk and sat down.

"Well, I'll leave that with you, then." She headed for the door.

The door slammed shut in front of her and she turned to face her brother again.

"You are in a hurry." He drummed his fingers on the desk. "Now where would a witch who has no friends or acquaintances be off to so persistently?"

"I thought, since I'm not needed at the moment, I would take a look at the city I've longed to see."

"Sightseeing?"

"Unless I am needed?"

He let the silence build between them.

Her heart beat rapidly. He liked to play games. Hywel's treatment of Ermentrude and Katryna showed the wizard was vengeful on anyone who betrayed his trust. And where Hywel led her brother would follow. She was going to have to tread very carefully if she was to survive and gain control over her own life. She was tired of being someone else's pawn, but she wanted to stay in the Magical Realm. She would honor her vow to Wilf to be on his side, but once he was back in Hong Kong, her obligation would be over. Finally, her life would belong to her alone.

"Be careful," Thiemus said, breaking into her thoughts. "Remember, you are an unclaimed witch. The patrols have orders to arrest anyone without a bracelet. You don't want to end up with the same fate as Ermentrude's."

"Thank you for your concern. I will be extra vigilant."

"Then, I look forward to hearing how you find the city at dinner this evening." He pointed his ringed finger at the door. It opened slowly.

She made good on her escape before her brother changed his mind. The small stones crunched under her feet as she walked towards the street gate.

That had been a deliberate threat, but he could easily have been delivering it for Hywel. It was going to demand all her powers of duplicity to keep everyone thinking she was working with them. The only side she cared about was her own, but until she had a clear route to gaining her freedom, she'd continue to play both sides. This had become a very delicate balancing act.

Her side ached. She put her hand into her pocket and her fingers caressed the pouch containing the three remaining vials of elixir. The gate swung open as she approached, and a wizard, in a purple robe with three golden bands on his shoulder, stepped over the threshold.

"You there," the wizard said, waving at her. "Take me to Hywel immediately."

She bit her tongue to stop the sharp remark she wanted to say, bowed her head, and turned back to the tower. At this rate, she'd never to be allowed to leave.

The wizard followed her down the footpath to the front door. She let him enter before her.

"Who should I say is asking for Wizard Hywel?"

"Councilman Tyrone."

Myra knocked on the study door and it swung open. The councilman pushed past Myra and entered the study. The door closed after him.

A councilman making a house call. That was irregular. She hoped Ermentrude had escaped already, but there would have been a platoon of guards in that case.

She hesitated. It would be interesting to learn why the councilman was there. But it was more important that she keep her appointment with Seldan.

Whatever the councilman was so agitated about, she'd find out from the housekeeper later. There may not be another opportunity to wander around the city alone. If the councilman had brought bad news, then Hywel or Thiemus might well stop her leaving. She stepped over the threshold and into the street. It was best to make use of her limited freedoms when they occurred.

# Chapter Twenty
## Wizard Tyrone's Visit

The journal lay open on the bed, next to Wilf. He'd performed the magical bond with Katryna and felt sure the journal would reveal more of its secrets. Perhaps there was no formula and his father had been misleading the two Councils. He tossed the book aside. A puff of smoke escaped. The journal flew open and pages rapidly turned, stopping on one filled with his father's spidery handwriting.

'*I have sent Griselda to Mathowytch. She had been infected on her last visit to Kureyamage. I can only presume that she is no longer of any use to the Wizard Council. On a separate note, Myra has been acting differently since her mother's return. Whatever the hold the Council has over this family has now been transferred to her. I believe she is the new spy in my home. I'll have to be extra vigilant over my research, as I'm so close to finding a solution for the Virus that I can't stop now. Perhaps, the Council thought I would use it on Griselda and that is why she was infected? I can't help her. I won't give the cure to a Council who would threaten the stability of the realm solely to hold onto power.*'

A diary. That's all this journal was turning out to be. His father had known Myra was a spy. Wilf didn't feel like he knew any of the members of his family.

"Why won't you show me the formula?" he yelled at the book.

The journal gave a sound of dry leaves rustling. It closed and opened in a different section.

'*The Pulch Virus vaccine requires the following ingredients:*'

"Finally." He placed his ringed finger on the page. The ring's ruby flared, and the words disappeared.

"No."

The journal slammed shut and locked.

He tried to pry it open, but it refused. "Damn you."

Loud voices echoed up from the hallway below. Wilf glared at the journal. It flipped over so the binding faced him. He huffed and stepped out onto the landing.

"You told me this couldn't happen," a deep voice shouted.

"That's not what I said, but the virus has obviously mutated," Hywel said.

"How are you going to stop this outbreak becoming an epidemic?"

"Gilvary's journal has an antiviral cure."

"So, do you have the cure, or is it still locked in that ridiculous spell associated with his lame-brained son?" the councilman said.

"The boy has never used magic before. I'm building his knowledge base so we can progress."

"Anyone who has ability but refuses to use it is either mentally deficient or a fool. If one wizard dies from this virus, there will be an enquiry."

"I'm doing everything possible to stop its spread," Hywel said.

"Frankly, I was against this method of controlling the witches from the beginning," the councilman said.

"That is not how I remember it," Hywel said.

Wilf edged forward, trying to catch a glimpse of the visitor.

"I remember you assuring the Council that there would be no danger to the balance of magic in the Realm. That assurance seems to have been rather empty, given the current situation," the councilman shouted.

"You're out of line." Hywel's tone sent a chill through Wilf.

"Some Council members are muttering about starting negotiations with the witches. A sort of amnesty." There was the sound of footsteps. "That will mean the seat you had your eyes on is going to a witch."

"So the Council is starting to panic?" Hywel said.

"The report on the ratio of wizard to witch magic is due tomorrow. If it shows a significant imbalance, and we have no vaccine, there will be a mass panic to evacuate. And Hywel, I will make sure you are held accountable for this total fiasco."

Wilf heard heavy footsteps across the hall's entrance.

"I want a vaccine on my desk in two days." Councilman Tyrone said.

The windows rattled from the slamming of the front door, followed by silence. He crept down the stairs.

Hywel stood staring at the door. His brows drawn together and his mouth contracted into a hard line. Wilf expected to see sparks flying from the wizard's eyes. He turned as Wilf reached the last stair.

"Eavesdropping. Not an activity I would recommend." Hywel's ring flashed.

All sounds disappeared. Then, a gentle whine started. It grew, and Wilf covered his ears with his hands, but the sound was inside his head. He collapsed to the ground.

Hywel waved his ring at him and the noise receded.

"You have a deadline of two days to learn magic and reveal the contents of that journal. You would be advised to concentrate on your studies instead of listening to private conversations." His ring flashed again, and Wilf was hurled into Hywel's study.

Thiemus stood by the fireplace.

"You're lucky I need you. I haven't forgiven you for that stunt you pulled with Katryna. But you are coming close to the end of my patience." Hywel sat behind his desk. "Get up."

Wilf winced as he tried to stand.

"Why would you bond with Katryna? You can't believe it's possible to ever return to Mathowytch."

"She'll come with me to Hong Kong," he said, struggling to his feet.

"Still longing to be a Normal. Tragic. So much talent wasted." Hywel turned to Thiemus. "Why don't you start today's lesson? I'll stay and view his progress. I might even find some ways to offer encouragement."

Wilf cringed. Another day of trying to light a globe and make it glide across the room.

The communication mirror lit up and pinged. Hywel spun round in his chair to face it.

"Wakefield here."

A wizard with a long nose and black, unruly hair, wearing a white laboratory coat, appeared in the mirror.

"Sir, I have to report that a test portal has not returned."

"Where was it last located?" Hywel pointed his finger at the bookcase and a chart flew across the room.

"That's the strange part. The data shows it arrived back in Kureyamage, but when the technicians arrived to download its information, it had disappeared again. The tracking device is no longer active."

Hywel leaned back in his chair. "Sabotage?"

"We're checking all avenues at the moment. I thought you would want to know," the wizard said.

"I appreciate your imaging me." Hywel waved his ringed hand at the mirror and the surface went blank.

The door opened, and Katryna came in carrying a soccer ball.

"What do you want?" Thiemus asked.

"I thought this might help. Wilf only uses magic through soccer." She threw the ball low at his feet.

He caught it on his right foot, bounced it a few times, before flicking it up into his hands.

"I was thinking, perhaps I can use the bond to show him how magic feels." She strode to stand next to him.

"Why not? Although, I'm not sure witch magic is comparable," Hywel said.

She took Wilf's ringed hand and placed it on her bracelet.

The world slipped a few degrees, and Wilf's peripheral vision blurred. He focused on the bracelet, and his name seemed to be calling him. The room disappeared. His head pounded, and he could sense a swirling pool of energy stored in his mind. He dropped the ball and broke contact with Katryna. "What was that?"

"I'm hoping you saw your energy store," Hywel said. "You need to feed that energy into any spell in order to add the magical element. It never occurred to me that you wouldn't know elementary biology."

"It might be elementary to you, but very few people in my world use magic."

"So primitive," Thiemus said. "I've seen bats who knew more about magic than he does."

"Don't you have duties to perform in the workshop?" Hywel asked.

Thiemus looked as if he would object but bowed his head and left.

"So how do you feed magic into a spell?" Wilf asked, after the door had firmly closed on Thiemus.

"Use an image," Hywel said.

"Like turning on water," she said.

"Some way that you can control the flow. It's amazing you've never been taught," Hywel said. "Why have you refused to use magic all these years?"

"Yes, Wilf. Why? I would have thought anyone with the ability would want to use it," Katryna said.

"Not everyone." He hugged his soccer ball.

"Perhaps that's the problem. You're still resisting," she said.

Hywel sat studying him in silence for a few moments, and then he quickly raised his hand.

Wilf couldn't move.

"What have you done?" Katryna faced her father.

"I don't have the patience for all this nonsense." Hywel walked around the desk. "It's time I found out what is really going on in that head of his."

"No." Katryna pulled on Hywel's arm, but he thrust her to one side.

"Leave us." Hywel waved his ringed finger at her.

Katryna obediently turned and left without a backward glance.

"Just you and me." The wizard sat on the edge of his desk. "Reginald thought he was being very clever putting that enchantment on his journal, but he always underestimated me."

Hywel collected the communication mirror and set it down on the desk.

"Sit in my chair."

Wilf walked around the desk and sat down. A tiny portion of his mind screamed, but he couldn't resist the order. The mirror filled with a green mist.

"I want you to look into the mirror, Wilf, deep into the mist, and clear a path for me to the reason why you refuse to perform magic."

He fought to gain control of his mind and stop the invasion. A shadowy figure appeared in the mirror. He focused on his father's evaporation. The guilt he felt about leaving his father that morning. He willed it to provide enough of an emotional block to prevent Hywel from penetrating his deeper memories.

The figure disappeared, and the mist began to clear. An image of his bedroom formed. He picked up a photo of his mother in her garden.

"What are you thinking?"

"That it hurts to look at her smiling eyes. I'd forgotten that she wore her hair tied back in a bun. She was forever tucking escaped strands back in place."

An image of his mother slumped in an armchair with a wizard action figure clutched in her hand sprang into his mind. He pushed it back. His father. He had to think of him. The mist swirled and Myra appeared in the mirror, running up the stairs to his room.

"Wilf, I'm so sorry about Reginald. It happened so quickly." She took his hand. "He came looking for you, but you'd already left. He was so upset when I told him you'd gone to soccer practice that he turned and hurried back down the stairs, and then there was a loud crash."

"He fell?"

"I tried to help him, but he took a deep breath and…" She wiped her eyes.

"I should have stayed." He stared at the ugly ring on his finger, tears slid down his face.

The mirror misted over again.

"What happened after your father evaporated?"

The swirling surface cleared again.

This time, he was in the store.

"I can't find it anywhere," Myra said from the closet.

"Find what?"

"Reginald's journal, or the entrance to his workshop." Myra banged her fist on the wall.

"What do you want them for?"

"For you, of course. It's your inheritance."

He gave a bark of laughter.

"What were you thinking?" Hywel prompted him again.

"I'm wondering why I would want a magical journal. What I really wanted was my father back, so I could tell him how sorry I was."

The mirror misted over again, and Hywel took it off the desk.

"Sit down in the chair next to the fire."

Wilf did as he was commanded. His soccer ball jumped into his lap.

Hywel took the seat opposite.

"The way to make your father proud would be to learn magic. That's what he always wanted. There will be no more resistance. You will embrace magic." Hywel's ring flashed.

"When can we start?" Wilf stood up.

"This has been a very illuminating discussion." Hywel raised his hand, pointed his finger, and his ring flashed again. "You won't recall anything else that took place in this room after Thiemus left, except your eagerness to help me in the workshop."

"Where did Katryna go?" Wilf glanced round the room. "I don't remember her leaving."

"You were absorbed in showing me your tricks with that soccer ball," Hywel said. "She slipped out when you were balancing it on your head."

Wilf rolled the ball over in his lap. Something wasn't right. When he performed ball tricks, he always felt happy, but now he had a suffocating sadness. All he wanted was to curl up in a corner and weep. That wasn't normal.

"It's good of you to want to help me in the workshop," Hywel said, standing.

"Happy to." Pleasure coursed through him, obliterating his confusion and unhappiness. He stood in the hallway and bounced the ball. A floral scent wafted over him, and a memory stirred that he couldn't grasp. The black and white ball vanished from his hand, and a green and purple one took its place. The floral scent grew stronger and the globes in the hallway began to flicker.

His ring flared. The ball became black and white and immediately disappeared again. It reappeared at the top of the stairs and bounced down to his feet, changing color on each step. Sweat beaded on his forehead, and he found it difficult to breath. He pointed at the ball.

"Stop," he shouted.

The bouncing increased until he couldn't distinguish the ball's shape. The smell of Peapod flowers filled the air. A swish of fabric sounded behind him.

The ball disappeared, and a single flower grew in its place. Its long leaves and stems twisted up from the tiled floor. A tiny cluster of bell-shaped buds with deep purple flowers swayed as if in a gentle breeze.

Hywel stepped out of his study. Wilf dodged around the plant, bolting for his room. The wizard's laughter followed him up the stairs.

He collapsed on the bed with his thoughts colliding into the memory he'd been blocking from Hywel. He'd buried it years ago, hoping it would never resurface, but now it began to play in full cinematic color behind his eyes.

A wizard had arrived to see his father, and Wilf had been dispatched to his room. His mother had told him not to come down until she came to fetch him. He'd dodged her hand and tried to make a bolt for the stairs. His action figures were still in the living room. But she'd caught him.

"I'll send up your figures, Wilf. It's very important that you don't leave your room."

He squirmed in her arms, but she sat him down on the carpet in his room.

"Do you understand me?"

He nodded.

"Say it."

"I'll stay here."

"Thank you." She stooped to plant a kiss on the top of his head as she left.

Seconds later, his action figures appeared. He picked them up and began placing them in teams. Super Striker wasn't there. He creased his brow as he counted the figures—nine. There should be ten. He glanced at the door. How could he have two teams now? He'd left all the figures together. He remembered they'd been next to his mother's chair when his father walked in. Then, she'd grabbed his arm and... his father had kicked Super Striker under the chair.

He put his hand on the doorknob and turned it. The door wouldn't open. But he needed that figure. Closing his eyes, he formed a picture of it in his mind. His palm began to grow warm. He could see the blue shirt and yellow shorts of the figure. The center of his hand tingled and he opened his eyes. The outline of the figure appeared in his hand. He scrunched up his face. A high-pitched scream of pain sounded from his mother as the action figure materialized in his hand.

The bedroom door flung open, and he rushed down the stairs. Reginald was bending over Shuai. She turned and smiled at Wilf, and then her body turned into a fine mist that floated up to the ceiling and vanished as she evaporated.

Sweat poured from his body and his stomach began to knot as the memory of his mother's scream filled his head again and again.

# Chapter Twenty-One
# Myra and the Spy Ring

Myra hurried through the crooked streets and alleys of Kureyamage as fast as she dared, trying not to appear suspicious. She didn't want to be stopped by a patrol.

Entering a narrow passage between two buildings, Seldan stepped out of the shadows in front of her. Nipits sauntered over to Myra and wrapped himself around her ankles.

"You're late," Seldan said.

"Couldn't be helped. Did you find out where Ermentrude is being held?"

"She has a room in Hywel's tower, of course."

"No. Really," she said. "I know you're pissed that you had to wait, but can we stop the games?"

Seldan smiled.

Since their first meeting, Seldan had become a regular feature in Myra's life. She didn't fully trust the young witch; however, the few times she'd followed Seldan, she hadn't detected anything suspicious. And now, she needed to rely on the young witch for help. Perhaps it had been selfish to bring her to Kureyamage, but her street smarts would be extremely useful. Besides, she had Nipits to keep an eye on Seldan and alert her if there was any danger.

"Your education on wizard law is sadly lacking, isn't it?" Seldan said. "As Hywel is the wizard who owns Ermentrude, he will carry out the sentencing."

"You're serious. She's in the tower?"

"There are tunnels that run between Wakefield Tower and the Palace. She'll be held in the cells down there, I should imagine." Seldan folded her arms and leaned back against the brick wall.

"Ever hear of anyone escaping from there?"

"The only witches who have are because the Wizard Council wanted them to. I don't think Ermentrude's going to have any joy from that quarter."

"What about you? Have you found somewhere to stay?" She didn't want the young witch captured by a patrol.

"I'm fine," Seldan said. "I'm in an abandoned building near the Veil. Wizards don't seem to like that view, for some reason."

"What about the patrols? Will you be able to dodge them all the time?"

Seldan rolled up her sleeve to reveal a bracelet with the name 'Qirko' etched in brown lettering.

"Is that real?"

"My father, Wizard Qirko, evaporated a few years ago. I ran away before anyone could claim me. It's inactive but useful. If a patrol caught me and tested it, then I would be in trouble; but otherwise, for general, everyday use it works fine."

"We should probably move. It will appear suspicious, two witches meeting in this area."

"The sooner we can return to Mathowytch, the better," Seldan said. "Has Wilf started using magic yet?"

"Very limited." She was silent for a few moments. "I've been wondering how Ermentrude was going to get Wilf back into Mathowytch."

"Why would she need him, once she has the vaccine formula?"

"I suppose you're right." She hadn't considered that Wilf would be abandoned here. "Have you managed to contact Ermentrude's spy ring and find out what they're planning, if anything?"

"I've tracked down one of their safehouses. I can take you there now, as long as we're careful."

Myra nodded. Seldan led the way out of the alley, pausing briefly at the entrance to scour the surroundings for signs of a patrol. She trotted across the street and ducked into another alley. Myra and Nipits followed.

They crossed two more streets before Seldan stopped outside a wooden fence. She looked around before placing her palm on a hidden panel. A section of fencing slid to one side.

"What's going on?"

"This is the safehouse."

"But, how do you have access?"

"I'm staying here. I told you." Seldan faced her. "It's best if we don't linger in the street. I promise I'll answer all your questions inside."

Nipits jumped onto the path and disappeared into the yard.

This had all the markings of a trap, and panic started to build. Myra glanced back. Could she navigate her way back to the center of the city without Seldan's help? Bat's blood, would she never learn that the only person she should trust was herself?

155

She took a deep breath and stepped into the yard. The fencing slid back into place behind them. The terrain reminded Myra of the trails in the New Territories after the opening of hiking season, when the thick vegetation was trimmed back on both sides of the concrete paths.

"Don't step off the path. Some of those plants are not advantageous to a prolonged life. They bite," Seldan said. She threaded her way along the path. Vines edged closer to the path.

"They can't penetrate the protective spell," Seldan said as a vine struck the invisible barrier. There was a zapping sound, and the vine disappeared back into the dense undergrowth. A splattered globule of yellow sap hung in the air where it had struck.

A door swung open as they approached, and they entered into a mudroom where a blue globe floated down in front of them.

"Don't make any sudden moves," Seldan said as it circled her, and then Myra.

"Place your hand on the globe. It needs to identify who you are. Next time, it will recognize you."

"What is it?" She placed her hand on the globe. "Ouch!"

"Oh, yeah. It takes a small sample of your blood. I always forget to mention that bit." A smile spread across Seldan's face.

Myra doubted the young witch forgot anything. The globe turned green.

"This way."

"Any more devices I should know about?" Myra glanced around the corridor.

"Probably, but I can't think of any right now." Seldan sprang up three steps.

"Who else lives here?"

"It's better if you don't ask too many questions about the group. They like to operate on a need-to-know basis. The fewer witches who know about us, the more likely we are to survive."

"I can understand that."

"Yes, I image you can. Come on." Seldan walked down the hall, passing two doors before opening the third.

Seldan threw her bag on a white, square fold-up card table that was surrounded by three chairs. The top was stained with mug rings, and there was a deep slash across its padded top. A set of cupboards ran along one wall, two were missing doors. On the yellowed countertop stood a plug-in kettle and a coffee machine. The smell of burnt coffee permeated the room. A chipped utility sink and small refrigerator were situated on another wall.

"Brew?" Seldan wriggled her fingers and the coffee jug floated over to the sink and rinsed out.

"I'm fine." Myra sat on one of the chairs. Any brew in this house was bound to have added ingredients.

Seldan flicked her hand at the coffee machine and the old grinds emptied out, the reservoir filled with fresh water, and the machine switched on. Coffee dripped and hissed into the glass jug.

"You've been part of Ermentrude's little gang all along, haven't you?" Myra asked when a steaming mug of brew settled in Seldan's hand.

"She expected you to arrive in Mathowytch after your little run in with her and asked me to keep a close eye on you." Seldan took a sip from her mug.

"Why am I here?"

"I'm surprised it's taken you this long to find out," Seldan said. "What we want to know is why are you trying to help us now? You've always belonged to Hywel."

"I don't belong to anyone. I thought you might need my help with Wilf, now that Ermentrude is incarcerated."

"That's very civic-minded of you. Not a characteristic I would have thought you possessed."

"Suit yourself," Myra said. "But, I don't think the wizards are going to reveal the vaccine's properties to the very people they're trying to manipulate."

"Once we know Wilf has transcribed the journal, I'm sure I will receive new instructions regarding him." Seldan took another sip and stared over the rim of her mug.

Myra leaned back in her chair and pinched her lower lip with her thumb and forefinger. It didn't seem that the witches were going to rescue Wilf and Katryna. They'd become collateral damage.

"Once Wilf's decoded the formula and you, somehow, acquire the journal. What happens to Katryna?"

"She's with her father," Seldan said. "The information I've received is that she's accepted his bracelet."

"Actually, it's Wilf's bracelet."

"If that is the case, then he should have more incentive to decode the journal, now that he's chosen a future mate with the Virus."

Myra didn't think Ermentrude had meant the trip here to be a one-way ticket for Wilf and Katryna. Her capture must have caused the change in plans.

"You're really not going to do anything to save Ermentrude?" Myra asked.

"She knew the risks that came with this job," Seldan said. "It's unfortunate. She's very good at what she does, but we all make sacrifices for the good of the cause."

"I can't believe you're willing to surrender her without even trying a rescue." Myra pushed back her chair and stood.

"Risk more of our group?" Seldan said. "There are too few of us already. The virus has reduced our numbers considerably. Not that we had many members in the first place. Witches with inactive bracelets are a scarce commodity."

"They aren't commodities. You're no different from the wizards."

"How dare you suggest we're like those tyrants? We are soldiers in the fight against oppression. Now sit down. I'm getting a crick in my neck."

"Why should I want to spend another minute with you?"

"Because I have a proposition for you." Seldan put down her mug.

"What?" Myra had underestimated Seldan, thinking her a mere runner for hire—a low-level witch. But, she was obviously more powerful than her features portrayed. The young witch must have spent a lot of time outside the Magical Realm.

"I agree that your unique position, living in Hywel's tower, makes you useful to us," Seldan said. "You could let us know what that Wizard's movements are, and keep us informed of Wilf's progress."

"What would be in it for me?"

"For the right information, you'll receive citizenship of Mathowytch." She leaned back in her chair, her eyes never leaving Myra's. "Isn't that what you want?"

Myra sat back down into the chair. As a citizen of Mathowytch, she'd be able to stay in the Magical Realm and never have to go back to Hong Kong.

"How do I know you have the authority to make me an offer? You could abandon me once you have the journal."

Seldan wriggled her fingers at the cupboards. A scroll floated over to Myra and unrolled. The document was headed with the crest of the Witch Council. It stated that Myra Picton had been awarded citizenship of Mathowytch for her services to the community. It was sealed, signed, and dated.

"But..."

"I know you want to remain in this realm. It was thought that once you'd experienced wizard rule, you would decide it wasn't a healthy environment for an intelligent witch." Seldan took the scroll out of Myra's hand.

"I..."

"Unfortunately, I can't give you time to think it over; given the circumstances, I must have your answer now."

Mathowytch. To be a part of that city and lifestyle... But it wasn't sustainable. The two Councils would eventually have to reach a compromise, or the Realm would be wiped out. However, she would be in a better position to control her own interests, maybe even influence the Council's negotiations once the Virus was no longer a threat. If she took this offer, she could also keep her promise to Wilf and help him escape to Hong Kong. That was important to her. She owed him for what she'd done to Reginald. This could be the opportunity she'd been waiting for. A chance to control her own destiny

Nipits placed his paw on Myra's leg, and she smiled at the cat.

"Alright, you've found a new recruit."

# Chapter Twenty-Two
## Magic Begins

Wilf grabbed the handle and stopped. He returned to his bed, bent down, and retrieved his soccer ball. He moved back to the door but again couldn't leave. He took down a black robe hanging on the hook. On his next attempt to exit the room, he was surprised that he could walk into the corridor and down the stairs without hindrance.

He entered the living room and sat down on the cushioned seat in the bay window. Sunlight lit the leaves of a rhododendron so the veins were visible. A squirrel-like creature with two tails scampered down a tree trunk.

He rolled the ball over in his lap—glad it had stopped changing color. Memories about the events in the study were hazy when he tried to fix on them. A vexing alarm, one he couldn't summon from the back of his mind, kept nudging him. It didn't feel as if the thought belonged to him. He sighed. It was like trying to inflate a punctured ball: useless.

He pulled his dead cell phone from his pocket. The team probably thought he'd abandoned them. Myra had told him she'd closed up the shop. If Enzo came to find him and saw the boarding, he'd think they'd done a runner.

"I've been looking all over for you." Katryna crossed the room and sat next to him.

"Do you remember me doing ball tricks for Hywel in the study?"

"I think so." She twisted the bracelet.

"Is that why you left?"

She pulled her sleeve down.

"To be honest, I don't know why I left. All I remember is using the bond to try to show you how magic felt. Next, I'm in my room."

"I'm having some trouble remembering details." He blinked in the bright sunlight shining through the window. Katryna's hair shone in the light. In his realm, she would be a stunner, which was exactly what she wouldn't want to hear, and he would never tell her. Sitting close to her made his pulse race. He wanted to touch her hand

160

resting beside him. He'd never noticed how long and slender her fingers were, or the perfect shape of her fingernails.

His ring flared and the strap of her dress slipped off her shoulder.

"What's happening?" Her eyes widened in surprise.

All the globes in the room shone on full capacity.

"I'm not sure." His voice sounded deeper even to him.

She sucked on her bottom lip, and his throat went dry as he stared at her moist lips. He shook his head, trying to clear his thoughts. He'd never felt this way about Katryna before. He cleared his throat and tried to remember what they'd been talking about. It was becoming increasingly difficult to concentrate on anything other than her closeness. He inched his hand closer to her's.

"So what do you think happened?" Dazzling sunlight made her blink and she shuffled nearer. Their fingertips touched and a shiver ran through him.

"No idea." He faced her.

"It's very strange." Her voice trembled.

He could smell the faint scent of soap and citrus shampoo waft towards him. She looked into his eyes, and he let the ball fall to the floor and roll away.

"Do you feel different?"

"Like there's a strong attraction between us? I think it's the bond." She placed her hand on his arm. "All I know is that I want to feel your lips on mine again."

"I don't think you two should be left alone together." Myra laughed and walked across the room. "Rituals are powerful magic."

Wilf and Katryna jumped apart. Myra bent down and picked up the soccer ball. She bounced it a few times before throwing it at Wilf.

"Did you manage to find anyone?" he asked, securing the ball.

"Apart from you two lovebirds?" she said. "Yes. I've managed to make contact."

"That's fantastic. When are they going to rescue Ermentrude?" he asked.

"I'm sorry. There aren't any plans. I was told it's too risky."

"What?"

"I didn't think they would." Katryna put a little more distance between herself and Wilf. "Mom told me once that they never risk the capture of other witches for the sake of one."

"But…" A buzzing sound came from his pocket. He reached in and pulled out a black flip mirror. "Where did this come from?" He flicked it open. "I've a lesson with Hywel."

Myra stood in front of him.

"Why so compliant? And what's with the wizard robe?" she asked. He dodged around her and met Hywel coming down the stairs.

"Good, you remembered the ball?" the wizard asked.

"I'm not sure why."

"I've an idea about how you've been using magic and how that might help us. Come along." Hywel continued down the hall, entering the tunnel to the workshop without a backward glance. His robe billowed out around him as he went.

"Great." Wilf tripped over his robe. "Why am I always running after someone?" he muttered under his breath. The ball flew from his hands and rolled under the hall table. He bent quickly to retrieve it; but when he stood, Hywel had disappeared.

He took the stone stairs two at a time trying to keep pace with the globe Hywel had left for him. The ball vibrated, and he let it fall to the ground. Using his toe, he flicked it over a few of the larger puddles and then maneuvered it around the rest as if they were practice cones. The globe bobbed along in front.

Ahead, he could see a faint light, and then it vanished. Hywel must have reached the workshop and hadn't even left a globe outside to mark the entrance. How was he supposed to remember what the door looked like?

The light appeared again. He sighed with relief and picked up his pace. It felt good to be running again. He'd missed the routine of daily soccer training. He slowed down as he approached the hovering globe.

The door swung open, but it wasn't the workshop. He paused at the entrance to a circular stone room. Numerous footprints and drag marks covered the dirt floor. On the opposite wall, a door stood ajar. He tiptoed towards it.

"What has she told you?" Hywel asked.

There was a muffled response from Thiemus.

"She can't hold out much longer." Hywel sounded irritated. "Ermentrude, tell us the location of the safehouse and this will all be over."

Wilf backed away from the door.

*Ermentrude!* Hywel was trying to discover information about the spy ring.

"Keep on her. Wilf's on his way down here. I have to go, but I want that address."

Wilf spun on his heels. Where could he hide? The room was completely empty. He ran back into the tunnel, skidded to a halt, and then began to slowly retrace his steps towards the round room.

Hywel stepped out.

"There you are. Come on." The wizard continued along the tunnel. Wilf caught a brief sight of the room before it disappeared back into the tunnel wall.

"Are there lots of rooms in this tunnel?"

"What? Rooms? Yes, quite a few storage rooms." Hywel appeared distracted. Wilf let the silence descend between them until the key unlocked the workshop.

"Have you heard anything about Ermentrude's sentencing?"

"Ermentrude? What made you ask about her?"

"The fact that we're under the Palace."

Hywel collected numerous items off the shelves. "I've been too busy with my own work to waste a thought on that traitor."

"I thought perhaps the councilman might have mentioned it yesterday." He sat on the bench.

"He was more concerned about you and your progress," Hywel said, directing an array of bottles, vials, bowls, and weights to the table. "Today, we are going to try another approach. You've been using magic on that ball." It bounced into the air and floated over to the wizard. "You can alter its flight. So perhaps we should start with having you try to move other objects as well. I'll tell you which object I want you to move. Do you understand?"

Wilf nodded. He got what the lesson was about, but he'd no idea how he made the ball move. He still held a nagging suspicion he used skill, not magic.

"You have to disregard the physical composition of the object and see it floating to the place you desire it to go."

That was easy for Hywel to say and think, but Wilf had his doubts.

"Let's start with the ball. I want you to float it off the ground."

"Right." His cooperation was beginning to annoy him, but he focused on the ball, trying to visualize it floating up. It couldn't be that hard. A ball was full of air, anyway, and the atmosphere was thinner here.

"Feed it a small stream of magic," Hywel said.

Ermentrude was right here and only a few meters away. He'd have to let Katryna know when he got back to the tower.

The ball bounced.

"Well. That's progress. At least, you managed to lift the thing off the floor. A longer span of attention would be better. You let your mind wander."

"Sorry." He'd made the ball move. But he hadn't felt the meld with the outside energy source that usually revolted him. He'd controlled the flow. It hadn't overwhelmed him. Usually, he felt as if it wanted to consume him. In the study with Katryna, he remembered she'd shown him how she felt using magic.

"Wilf," Hywel said. "The ball."

Wilf looked at the ball and ducked as it went spinning around the room. He brought it back under control, gently floating it to the ground.

"Finally," Hywel said. "But controlling your thoughts is the secret to good wizardry." The room shook. Books and bottles crashed to the ground.

"Was that me?"

"Another quake," Hywel said, his face turning ashen. "That's the second one this week."

"Is there nothing you can do about it?"

"This is another consequence of that Virus and your father's arrogant behavior." Hywel pointed his dominant finger at a bowl, catching it before it hit the ground. "Reginald should have shared his formula with the Council, then none of this would be happening." He leaned forward and pointed at Wilf. "Now, shall we get on? I want you to pick up that book and hurl it at the door as hard as you can. Think of it as filled with air, like the ball."

A large leather-bound book had fallen off the shelf. Its binding lay splayed and its pages crumpled. It looked heavy, but he couldn't think of it that way. He had to imagine the binding was hollow; a fake book that weighed nothing at all, less than a feather.

He added a small amount of magic to the thought and the book hovered in the air.

"Use your dominant finger to hurl the book," Hywel said.

Wilf pointed at the book, his ring flared, and he flicked his wrist. The book hit the door and clattered to the ground.

"Good," Hywel said. "Put all these objects back on the shelves without breaking a single item."

Wilf sighed. There must have been ten items on the table, and they all looked delicate. He focused on a jar containing a bright-green liquid. He didn't want to know what would happen if he smashed that one.

"Well," Hywel said, "What are you waiting for?"

Wilf tried again, but the jar remained firmly on the table. "I'm trying," he said.

"Perhaps you need a little persuasion?"

Wilf's ball floated over to the fireplace and hovered above small flames. He tried again, but the jar still refused to float. The flames grew higher.

Beads of sweat covered Wilf's forehead as he tried again. He had to stop wondering what that liquid could do. There was nothing in the jar. Only air. It was a green-colored glass jar filled with oxygen.

The flames grew higher. "No," he said. Luckily, there weren't any scorch marks on the ball yet. The jar was filled with the same contents as a ball, so it could float. That's what he had to imagine.

It jumped off the table and banged down on the shelf. The flames extinguished, but Hywel kept the ball hovering in the fireplace.

"All the objects," Hywel said.

Wilf groaned. He was never going to be able to rescue his ball or... Ermentrude. But he had to tell Katryna and Myra about the witch's location. There were so many objects on the table. It would take forever. He focused. He had this.

The next object was a small figurine of a toad. It floated slowly off the table, and he pointed towards the bookshelf. The ruby flashed at the center of his ring. He glanced at the next object. This was taking too long. He concentrated on all the objects at once. Nothing happened. He tried again, and several lifted off the table, then all the objects floated inches off the surface. They bobbed up and down as he struggled to keep them from clattering back down. Then, he pointed at the bookcase, and they obediently floated across the room and gently settled. All except for a vial of black powder, which missed the bookcase and crashed in front of it.

Wilf turned to look at Hywel, and then back at his ball. The flames shot up to surrounded the ball.

"No," Wilf said. He reached out for the ball. It came spinning out of the flames and landed, smoldering, into his arms.

"Well done," Hywel said. "It's amazing what you can achieve with concentration and the right motivation."

Wilf hugged his ball. He felt empty inside, totally drained.

"That will do for the present," Hywel said. "Go back to the tower. Bring the journal with you to dinner. It should have revealed more pages."

Wilf left the workshop, and a light globe bobbed along beside him. He walked slowly down the tunnel, trying to see any indication of where the hidden door to the round room might be. He pictured the room. Seeing the door with its four knots and large circular handle. He opened his eyes to darkness.

The globe was missing. He needed to control the thing better. But what was that light? He ran down the tunnel, and the globe brightened as he approached.

The outline of a door with the four knots on it showed in the tunnel wall. He pictured the door opening, but it didn't. He grinned. That would have been too easy. At least, he knew he could find the door again. Myra would help rescue Ermentrude; he felt sure of it. Perhaps, they could smuggle her through the Veil and back to Mathowytch. It had to be worth a try.

It was worth the risk of Hywel catching them. Besides, he still needed Wilf, and Hywel wouldn't let anything happen to Katryna. Myra could take Ermentrude to Mathowytch, and then she would also be safe.

He set off down the tunnel, again, towards the tower. Tonight, when Hywel slept, Myra and he would return. She was bound to know how to open the door. They'd rescue Ermentrude. Katryna would be amazed at his daring. She'd cling to him and...

The globe exploded, plunging him in darkness except for the glowing ruby at the center of his wizard's ring.

# Chapter Twenty-Three
# The Rescue of Ermentrude

Myra wriggled her fingers at the fireplace, and flames sprang to life. The fading light outside sent shadows around the yard. The sun no longer bathed the room, and its temperature had chilled.

She moved over to one of the plush armchairs, snuggled up into it, and watched the flames dancing around the logs.

"Myra?" Wilf asked.

"Yes." She opened her eyes.

"Do you know where Katryna is?" He sat in the opposite chair.

"Went for a lie down. Said she had a headache."

"Good." Wilf sat on the edge of the chair, opposite her.

"That's a little unfeeling." Myra untucked her legs and straightened them.

"I don't mean it's good she's got a headache. I mean, it's good because I want to talk to you alone." Wilf stared at the fire.

"Well?" Myra asked.

"I just heard Hywel talking to Ermentrude, down in the tunnel."

"You did what?" She sat on the edge of her chair.

"I entered this circular room. Hywel was talking to someone in there who I'm pretty sure was Thiemus. Hywel was unhappy, because Ermentrude still hadn't told them the location of the safehouse." Wilf's words came out in one long breath.

"And you can find this room again?"

"I think so."

Myra stood up. "Show me."

"Shouldn't we wait until everyone's asleep?"

"What difference would that make?"

"If we manage to release her, we'll have to bring Ermentrude through the house. It would be better if we don't bump into Hywel or your brother."

"I think the longer Ermentrude is held down there, the more likely it is they'll break her."

"I suppose so." He didn't sound convinced and looked into the flames again. Myra tapped her foot. They should go now. It was clearly the right thing to do.

"Okay," he said, standing up. "But, I left Hywel in his workshop. If he comes out, we'll have no place to hide."

"It's worth the risk."

"I hope you're right." He led the way down the steps and into the long, dank tunnel. Myra summoned a globe and handed it to Wilf. It spun three times and then took off down the corridor.

"Can't you slow it down?" she asked, running beside Wilf as he splashed through puddles.

The globe stopped, and a door materialized.

"How did you get in last time?" she asked, placing her hand on Wilf's arm. She couldn't let the globe shine very brightly. It was making it difficult to see.

"The door was open."

"If it has a palm panel, we'll never gain access," she said.

"Isn't there some magic you can do to open the door?"

"No. Panels prevent other spells from gaining access."

"Then what are we going to do?"

"Step up to the door. See if a panel appears, but don't touch it," she said. "It will take a print of your palm and show Hywel who tried to gain access."

Wilf approached the door. No panel appeared.

"Perhaps there's no need for that type of security down here," she said. "Good news for us. Can you open it?"

"How?"

"Visualize it open, as you saw it the last time you were here. I've never been inside, so I can't."

She kept guard while Wilf closed his eyes. Peering down the corridor, a faint pinprick of light appeared at the end of the passage, or at least she thought it was one. The light expanded. It was another globe heading towards them.

"Someone's coming," she said, extinguishing her globe. "Hurry up. Get that door open."

"It's no use. I don't know how."

"Of course you do. You found the door. Therefore, you can find the room it belongs to."

He turned back to the door again. The other globe advanced on them and she moved closer to the corridor's wall.

"Come on, Wilf. Get that door open."

If Hywel found Myra down here, he would know she was playing both sides. He would probably throw her in one of the dungeons and torture her too. She glanced back down the tunnel, towards the tower. They might have time to retrace their steps before they were spotted. It would be difficult to negotiate the puddles without alerting whoever that globe belonged to. They should move now. There were only a few minutes before the globe illuminated them like a building in the Hong Kong evening light show.

A click sounded behind her, and the door to the circular room opened. She breathed a sigh of relief, pushed Wilf into the room, and closed the door behind her.

Myra relit the globe, and it cast a dim light that elongated their shadows across the room. The door to the inner room stood open. Silently crossing the dirt floor, she stood on one side of the doorframe and peered in.

Ermentrude sat, slumped over, in a chair facing the door. Her arms were suspended behind her, but the bindings were invisible. In the corner, a robed man appeared to be asleep. His chair balanced against the wall on its back legs. The room echoed with the sound of his open-mouthed snoring. Several globes hung in brackets at regular intervals along the walls. A closed wooden cupboard stood in the far corner.

Myra placed a finger on her lips and motioned for Wilf to follow her away from the door. "Ermentrude's restraints prevent her from using magic, so they didn't need to shield the room."

"How do you know that?"

"Because otherwise they wouldn't be able to use complex magic, would they?" she said.

"Of course. So what are we going to do?"

"How far have you come in your training?"

"I can move objects around and throw them," he said.

"And?"

"Find doors."

"Oh, great," she said. "Well, if that guard wakes up, start throwing heavy things at him. Hopefully, you'll manage to knock him out. However, let's try not to disturb him."

Myra touched Ermentrude on her shoulder and the witch raised her head. Myra placed her finger on her lips and pointed at Wilf. Ermentrude's eyes opened wider and she nodded. She stepped around Ermentrude. The air shimmered in a band around the witch's wrists. She altered her vision and saw a pulsing strand of magic leading to the guard. If she tried to disable it, he would wake. She stepped back in front of Ermentrude. The witch shook her head.

Myra brought her mouth close to Ermentrude's ear. "We have to get you out of here."

"As soon as you break the strand, the guard will know," Ermentrude said.

"I realize that. Any suggestions?"

"Leave me."

"We can't do that. Sooner or later, you're going to divulge every secret you know. And by the look of you, I don't think you can hold out much longer."

"Is that why they've sent you in here? Does Hywel think I will believe that you're here to rescue me? I bet he'll even let me leave, hoping I'll take you to the safehouse."

"I've already been to the safehouse. I spoke to Seldan. They don't have plans to rescue you."

"Of course not," Ermentrude said. "The protection of the ring is what's important, not one member."

"Katryna needs you. The Virus has nearly destroyed all her magic. You must get her to safety."

"There's nothing I can do for her. It's up to Wilf to save her."

"If I cut this thread, will you be strong enough to help us get you out of here?"

"I told you to leave me," Ermentrude said.

"That's not happening. Wilf has a little control over his magic, but he'll need your help."

She stepped back around Ermentrude, raised her hand, and wriggled her fingers. Sparks flew from the thread. The guard's chair banged onto the floor.

"Hey!" he said.

Wilf hurled a light globe, and it hit the guard square in the forehead. The guard pointed at Wilf, and he had to swerve to one side as a bolt of magic smashed against the wall. He kept on his toes, dodging and weaving in front of the guard to distract him, before throwing another larger globe. It exploded on the side of the man's head and he staggered.

Myra kept a steady stream of magic cutting at the band securing Ermentrude. Part of the room plunged into darkness as Wilf extinguished globes. The only light came from a globe that hovered in the doorway, ensuring they could see the exit.

The guard sent a bolt of magic at Myra, and she paused to create a shield over Ermentrude and herself. The cupboard in the corner rattled and shook. She glanced at Wilf. He was biting down on his tongue as he concentrated. The cupboard came free, flew across the room, and crashed into the guard.

The band securing Ermentrude disappeared as the guard fell beneath the heavy oak cupboard. Ermentrude stood slowly and held onto the chair for support. Wilf slung her arm over his shoulders.

"We'd better move," Myra said. "I'm sure this place is alarmed."

Thiemus stormed into the circular room, blocking their escape. He carried a small metal tray holding a hypodermic syringe and vial.

"Not one, but three traitors," Thiemus said. "Thinking of escaping?"

Ermentrude straightened up.

"Now," Myra said as she and Ermentrude blasted Thiemus together, throwing him back into the corridor. He lay slumped against the wall. The tray and its contents crashed to the ground.

"He always underestimates me," Myra said, glancing down at her brother.

Ermentrude picked up the syringe and vial. "You were going to infect me with the Virus?" She unwrapped the syringe and loaded it with the contents from the vial. "Let's see how you deal with losing all your power."

"No." Myra rushed towards Ermentrude. "Don't."

Ermentrude plunged the needle into Thiemus's arm. She sagged from the effort, but Wilf caught her.

"How could you do that?" Myra blocked Wilf and Ermentrude. "You're as bad as they are."

"We need to get out of here," Wilf said, placing a hand on her arm.

"He's my brother. I came to rescue you, and this is how you repay me?"

"It has nothing to do with you." Ermentrude glanced down the tunnel. "But, this won't be much of a rescue if we stand here in this corridor, waiting to be caught, will it?"

Wilf navigated around Myra and set off along the corridor, half-carrying half-dragging Ermentrude. Myra went over to Thiemus.

"I'm sorry." That was all she seemed to say to him these days. She took a deep breath and then ran to catch up with Wilf and Ermentrude.

# Chapter Twenty-Four
## Escape and Capture

Katryna woke to Myra shaking her. The pain in her head throbbed, but she forced her eyes open only to snap them shut again.

"Please, leave me alone." She turned over and hugged her knees. The headache was worse than it had been hours ago.

"Ermentrude's downstairs. It's vital you and her leave now for the safehouse."

"You have my mom?" She opened her eyes and winced as shimmering lights frayed the edges of her vision.

"Yes." Myra tugged on her arm.

Katryna raised her head and groaned. Myra helped her to stand. Her stomach wrenched and a powerful wave of nausea hit her. She stumbled over to the sink and vomited.

"I can't go anywhere." She wanted to lie back down on the bed.

"You don't have a choice." Myra steered her across the room.

"I can't see very well." She held her hands out in front until her fingers made contact with the doorframe.

"Lean on me. I'll guide you."

She stumbled along the landing, behind Myra.

"Ouch!"

"I'm sorry," she said each time she stepped on Myra's heels.

"We're going downstairs." Myra placed one of Katryna's hands on the railing and linked the other hand through her arm. They took the stairs one at a time. She had to feel for the edge of each step before she climbed down. She felt the tension in Myra's muscles as they progressed.

"Mom?"

Ermentrude folded her into an embrace.

"Later." Myra handed out hooded cloaks. "Thiemus won't stay unconscious for long. It's crucial we put a large distance between us and this tower before he comes storming out of that tunnel."

Wilf opened the door.

"Ready?" he asked.

Myra nodded. He stepped forward and hit an invisible solid wall. Myra pushed past him into the garden. "I thought Hywel had set up a barrier."

"Hopefully, it only prevents me from leaving. Ermentrude, you try next," Wilf said. She followed Myra outside.

Wilf turned to Katryna.

"I need to stay and complete my training, but you have to leave."

"Thiemus isn't very forgiving," Myra said, stepping back into the tower.

"Do you think Hywel will allow you to continue when he knows you helped us?" Katryna asked

"He needs the journal translated, and I'm the only wizard who can do that." Wilf backed away from the front door.

"We need to leave," Ermentrude said.

"She's right. I'm sorry, Wilf." Myra hugged him. "I'll find a way to let you know we're safe."

"Thanks," he said, turning to Katryna. "You look awful. How's your headache?"

"My head feels about two sizes too big for my neck, and it's pulsing to a very loud beat." She hugged Wilf and wanted to stay with her head supported on his shoulder. She gave him a weak smile.

"I'll find the formula," he said.

"I'm relying on it."

Myra ushered her out of the tower, along the gravel path, and out of the street door. Rain lashed at them when they crossed the threshold. Mud-colored water gushed down the hill concealing the street and covered their shoes.

Katryna groaned with the extra weight on her head from her rain-soaked hair and struggled to pull up the hood. The shimmering lights receded from her sight, but the pain in her head increased. Myra linked arms when Ermentrude stumbled with the force of the water.

"Where did this come from?" Katryna pushed through the fast-flowing torrent of water the street had disappeared beneath. Struggling down the center of the road seemed the safest option. She didn't remember any serious potholes in its surface.

"Hywel," Ermentrude said, breathing deeply. "This is the same type of storm he produced the last time I ran away."

They watched a couple of wizards struggling up the hill and then entering a house.

"He can do this?" Myra asked. "The Council allows him?"

173

"It's not the whole city, just this hill," Ermentrude said. "They won't be pleased, but they need him."

"Won't this hinder him catching us?" Katryna said.

"Our wet footprints will show him the route we've taken," Ermentrude said.

"Argh," Katryna said, doubling over.

"Is your head hurting that badly?" Ermentrude wrapped an arm around her.

"Yes, but… sharp pain… in my stomach," she said.

"Wilf," Myra said, glancing back up the hill. "You're feeling his pain."

"If I can feel his pain, why didn't he have a raging headache?"

"Why would either of you feel each other's pain?" Ermentrude asked. Katryna rolled up her sleeve and showed her mother the bracelet.

"No," Ermentrude said. "I told you not… But what has that to do with Wilf?"

"We don't have time for this," Myra said. "We'll exchange stories when we get to the safehouse. If someone is attacking Wilf, we know it's either Hywel or Thiemus, and that means they won't be far behind us."

Katryna shuddered as she plunged through the cold, muddy water. A floating branch snagged her cloak and she lost her balance, tugging her cloak free. The water pushed her downhill. She flailed around trying to grab anything that would stop her momentum. Arms caught hold of her shoulders and dragged her up.

"Thanks," she said, panting. The pounding of her heart matched the noise in her head. She wobbled when she tried to step forward.

"Careful," Ermentrude said. "We don't want to go fishing for you again."

At the end of the hill, the water branched into two storm drains. The road ahead was bone-dry with a layer of dusty mud over it.

Katryna's shoes squelched with every step. A few wizards and witches turned to look at them. Myra glanced back and saw the trail their wet footprints were leaving.

"Hywel will have no difficulty finding our route," Katryna said, wringing out the bottom of her cloak.

"If we stay on the busy streets, our footprints will soon be covered," Myra said.

"But won't we stand out in these wet clothes?"

"Do you have a better suggestion?"

Katryna would have shaken her head if she could.

"We'll stand out more if we don't move," Ermentrude said, walking forward. "We're three witches together, and that means we're already breaking about a dozen laws."

She caught up with her mother as they turned the corner into the market square. This late in the day, only a few stallholders still conducted business; most were clearing away their wares for the day. Ancillary wizards and witches were clearing up the debris from the day's trading. Staff wheeled large industrial trashcans and directed brooms and shovels to clean the square.

Katryna kept her face down as she traversed the square, steering clear of the cleaning crew. She followed Myra into the narrow streets at the other side. They seemed familiar, and she had a dim recollection of walking some of these streets after they came through the Veil.

Ermentrude struggled on, but her steps were becoming more erratic. Katryna wasn't sure how much longer her mother could keep up this pace. Ermentrude stopped and leaned against a wall, catching her breath.

"How much farther?" Katryna asked, wanting to lie down and sleep. Even the ground seemed inviting.

"We're almost there," Ermentrude and Myra said together.

Ermentrude pushed off the wall and staggered forward.

"What a sorry-looking team we are!" Katryna said.

They crossed over two more streets.

"Hold it right there."

Katryna spun round and blinked rapidly as her vision blurred.

"What can I do for you?" Myra asked.

"Explain what three witches are doing together and in this part of town." the patrol wizard said.

"Is that a problem?" Myra stepped in front of Ermentrude.

"The unlawful gathering of two or more witches is strictly prohibited," the patrol wizard said.

"I'm sorry." Myra raised her hands. "I'm from out of town." A blast of white magic surged from her palm. The wizard shielded the blast, but Ermentrude retaliated before the officer had time to recover. The patrol wizard collapsed to the ground.

"Run," Myra said. "I'm sure that will have alerted his patrol."

Katryna sped into the next alley and rounded a corner. A bolt of magic hit the wall above her head. Myra sent another blast of magic as Katryna kept pace with her mother.

"We can't go to the house with a patrol following us," Ermentrude said, breathing heavily.

175

"You two go on. I'll keep the patrol busy." Myra turned to face the direction of the last attack.

"Thank you," Ermentrude said.

"Just go. I'll see you in an hour after I lead this lot away." She sent another blast of magic down the alley.

"Be careful," Katryna said, running to catch up with Ermentrude.

At the end of the alley, she stopped, checked the street, and then darted across the open ground into the next one. Ermentrude paused at a wooden fence. She placed her hand on the palm reader. A panel slid open, and they stepped inside. The entrance closed behind them.

Katryna glanced around at the concrete path edged in overgrown vegetation.

"Don't step off the path," Ermentrude said.

"I hope Myra makes it."

"So do I," Ermentrude said. "Especially since she says she knows the location of this house."

The kitchen door opened, and Seldan stood in the doorway.

"Ermentrude," she said, beaming.

"Where is everyone?" Ermentrude entered the house and the blue security globe circled her. "Place your hand on the globe, Katryna. It will need a sample of your blood to register you."

"Ouch," Katryna said. The globe turned green.

"The members are waiting inside," Seldan said. "We got your message."

"What message?" Ermentrude asked. "I didn't send any message."

Ermentrude pushed past Seldan and strode into the meeting room. Katryna followed. 12 witches turned to face them and went silent.

"What is everyone doing here? The rule is we never meet all at once."

Seldan stepped forward. "Since you were captured, we thought this house might be compromised soon. Decisions involving us all have to be made."

"So you sent out a message in my name?" Ermentrude asked.

"It was the only way to get everyone here. We need a more radical approach in our campaign against the Wizard Council."

"What exactly are you proposing?" Ermentrude leaned on the back of a chair.

"We destroy the Palace and all those inside," Seldan said, addressing the assembled witches.

"But there are prisoners—witches—held in the dungeons under the palace," Ermentrude said.

"Sacrifices have to be made," Seldan said. "The wizards have made a Virus that is destroying our realm. What else are they capable of? I say we put a stop to them now."

"Do you have backing from the Witch Council?" Ermentrude asked. "Or is this plan all your own invention?"

"We have some support from the Witch Council." Seldan didn't meet Ermentrude's gaze.

"But not full support."

"There are some, like you, who think we should play the political game. Negotiate a settlement," Seldan said. "But that isn't working. Witches are dying, and our realm has been compromised. It's time for action, not words." Her voice became a rallying cry. Many of the witches shouted their support.

Katryna stared around at the group and back at Ermentrude. A few of the witches looked shocked at Seldan's proposal, but the majority were nodding their agreement.

"This group likes action. No more attacks from the shadows. Let's show the wizards real witch magic."

"And just how do you propose to destroy a palace that's protected by a copious amount of spells?" Ermentrude asked. "Not to mention the possibility that, by destroying many witches and wizards, you could bring about the destruction of the very realm you hope to save."

"Actually, we think it might be the one action that could save it. The evaporation of many wizards and a few witches might be enough to re-establish stability," Seldan said.

"This is unbelievable," Ermentrude said. "It might. It could. You have no scientific evidence that your actions won't cause irrecoverable damage."

"The Wizard Council has already done that," Seldan said. "At least this way, we can also stop the manufacture of the Virus."

"But you don't know that," Katryna said. "Wilf will be down there, and he's the only hope we have of stopping the Virus."

"Quarantine that witch. Get her out of here," Seldan said, pointing at Katryna. "The way to stop the Virus is to stop its production and isolate anyone suffering from it, so they can't spread the disease."

Witches moved away from Katryna. A protective bubble appeared around her with two thick strands, like rope, attached. Two witches stepped forward and each one took a strand. They pulled the bubble out of the room.

"Seldan you're going too far." Two witches restrained the shocked Ermentrude.

The witches pulled Katryna along a passage and down steps into the basement. One of the witches placed a hand on a wall panel and a hidden door swung outward. The witches pushed her inside. The door closed, and the bubble disappeared.

Katryna banged on the door. Then, she felt around the wall for another panel, but nothing appeared.

A globe stood in a wall bracket beside her and she tried to light it. It flickered and died. If she couldn't get out that way, she would have to follow the tunnel and find out what was at the other end.

The tunnel wall felt rough as she trailed her hand along it. Her fingers came into contact with strands of a wet, slimy plant and sharp rocks that sliced her skin. Roots and boulders littered the floor of the tunnel, causing her to stumble.

She rounded a bend and gasped. A pinprick of light shone far in the distance. She inched her way cautiously towards it. Water bubbled close to the trail as it started to incline. The pinprick expanded. Dim light illuminated the tunnel, revealing a rocky wall sparkling with quartz. On the other side, the path fell away. She peered over the edge at an underground river. It meandered through the gorge like a giant python approaching its prey.

The closer she moved towards the light, the faster the river flowed. It's babbling changed into a low roar as it plunged into an underground tunnel and disappeared.

The ceiling sloped lower, and she had to bend at the entrance to the light source. The distance between the floor and roof narrowed until she was forced to crawl. Rocks blocked her path, but she dug her way through to a narrow ledge that led to a large cavern.

The river resurfaced to cascade in a loud, triumphant roar down a waterfall, into an underground lake. Miniature rainbows arched around the falls as the spraying water hit shafts of light entering the cave through its chimney roof. Three fires burned on the cave floor. Katryna carefully made her way down a narrow path to the sandy beach. Two witches watched her approach.

"Where am I?"

The witches were pretty, with not a wart or hooked nose between them. "Quarantine," one of them said. "Those of us with the Virus have all been captured and sent here."

"How many are you?"

"30," the witch said.

"All from Kureyamage?"

"Kureyamage?" one of the other witches said. "No one catches the Virus there."

"But I came from there."

"That explains why you arrived from that direction." The first witch pointed at a steep path leading up in the opposite direction. "The rest of us came from there."

"You're the first from Kureyamage," the other witch said.

"So, the Virus is there too?" the first witch asked.

"I contracted it in Mathowytch, but I think it's also attacking wizards now," Katryna said.

"Good," said the second witch.

"You'd better come and join us," the first witch said, leading the way to one of the campfires. She pointed at a small cave in the rear. "Don't go in there. That's where we're putting the dead."

"The dead?"

"Five so far," the second witch said, sitting on the sand next to the fire.

"All from the Virus?" She stared down at the upturned faces of the other witches.

"Malnutrition and depression," the first witch said.

"Oh." Katryna collapsed on to the sand.

"I'm Olga, and this is Rytan," the first witch said.

"Katryna."

The other witches around the fire mumbled an unenthusiastic welcome.

"Do you know a witch named Griselda Picton?"

Rytan gestured over to the cave. "I'm sorry."

Katryna hugged her knees. She had to believe the bond with Wilf would let him know where she was. Her mouth went dry, and her gaze wandered over to the cave. She might never be found.

She had to believe he would find her. But perhaps she didn't have enough magic for the bond to still work. The black depths of the death chamber called to her. She placed her hands over her ears and bent her head. The pounding in her head increased, blocking all other sounds. She vowed not to answer the call—not yet.

# Chapter Twenty-Five
# The Dungeons

Thiemus stumbled into the hall. Blood dripped from a large gash on the side of his head. "Where are they?"

"Gone," Wilf said.

Thiemus pushed past him, ran into the courtyard, and opened the threshold door. A curtain of rain fell so heavy it hid the street from view.

Hywel appeared. "Send out a patrol. Advise them to follow any wet footprints leading from this hill."

Thiemus careened back into the tower, slamming the door. He stepped over to Wilf and punched him in the stomach. He doubled over and dropped to the ground, where he lay coughing.

"Those witches very nearly cracked my skull open," Thiemus said.

"That will do. We still need him," Hywel said.

Thiemus kicked Wilf before following Hywel into the study.

Struggling to his feet, Wilf stood in the entrance. He needed to stay and listen, but his instincts told him to flee to his room and barricade the door.

"They'll lead us to their safehouse." Hywel leaned forward on his desk. Thiemus was already yelling at a uniformed wizard in the mirror.

"That's correct, three witches. One of them is the traitor, Ermentrude Wakefield."

"How did she manage to escape?" the uniformed wizard asked.

"That's not important," Thiemus said. "Send out a patrol. Hywel used the rain charm, so you should easily be able to track them."

"Very well." The surface went blank.

Thiemus stepped away from the mirror and collapsed into the chair. He glared at Wilf with murder in his eyes. "Why are you still here?" he said, placing his dominant finger on his gashed head and closing the wound.

"Where else can I go? I seem to be rather attached to this place."

Hywel steepled his finger and regarded him. "You believe they will escape me?"

"They have a good chance. I wish I could have joined them." His stomach curled in knots. His words were braver than he felt.

"Despite your optimism, I believe you will see them again soon." Hywel sent a stream of magic at Wilf that secured his arms behind his back. "I've been very patient with you, but that is about to change. Follow me."

Wilf's legs moved to obey Hywel. He fell down the stairs to the tunnel, landing on his side. With his hands tied and his legs not under his control, he lay helpless until Thiemus jerked him upright. He splashed through puddles he normally avoided.

Hywel stopped at a portion of the wall and a palm reader slid into view. Wilf was pushed inside. The room was an antechamber with a door in two walls and a large dormant fireplace occupying the opposite wall. A squat figure approached, and Wilf recognized the guard from Ermentrude's cell.

"Bring him," Hywel said, stepping towards a closed door beside the fireplace. The guard grabbed Wilf's arm and propelled him forward.

"Is this where you made the Virus?"

The large room looked like a laboratory from his science classroom. "It's the place where we've made some of the greatest discoveries in magical science," Hywel said.

"And did you experiment on witch magic here too?"

"When it was necessary." Hywel pointed his finger, and two chairs moved to create a large space in the corner of the room. "You sound like Reginald. He tried to regulate all experiments involving anyone with magical ability. He didn't care that it would have put our programs years behind."

"Is that why he went to live in the other realm?" His father had never mentioned life in Kureyamage, but then Wilf hadn't shown any interest in Reginald's past. Another regret he had to carry.

"He was made to leave Kureyamage," Hywel said. "Reginald upset a lot of important wizards with his views on equality." Items from the shelving around the room flew to the table in front of Hywel. "Reginald went into hiding, but he wasn't one to keep quiet. He made contact with the renegade witches' movement about some of the experiments he'd witnessed." A small cauldron appeared on the workbench. "It's believed he taught the witches how to create the Veil around Mathowytch, but I think that monstrosity is pure witch magic."

"That's why your mother ended up dead," Thiemus said, malice dripping from every word.

"What?" Wilf leaned forward, but the guard pulled him back.

"It was regrettable," Hywel said.

"But…"

"You thought you'd killed her," Thiemus laughed. "You believed that a small, insignificant boy could wield that amount of magic. You're pathetic."

"You bastard," Wilf yelled. His ring flared and he could feel magic building up inside.

"Reginald needed a warning that showed him he wasn't beyond the reach of the Council. Her death reinforced to Reginald what would happen to his son if he didn't cease all contact with the Mathowytch witches."

"You killed her." He struggled against the guard's hold. His tattoo burned and his ring blazed.

"I'm surprised Reginald never told you," Hywel waved his finger over the small cauldron and the ingredients lined up next to it. "Move to that space." Vials hovered over the pot and emptied into it.

Wilf tried to dig in his heels, but his legs still followed Hywel's instructions. He twisted and turned against the guard. A stream of white magic blasted from his palm and hit the wall.

"Don't be difficult," Hywel said. "This won't hurt at all."

"What are you doing?" Power built up again as rage coursed through him.

"It's a new prototype of mine. It's still in the experimental stage, but I think it is ready for the next stage of trials." Hywel stirred his finger above the cauldron. "It's called 'An Advancer'." Thiemus secured Wilf's legs together. Then, he dove backward, narrowly escaping being hit by a white blast of escaping magic.

"He's becoming volatile," Thiemus said.

"You should have thought about that before you brought up his mother." Hywel sent a lash of fizzing light to strike Thiemus. It cracked across his back, and Thiemus bit his lip.

Hywel turned back to Wilf. "You're not the only young wizard who has difficulty in accessing his magic. All you needed was control over a few basic spells. Once that was achieved, this little device of mine could transfer knowledge appropriate for your wizard class and age. Then, you will no longer be a threat to society."

"I think I'd rather take the longer route." He struggled to control his magic as heat once again built up in his palm. The last of the ingredients tipped into the cauldron.

"I hope it doesn't overpower you, because then a little scrambling could happen." Thiemus leered at Wilf.

"A little scrambling?" he said, through gritted teeth. Sweat beaded on his forehead and dripped into his eyes. The power surged through him again, but he tried to tame it.

"Nothing to worry about, in your case. I understand you have the potential for greatness," Hywel directed a steady stream of magic into the cauldron. A bubble began to grow and stretch out towards Wilf.

"Hywel. Don't. Please." He pushed back into the wall. The bubble slithered along the floor until it touched his feet.

"What if it doesn't work? What about the vaccine?" His chest tightened. He wanted to run, screaming.

"It will work," Hywel said. "Relax."

The bubble grew to engulf him from the ground up. His feet, legs, and abdomen disappeared. The density of the bubble pressed in on him. He gulped air as it traveled up the rest of his body, restricting his chest and breathing. He struggled, twisting and lengthening his neck. The bubble halted. A surge of magic flashed across the room, and the bubble enclosed him.

He breathed deeply, relieved his lungs worked. The bubble continued expanding. Strands emerged from its walls and floated towards him. They uncoiled to reveal sharp needles at the ends. They drove into the skin at his wrists and ankles. He cried out. Hywel was killing him with magic.

The pain increased as the strands pulled tight, so he no longer stood on the ground. His shoulders burned as he hung suspended, arms and legs spread-eagled, within the bubble. Random thoughts swirled through his brain.

Reginald stood next to the shattered Mage Crystal. "Control," he said.

"Control," his mother said, floating towards him, holding out the Super Striker action figure.

Ermentrude waved a broom at him. "Control."

"Control," Katryna screamed at him.

Myra held out the bean stew covered in fungus. "You have to control your magic."

Soccer balls flew at him and disappeared centimeters from his face. Katryna's voice screamed again. Hywel must have forgotten about the bond Wilf shared with her.

"Control," he whispered as his body vibrated with a jolt of power. A high-pitched buzzing sounded before the pain's intensity increased. A searing heat shot up his body, from the strands, into his brain. Images of flames playing behind his eyes blocked out every other thought. He shrieked in terror and his body convulsed. A blinding white light filled the bubble, blocking his view of Hywel, Thiemus, and the room. He was back in the Veil. No. This time, it was wizard magic attacking him.

Agony pulsed through him, and his mind screamed as his whole body became consumed with pain. He could feel his and the Advancer's magic meeting like a head-on collision. His body jerked and convulsed. The buzzing grew louder, and the strands pulled at his limbs. He opened his mouth and howled in agony and rage.

Hywel had killed his mother. Reginald had been protecting him by placing the enchantment on the journal until he could defend himself. He'd assumed his father had meant to punish him. For years, he'd blamed himself for Yan Shuai's death and fought with his father, but it had all been Hywel's fault. He would survive, and then he'd show them the full extent of his Wizard Gilvary power.

# Chapter Twenty-Six
## Myra's Dilemma

Myra entered the meeting room of the safehouse and stopped. Angry voices filled the air as witches shouted at each other. Hands were raised and lowered, thankfully without sparks flying, but it seemed only a matter of time.

"There you are." Seldan moved to stand next to Myra. "We were beginning to mourn your capture." She would have loved to wipe the smug look off Seldan's face. The young witch exuded self-satisfaction like a cat lapping up the last drops of cream.

"Thanks for the vote of confidence. You should be glad of my diligence in making sure I'd lost the patrol before I returned."

"It won't matter soon," Seldan said. "We're about to abandon this house. We can't trust that Ermentrude managed to hold out under interrogation."

"Where is she?" Myra glanced around the crowded room.

"Over in the corner. Her fate is the subject of all this discussion," Seldan said. "Some want to ship her back to Mathowytch. A few loyalists want her to remain part of the group, but others think we should permanently remove her. She could be working for the wizards, they claim."

"And you?"

Seldan smiled maliciously. "I think she should join her daughter."

"What have you done with Katryna?"

"She's been sent to join the special enclave for virus sufferers," Seldan said. "If she survives the journey."

"What?"

"We've never sent anyone from Kureyamage before, but it's thought to be possible."

"Explain." Myra folded her arms.

"We discovered the place far beneath the Veil where the Witch Council quarantines its virus sufferers."

"I don't understand."

"It's quite simple. When the first cases of the Virus happened, the Council panicked. They weren't sure how it was contracted, and so they isolated any sufferer. Then, the numbers of new cases increased. They wanted to prevent widespread panic. So, a decision to avoid the real number of sufferers being known was made. After that, any witch showing symptoms was quarantined immediately beneath the Veil."

"And Katryna?"

"She's made history as the first witch sent from Kureyamage to join the enclave."

"I see," Myra said. "But then, how is it possible that wizards are being infected?"

Seldan's smile spread across her whole face.

"We discovered a batch of the Virus being delivered and returned it to a few senders."

"The wizards think the Virus has mutated and is able to infect randomly," Myra said. "But actually, both sides could stop any new cases from happening."

"Excellent, isn't it?" Seldan laughed. "Wait here. I need to count votes." She sauntered to the middle of the room, and a paper appeared in her hand. "Enough." Her voice was amplified above the din, and silence fell over the room. She read the paper, "The majority vote is to return Ermentrude to Mathowytch."

"Seldan, don't do this," Ermentrude said. "It's suicide to go up against the Wizard Palace." A low mummer filled the room again.

"Ermentrude, you've been a brave leader in the past, but you've become weak. There can be no negotiation with the Wizard Council until they accept witches as equals. This is a time for action, not rhetoric. Wizards have declared themselves the enemy by infecting witches. They are willing to sacrifice the very realm we live in. They are no longer fit to rule. It's time to take back our realm before it's totally destroyed. With witches in charge, we will be able to re-establish the balance."

"How?" Ermentrude struggled against the witches who held her.

"By scaling back the amount of wizard power in the realm until it equals witch power," Seldan said, addressing the assembled witches. The witches applauded and cheered.

"And tell me, Seldan. How are you proposing this equalization happens?" Ermentrude asked.

"They will be offered the chance to leave the realm," Seldan smiled.

"But they would still draw on this realm's power," Ermentrude said. Seldan glared at her.

"You're going to kill them," Ermentrude shouted.

Seldan raised her hand and wriggled her fingers.

Ermentrude tried to speak, but no sound came from her moving lips.

"Gather the supplies from the armory. We attack the Palace tonight, as planned."

The witches cheered and filed out of the room. Seldan placed a hand on a witch's arm, drawing her aside. "Hold Ermentrude until I return. We can deliver her to Mathowytch later."

The witch nodded and jerked the silently protesting Ermentrude out of the room.

"Myra," Seldan said. "I need you to return to Hywel's tower."

"Return? Are you insane?"

"We need to know Wilf is safe," Seldan said. "Hywel's workshop is in a tunnel connected to the Palace, therefore you're the only one who can bring him out."

"Why do you want Wilf?" Myra said.

"The same reason as the two Councils: access to that journal," Seldan said. "Once we've balanced the magic in the realm, we need to ensure that the Virus is never a threat again, and for that we need Wilf." Seldan laid her hand on Myra's arm. "Give Hywel this safehouse. We're not coming back here."

"Then where am I to bring Wilf?" Myra asked.

"Once you have him, we'll contact you."

This was the most ludicrous plan Myra had ever heard. Seldan had a bizarre notion that she could take control of Kureyamage. And Myra was supposed to return to the tower and convince Hywel of her loyalty. And there was Thiemus. She shuddered. She didn't want to know how, with his sadistic inclinations, he'd deal with her return.

Myra took a deep breath. This wasn't how she'd envisaged this escapade turning out. There didn't seem to be an angle she could use to her own advantage. She had no intention of this being the last trick she tried to pull off, but there didn't seem to be any other options.

"Alright," she said.

"Good luck." Seldan patted her on the back. "Take Nipits with you. Send him to find me once you have Wilf. That cat is one of the smartest I've ever met."

Nipits came out of the shadows and rubbed himself around Myra's legs in greeting. It was good to see the cat again. Myra left the safehouse and Nipits trotted through the city on point duty. He altered her to several patrols until they arrived back at the tower.

"Stay in the garden, out of sight," she said.

The cat meowed and jumped into the undergrowth. Myra took out the pouch of vials and drank one. The elixir's warmth spread through her body as she entered the tower.

Hywel's study was empty, but as she turned to leave, she heard him approaching, talking to Thiemus. She sat in a chair waiting for them. Her heart pounded and she hoped her voice wouldn't betray her fear.

"I've news that the spy ring is going to attack the palace," she said as soon as Hywel entered the study.

"And the safe house? Do you know its location?"

"Yes."

Thiemus stood by the fire, examining his fingernails.

"Excellent. I'll send over a couple of patrols to capture it."

"There's no one there. They've abandoned it. The Palace needs warning," she said.

"They won't attack. It's impossible to disable the warding spells protecting it," Hywel said.

"I bet that's what you said about Mathowytch before it was captured."

"That was different," Hywel said.

"Where's Wilf?"

"Safe," Thiemus said. "We've locked him in one of the workrooms."

"Under the palace? The Palace that's about to be attacked."

"I'm telling you, there is no danger from that little spy ring," Hywel said with a note of annoyance.

"These witches are a real threat, and you need to take them seriously." Her hands trembled. She shouldn't have taken the elixir with the amount of adrenalin pumping through her.

"Captain, I have news of the location of the witches' safehouse, it's…" Hywel said into the communication mirror. He glared at her as he spoke.

She gave the captain precise directions. "…And be careful of the vegetation in the backyard, its carnivorous."

Hywel barked out further instructions into the mirror for several minutes. Thiemus stood, never taking his eyes off her.

"This is all a complete waste of time," Myra said, when Hywel finished his call. "The witches are long gone."

"But if we secure the house, and they return, we will have them," Hywel said.

"Or you could try capturing them before they destroy the Palace. Why won't you take this as a real threat?" Myra said. The exasperation she felt punctuated every word, her usual caution disappearing.

"You actually believe them capable of..." Thiemus said and laughed. "...It's too absurd to even contemplate."

"If it will make you feel better, I will alert the guards at the Palace," Hywel said, using the mirror again. Thiemus's suspicious look made her want to shrink into the chair. She needed to persuade Hywel to take her to Wilf, but she wasn't sure how to begin.

Hywel leaned back in his chair and regarded her over his steepled fingers. "You're very agitated," he said. "Ermentrude infecting Thiemus wasn't part of your plan, I suspect, but playing both sides is always tricky."

She jumped out of her chair, stood in front of the desk, and stared down at the wizard. If Hywel knew all about her, then she was in danger of becoming a prisoner for Thiemus to practice his skills on.

"You sent me to Mathowytch to watch over Wilf and the witches."

"Yes," Hywel said. "But I don't remember telling you to join Ermentrude's spy ring. I remember telling you not to contact them."

"How else could I gain their confidence and glean information?"

"You're saying that, in order to maintain your usefulness, you attacked me and the guard?" Thiemus rubbed the red welt on his arm. "You let that old crone infect me."

"I didn't know she was going to do that. Look, I've discovered their latest plan." She put her hands behind her back, spreading her fingers. Hywel seemed deeply suspicious, which was only to be expected. She had to convince him that she still worked for him if she was going to get out of this alive.

"Where are Katryna and Ermentrude now?" Hywel asked. "I suppose their escape is also in my best interest?"

"Ermentrude was never going to reveal the safehouse's location," Myra said. "And now you have it."

"Go on." Hywel still peered at her over the tips of his steepled fingers. His eyes sparkled; he appeared amused by her discomfort.

"You can easily find Katryna using Wilf. She can't leave Kureyamage without him." She moved closer. "I needed to show the new leader of the spy ring that I'm trustworthy."

"Why have you come back?" Thiemus asked. "What's in it for you?"

"The same as it's always been," Myra said. "Staying in the Magic Realm."

"But in which city?" Thiemus asked.

"Kureyamage, of course," Myra said.

"Umm," Thiemus said. "So you profess."

"I've told you their plans, and their location. What more do you want?"

Hywel sat in silence.

"If the witches' attack is successful, what will happen to Wilf?" Myra asked. "Shouldn't we bring him here?"

"Wilf, of course," Hywel said. "He's what this is all about. You're here for him."

"I want him safe, that's all," Myra said. "He is my stepbrother." All she really wanted was to bolt for the door and escape. But she needed Wilf. Without him, she had no negotiating power. With the journal in her hand, she could decide which faction to empower, and that would be whichever society offered her freedom to control her own destiny. She wanted a life where she no longer had to placate a wizard, or witch, who was threatening her survival.

Thiemus laughed mirthlessly. "Such a concerned sister," he said. "Not a role you're good at. I can testify to that." He shook his withered arm at her. "Is he to be your bargaining chip? Are you thinking of offering him to the highest bidder?"

"I've no idea what you are talking about," Myra said. "I'm worried he will be captured, or killed, if the attack is successful."

Hywel stood up. "Then let's go and visit him, shall we?" He motioned for Myra to lead the way.

She hesitated. Once in the dungeons, she'd be at Hywel's mercy. She took a deep breath and hoped it wouldn't be one of her last. Then, she walked out the door and turned towards the tunnels.

# Chapter Twenty-Seven
## Under Attack

The pain receded, but Wilf's veins throbbed as magic pulsed through him. He cracked open his eyes. The bright white light had dissipated. He could see into the room beyond the bubble, although the air reminded him of water rippled by wind.

The guard sat close by with his chair leaning on its hind legs against the wall. He appeared asleep. Wilf couldn't see Hywel and Thiemus. He flexed his stiff, swollen fingers. A golden shooting star blazed on the back of his right hand where his red one used to be. The pressure in his skull felt as if his brain had expanded to fill every gram of space. Strips of his singed clothing lay on the bottom of the bubble.

The door opened, and the hazy outlines of two wizards and a witch entered the room. Through the distorted bubble wall, he saw one of the wizards kick the legs from the guard's chair. The guard jumped up.

A clear window appeared in the bubble wall as they approached. Wilf registered Hywel, Thiemus, and the shocked expression on Myra's face. They'd managed to capture her. He'd felt Katryna's pain earlier, so they must also have her and Ermentrude.

A small hole appeared in the window.

"Can you hear me?" Hywel asked.

He tried to speak, but his voice sounded hoarse and gravelly. He nodded.

"Good," Hywel said.

"What have you done?" Myra's face was deathly white.

"It's an experiment of mine," Hywel said. "It advances ability by sending an amplified stream of magic and knowledge."

"Experiment! How much success have you had with this... device?"

"It's been varied, I must admit," Hywel said. "A wizard with Wilf's potential should survive the process."

"Let me get this straight. You applied a risky piece of apparatus to Wilf, not knowing if it would kill him or not? Am I missing something here?"

"It wasn't that much of a risk," Thiemus said. "We'd performed lots of tests. And see, he's alive."

Myra opened and closed her mouth.

Wilf noticed the rage burning in her eyes. That was an expression he'd witnessed and suffered from before. By the way she was talking to Hywel, it seemed they were working together. He couldn't trust her. She said she was there for him, but it was more likely she was there for her own self-interest.

"Would you like to see what he can do?" Hywel asked.

"You make him sound like a dog doing tricks." She folded her arms.

"I won't do anything." His eyes watered with the pain of speaking.

Thiemus picked up a small hand mirror off the table and Hywel nodded at him. He ran his finger over the mirror's surface.

A pulse of magic ripped up Wilf's left side. He screamed, arching with pain, and his vision blurred.

"Stop it." Myra tried to snatch the mirror away from Thiemus.

"How else would you suggest I entice him to demonstrate his new powers?" Hywel asked.

"I won't," he said, through gritted teeth. Finding the swirling mass of magic inside his mind, he began to form an image of a defenders' wall being erected, one player at a time.

Thiemus held the mirror out of Myra's reach and ran his finger over its surface again. Wilf howled in agony. A hole appeared in his wall as a player fell to his knees. He focused back on the image and more defenders rushed to secure the wall.

"You're killing him. How will that help you?" Myra stepped towards Thiemus again.

The guard blocked her and held onto her arms.

"Get your hands off me," Myra yelled.

Hywel nodded, and the guard released her but remained close.

The room shook. Vials and bottles rattled on the shelves. Several books thudded to the floor.

"What was that?" Myra stared at Wilf.

"Don't worry. It wasn't him, probably another quake. They are becoming stronger and more frequent lately," Hywel said.

"Or it could be the attack I was telling you about." Myra glanced at the door.

"Attack?" Wilf's voice was little more than a whisper.

"Nonsense," Thiemus said.

"Wilf, I want you to transform this mouse into a toad," Hywel said.

Thiemus walked over to a cage on the bookcase containing several mice. He selected one and placed it in a glass flask.

"All this for party tricks?" She gestured at Wilf and the bubble.

"It is more than Wilf could do this morning. Transformation is actually a very difficult skill," Hywel said.

Wilf shook his head again. Hywel sighed and nodded for Thiemus to increase the pulse. His body vibrated until the pulse stopped and he hung from the strands with his head bent. He couldn't take much more, but he'd be damned rather than become Hywel's puppet.

Thiemus placed the flask on the table. He picked up the hand mirror again. Wilf focused on the image in his mind and his players' linked arms. Wilf had control. The goal was secure. He stopped fighting and embraced the pain. It began to recede, becoming a mere nagging twinge. The strands pulsated, but he raised his head to stare at Hywel.

The wizard snatched the mirror from Thiemus and ran his own finger over its surface. Wilf blocked the pulse. The strands dangled limply and he fell, hunched, to the ground.

"Amazing," Hywel said in hushed tones.

"What?" Myra asked.

"He's blocking the pulse," Thiemus said, awe in his voice. "That's incredible."

Wilf concentrated on the strands of magic attaching him to the bubble. He could sense the sharp ends within his veins. Taking a deep breath, he began to force them to retract slowly from his body. Sweat trickled down his forehead. The strands resisted, but as he battled on, they began to move. Inch by inch, they loosened their hold on him, until finally, with a snap, they exited and melted back into the bubble's wall.

Wilf took several breaths, and then stood on his trembling legs. Placing his hands on the sides of the bubble, he closed his eyes. Concentrating fully on the ebb and flow of the magic, until he felt its connection to the source, the spell's attachment to the Realm's energy. He grabbed hold of the magic and shattered it. The bubble disappeared.

He brought his full attention back to Hywel. The wizard backed away. A shocked expression crossed his face.

"How did you do that?" Thiemus asked.

Myra placed a hand on Hywel's arm. "I don't think Wilf will be answering any more of your questions. I'm not sure he can hear us anymore."

"I can hear you." His voice sounded unusual even to him, deeper and stronger.

"Your skin is shimmering," Myra said.

He held his hands up and looked at the ripples of magic coursing up his arms. He pointed his finger at the guard. The man flew against the stone wall and became embedded, until all that remained were his head, hands, and feet. The guard screamed, soundlessly.

"Wilf," Myra said, panic in her voice. "Control your magic. Don't let it overpower you."

The guard's face turned blue. Wilf could feel the stones crushing the guard, snapping his ribs.

"Release the guard before he dies," she begged.

His gaze fell on Hywel backing towards the door. He stepped over to Thiemus and took the mirror out of his fingers. He crushed it to powder. The room shook again. A crack appeared in the stone around the doorframe. Dust fell from the ceiling. Hywel ran from the room, followed by Thiemus.

"Whose side are you on, Myra?" Wilf asked.

"Yours." She took down the guard's cloak from a peg beside the door and threw it at Wilf.

"Where are Katryna and Ermentrude?" He put on the cloak and secured it with a cord that appeared in his hand.

"We need to get out of here first," she said.

He surveyed the damaged room, surprised that they were still in the dungeon. He shuddered and released the guard. The man fell to the ground and took several shallow breaths.

Wilf stepped towards the door, not taking his eyes off the huddled form of the guard. He'd put a living man into a wall to die. It had been a thought, an image he'd created and that had become an action. If the Wizard Council had thought him a danger before, they were in for a very unpleasant surprise at his new ability. This new power gave him access to the very pulse of the Realm. It had become part of him.

A door stood open in the tunnel wall.

"Do you know where that leads?"

"No," Myra said.

He pointed at a globe, and it floated down from its bracket. He went through the entrance and up the steep spiral staircase. The dust-covered steps showed recent footprints. Myra grasped the rope handrail and the metal rings clanked. He glared at her, and she released it.

He climbed, but the steep twist of the staircase restricted his view to only a few steps in front. He softened the light from the globe to reduce their shadows' lengths. Weak from Hywel's Advancer, he needed to stop now and again to catch his breath. He leaned against the wall. His heart pounded. He struggled, trying to suppress his thoughts. The amount of magic rushing through him was frightening.

He rounded a bend and a barred window shone light on the steps. A faint breeze cooled his face as he peered through its bars. He studied the inner courtyard. A large pool stood in the center, reflecting the imposing towers of the palace and its galleries. Shallow basins fed the pool at its narrow end. Four small lawns, boarded with flowering shrubs, lay in between the pools. The building surrounding the courtyard had a large door on each side. They were decorated with symbols and painted in colors of the different seasons from Wilf's realm. He could see spring, summer and fall.

Wilf moved, allowing Myra to see through the window.

"I've heard about this courtyard. It's in the Wizard Palace.

Wilf continued to climb the remaining steps until they ended in front of a locked iron door. He laid his hand on the door and closed his eyes. His mind could visualize the metal and its welds. Running his hands up and down the edge, he found the bolts securing the door.

He opened his eyes and stepped back. Placing his ringed finger on the door, he drew it across. The bolt slid back as if his finger were a powerful magnet. He did the same with the bottom one. Then, he unlocked the door with the thought that it should be open, and it swung outwards, allowing him access to the courtyard. Myra followed him through the winter door. Glass windows rattled and the ground shook from an explosion.

"Ermentrude's not in charge of her spy ring. A witch named Seldan is leading an attack on the Palace," Myra glanced around the inner courtyard. "Which way now?"

Footprints appeared in the gravel path running around the edge of the garden. Wilf set off at a sprint towards the summer door; he opened it and stepped inside, Myra following him. He pulled Myra violently to the left. A large chunk of masonry landed where she'd stood.

"That was a little too close," she said.

Murals decorated the large room. All the scenes were of summer pastures from different continents around his realm. But through them all ran a river that reminded him of the Thermals. A domed, stained-glass ceiling sent colored lights dancing around the tall, vaulted room.

"This isn't a safe place." He gestured towards the ceiling. Spider cracks spread across the plaster of the murals. Myra nodded and followed him around the edge of the room and into a wide corridor.

"Now where?" she asked. A grand staircase, covered in a red-patterned carpet, graced the end of the corridor. Wilf saw the edge of a cloak disappearing.

"Up there."

He ran forward and bounded up the stairs two at a time. All signs of his past weakness left him as he used magic to increase his speed. He reached the landing before Myra had climbed three stairs and sped after Hywel and Thiemus.

He turned the corner as a door began to close near the end of the landing. He raised his finger and forced it to remain open. He surged on and dived into the room. The room had no windows. It contained a small table, one chair, and a trundle bed. A large mirror ran the length of one wall, dominating the space. The mirror glowed. Hywel appeared in it with Thiemus grinning behind him.

"It's remarkable what that machine has achieved in you," Hywel said. "However, I think, for both our sakes, it might be better if I put a little distance between us until you have adjusted."

"Come back, and I'll be happy to demonstrate how well-adjusted I am." Wilf ran his eyes around the edge of the mirror. Myra ran into the room.

"How does it work?" He pointed at the mirror.

"I don't know." She stood in front of it.

Thiemus reached through the mirror and dragged her through.

Wilf banged on its surface, but it remained solid. He visualized it as a window and tried the surface again. It remained unyielding.

"Open Reginald's journal and show me," Hywel said.

"I don't…"

A handle appeared under the mirror. Wilf took his father's journal out of a drawer. The handle disappeared.

"Show me," Hywel said.

"Don't," Myra said.

Thiemus slapped her face. Blood trickled down her chin from the cut on her lip. Wilf opened his father's journal.

'*The Pulch Virus Vaccine requires the following ingredients:*'

Words, drawings, and symbols appeared on the page.

"Excellent," Hywel said. The room shook. Hywel turned to speak to Thiemus.

"I thought you might like to know that the witches have been captured," Hywel said. "This little stunt of theirs has cost them dearly. In one action, we've been able to put an end to their resistance in our city. Tomorrow, you can start to transcribe the vaccine for me if you want to see Myra again."

The mirror went opaque. Wilf banged on the surface again in frustration. Running from the room, he tore open doors along the corridor. They had to be here. The last room contained shelves filled with servants' uniforms in various sizes. He dressed. Then, carrying socks and shoes, he walked slowly back to the mirrored room. He sat down on the bed, dropping the shoes to the floor.

His vision flickered, and he fought to keep his eyes open. A wave of fatigue hit him. All he wanted to do was lie down and sleep. He couldn't fight anymore. He'd been through so much. His body trembled. He slid back onto the bed. A blanket appeared and covered him.

Myra. He had to find her.

His eyes closed, his head sunk into the pillow, and the dreams started.

# Chapter Twenty-Eight
## Katryna's Escape

Katryna woke with a start. She rolled onto her right side and sat up. Only Olga and Rytan remained near her.

"You're awake," Rytan said. "We weren't sure you would."

"My headache's gone," she said. "For the first time in days, I don't have the pounding to deal with."

"You were shouting and writhing on the ground," Olga said. "We tried to rouse you, but…" She held up her hand to show a burn mark on her palm.

"I did that?" Katryna asked.

"Yes," Olga said, cradling her hand once more.

"And that." Rytan pointed at the rock face.

"But how?" She ran her fingers over the jagged edges of a deep scar in the cave wall. "My magic's gone."

"You've given us all hope," Olga said. "If one witch can fight the Virus, perhaps we all can."

"I'm not so sure." Rytan shook her head. "Look at her arm and neck."

Katryna rotated her arm. A wizard's golden shooting star blazed and pulsated on the back of her hand. A vein of gold ran up her arm. "Wizard power?" She ran over to the pool's reflective surface. Witches backed away from her, muttering.

The vein continued up her arm, disappearing under her sleeve, only to reappear on her neck, behind her ear.

"How?"

"Don't look at us," Rytan said. "I've never heard of a witch with a wizard's mark. Do you feel different?"

"Apart from the joy of no pounding headache, I'm the same." She stared back into the pool, turning her head from one side to the other. "Not one wart, though."

"What about the magic?" Olga asked.

Katryna paused, closed her eyes, counseling her thoughts. She found a spark of magic in the recesses of her mind. She laughed. It looked like a gas fire's pilot light flickering its blue flame, waiting to ignite and burst into flames. She opened her eyes, raised her hand, and wriggled her fingers. Nothing happened. She pointed her finger and power surged through her. A blaze of white energy streamed across the lake. Rocks shattered and plunged into the churning water.

"Yesterday, I couldn't light a globe." She giggled from the power rush.

"That's amazing," Rytan said in a hushed tone.

"It must be because of the imbalance," Olga said, wringing her hands. "We're trapped below ground in a realm gone mad. We're going to die, either from the Virus or a quake."

"Get a grip on yourself," Rytan said. "No good comes from thinking that way." She pointed at Katryna. "And there is hope."

"Has anyone tried to return to Mathowytch?" Katryna asked.

Both witches nodded their heads.

"There's more than one way to die down here." Olga reached out to put a hand on Katryna's arm but stopped midway.

"You probably can't enter Mathowytch without setting off all the alarms in the city with your magic and that bracelet," Rytan said.

Katryna focused on the shooting star. There had to be a connection with Wilf. She turned to face the route to Kureyamage. "Then I'm heading that way," she addressed all the witches. "Who wants to join me? Or are you happy to wait here and die?"

Olga and Rytan walked over to stand next to her. The muttering sound of discussion grew amongst the other witches. "We're with you," Rytan said. Olga nodded.

"What makes you think you can get us into the city?" one of the witches shouted.

"What if we can't open the door? There's no water or food at the end of that tunnel," another shouted.

"Some are too weak to travel. Are we to abandon them?" asked another.

"Each witch has to make her own decision," Katryna said. "I'm giving out no guarantees, but I'm not prepared to wither away down here."

"Easy for you to say," said the first witch. "Now that you have magic."

"If we make it through, I will try to send you word." Katryna strode towards the path leading to Kureyamage. Olga and Rytan guided a small group of witches to join her. The majority herded together next to the lake. Katryna headed up the narrow path, amazed that she'd managed to travel this treacherous route in the dark. She peered over the edge at the rushing water. There were advantages to not knowing how perilous this trail was. A globe bounced next to her. Magic—how she loved it.

The weakened witches made the pace slow and ponderous. It took a long time before the locked door loomed into sight. She wasn't expecting a warm reception when they entered the safehouse.

There were no visible handles or rivets for her to manipulate on the heavy metal door. She placed her hands on the door's surface and flinched.

"What is it?" Rytan asked.

"I can feel the metal," Katryna said. "It's so strange. I've never been able to do that before." Working her hands over the metal surface, she located the lock. The door clicked open, swinging inwards.

She grabbed the edge of the door to stop it from crashing against the wall. Peering up and down the corridor, it seemed to be empty. She waited, listening. Olga placed a finger on her lips and motioned the group to stay quiet.

"Rytan, you come with me. Olga, stay here and keep the rest silent while we check the corridor and meeting room," Katryna said. "If we're not back in ten minutes, you'll have to decide whether to go back to the cavern or come after us." Olga nodded.

Katryna and Rytan hugged the shadows as they made their way along the corridor to the meeting room. Furniture lay in splinters. Paintings slashed. Pottery and china smashed. At least, there appeared no evidence of blood in the ransacked house. The damage seemed to emanate from malice, rather than a fight. A cold sensation stretched out from the meeting room.

"What's the matter?" Rytan asked when Katryna stopped.

"Sensors are covering the opening. I can feel them."

"What is this place?" Rytan peered over Katryna's shoulder and into the room.

"It used to be a safehouse for the resistance movement."

"Doesn't look very safe anymore," Rytan said.

"How did you escape the tunnels?" Seldan asked.

Katryna spun around to face Seldan, her finger out in front of her. Nipits hissed at Katryna.

"What happened here?" she asked.

"Wizard patrol." Seldan carefully placed her hands on her hips. "Myra probably told them where to find us."

"Myra?"

"I think she's playing both sides," Seldan said. "Now answer the question. How did you get back in here?"

"Magic." Katryna revealed the shooting star on the back of her hand.

Seldan's eyes widened. "That's not possible."

"Is Wilf still being held in Hywel's underground workrooms?"

"As far as I'm aware, unless he's been crushed," Seldan said. "We set off a number of explosions around the Palace last night."

"I would know if he were dead or injured. He's not in pain any longer."

"Then, we'd better start for the tower. If he's not there, then he could be in the palace," Seldan said, taking a couple of steps into the corridor and then stopping. "What are you both waiting for?"

"You think I would go with you?" Katryna asked. "Trust you? Olga, put this witch in the tunnels."

Seldan spun round. Olga and the rest of the witches came around the corner of the tunnel. Seldan raised her hand too late. Katryna's magical strands secured them.

"You need me," Seldan said. "These witches can't do magic."

"Where's my mother?"

"Back in Mathowytch for reassignment. She's no longer the leader here."

"Take her," Katryna said.

Olga nodded to two witches. Seldan struggled, but they held her firmly and dragged her to the tunnels. Nipits escaped down the corridor.

"What now?" Rytan asked.

"We find Wilf." Katryna turned to the group of witches. "If we stay together, we'll look very suspicious. A patrol is bound to find us. We need to split up. I'm sorry, but this is as far as I can take you."

"But, we're witches with no power in Kureyamage," Olga said.

"Then stay here," Katryna said. "Don't go into the meeting room. There are sensors. Interrogate Seldan. She travels between the two cities. Find out how. Perhaps, you can convince her to help you return to Mathowytch. Only, I'd be careful about trusting that witch."

"You're going to leave us?" Olga asked.

"I have to find Wilf." Katryna headed for the door.

"I'm coming with you," Rytan said, following her. "Two witches walking the streets can't cause a problem."

"Thanks." She headed into the garden. "Don't step off the path. These are not friendly plants."

The gate stood open to Hywel's tower. A film of dust covered the entrance and its furnishings. She opened the door leading to Hywel's workrooms. The staircase had collapsed. She sent a globe floating into the void. It bobbed above a deep hole. The tunnel was destroyed.

A screech pierced the tower. "What have you done?" the housekeeper yelled, running down the corridor.

Katryna pointed her finger at the servant, freezing her in mid-run. "Where's Wilf?"

"You've killed him, the master, and Thiemus." Tears ran down the housekeeper's cheeks.

"Wilf isn't dead, I'm still connected to him." Katryna stepped closer to the witch. "Where would Hywel take Wilf?"

"I'll never tell you. I'm no traitor," the housekeeper said.

"Must be the Palace," Rytan said. "But we'll never get in there. Not after a witch attack."

"Bring her." Katryna led the way to the kitchen and secured the housekeeper to a chair. The smell of cooked food caused her stomach to rumble. It had been days since she'd had a substantial meal.

Rytan scoured the kitchen, throwing open cupboard doors as she went. She collected two large plates and heaped them with food. Katryna sat next to Rytan and grinned at the mountain of food.

"We could wait for Hywel to return and force him to take us to Wilf," Katryna said.

"You might have enough power to challenge him, but I don't," Rytan said. "If your father is as powerful as you've said, I don't see how we can make him do anything. What if he's not alone?"

She shrugged her shoulders, her mouth full of bread and cheese.

"I'm not alone," Hywel said, walking into the room ahead of a company of guards. "Nice of you to return, Katryna. And you've brought me a guinea pig for the first batch of the vaccine. Very kind of you."

Katryna stood and her chair crashed to the floor.

"Wilf will transcribe the journal for me," Hywel said. "When he's finished, I will need a witch, or several, to test the new vaccine on. If it works, then we can vaccinate enough witches to restore the magical balance."

"And what will happen to those witches?" Katryna asked.

"They will receive a bracelet in return for a dose of the vaccine," Hywel said. "What is that?" He grabbed hold of Katryna's hand. "It can't be." He pulled her closer, examining the vein trailing up her arm and neck. "You're a wizard? But how is that possible? Wilf did this. That's very impressive. You and Wilf are about to spend the rest of your lives under my microscope and very heavy shielding."

"The Witch Council won't let you get away with this."

Hywel laughed. "What Witch Council? They're finished."

A guard stepped forward and released the housekeeper. She rubbed her wrists and glared at Katryna.

"Political power can make strange friends. The Witch Council has prudently opened negotiations for their survival," Hywel said. "They've agreed to hand over Mathowytch for the vaccine. I intend to be in the front row to watch the Veil being dissolved."

"It can't be true." Katryna leaned on the table for support.

"But it is," Hywel said. He pointed at Rytan, "Guards, escort this witch out of my home and into the cells." He took Katryna by the arm. "Let's visit Wilf. I'm sure he's going to be happy to broker a beneficial deal for your release."

# Chapter Twenty-Nine
# The Wizard Palace

Wilf woke in the mirrored room. His shoulders ached and his neck had a terrible crick on the right side. He groaned as he stood up. There wasn't an inch of him that didn't feel sore and bruised.

He staggered over to the mirror's surface. It held no reflection. Pointing his ringed finger, he began to imagine a doorway through the glass. His ring flared and a flash fizzed on its surface.

Hywel appeared.

"Did you sleep well?"

Wilf sat down at the table and folded his arms.

"This is important." Hywel ran his fingers through his hair. "Were your dreams particularly vivid?"

Wilf glared at Hywel. The mirror went opaque. Then, a pad of blank paper and pens materialized on the table. Wilf sent a bolt of magic at the mirror again, but it fizzed out. A satisfying, small scorch marked the surface. He rubbed the gold shooting star on his hand. His dream last night had felt so real of Katryna lying in a deep cavern, next to a lake.

When he'd tried to contact her through the bond, pain had swelled in his head from her. He'd sent a pulse of magic trying to ease it. It worked, and a soothing sensation, calm and loving, flowed back through the bond. His pulse raced as it washed over him. He caught his breath. The image grew of her sitting on the window seat in Hywel's tower and filled his thoughts. He moaned as his body began responding to the remembered smell of citrus lingering in the air. A desperate craving to touch her grew in him, to feel her lips on his. The magical stream filled with waves of longing as he gave in to his thoughts. The image had been so vivid, he'd reached out and felt his fingers touch her hair. His magic flared, and he'd struggled to control the flow. A scream developed in his head that wasn't his. Katryna had begged him to stop, but he couldn't break the connection. He'd woken. His heart was racing and his clothes were damp with sweat.

He held his head in his hands. Then, he quickly glanced up at the mirror. Hywel must have been trying to tell him that he'd injured Katryna. But Hywel wouldn't know about her. So what was the wizard trying to blame him for?

The mirror cleared. Hywel stood next to Myra… and Katryna. Wilf let out a sigh of relief at seeing her.

"Can you read the formula?" Hywel asked.

"Katryna, last night, I thought…"

She held up her arm. A golden shooting star started on her hand and ran up her arm. He'd done that to her.

"I'm sorry," he said.

"Enough of this," Hywel said. "Answer the question."

"I haven't tried."

"It's probably beyond your comprehension. Use the paper and ink to make me a copy," Hywel said.

"Wilf!" Katryna said.

Hywel waved his hand, and her mouth opened and closed without sound. "Once Wilf has transcribed the vaccine formula, you can talk all you want."

"You'll let us go?" Myra asked.

"I'll let them be together," Hywel said, signaling to a guard.

"I don't think we're talking the same outcome," Myra said.

"I want that formula by the end of the day," Hywel said, turning back to Wilf.

"And if I refuse?"

"That would not be in the best interest of anyone associated with you."

The mirror went opaque again. Wilf took the journal out of his pocket. The page containing the formula shimmered. It was covered in magic and chemical symbols he didn't understand. He flicked over to the next page. Lists of how the substances were to be prepared and the dosage to be given to each patient appeared. Chemistry had never been his favorite subject.

Wilf leaned back in the chair. Enzo and the team would have played the championship by now. He'd rather be running up the field with his only problem being how to dodge defenders and score a goal.

The air moved next to him, and a soccer ball materialized. It bounced next to him until he trapped it with his foot and rolled it backward and forward.

"A stupid ball." He kicked it, and it bounced off the wall. He ducked as it headed back towards him. All he could do was produce a ball of pure energy when he was angry, hurl objects around, or materialize a soccer ball that thought it was a puppy. He was pathetic. Magic surged through him.

He pointed at the pen. It jumped off the table and into his hand. Fixating on the journal, he fed magic into the image of it floating above the table. The pages rustled, and the table rose a few inches off the floor. Copying out his father's journal would feel like detention, unless he could use magic. He tried an image of the words highlighting and copying themselves. The table banged back down. The journal sent a puff of smoke into the air. He picked the book up and examined it. The formula was still there. He sighed.

Thankfully, Katryna hadn't appeared hurt. He should have known that it had been a dream. Although, she did have a tattoo on her hand and arm. He'd been able to use the bond to reach her, so that must be good news. But, how had Hywel managed to capture her, and did he also have Ermentrude?

They were back at the center of the field, nothing achieved, but with the other team well ahead. Hywel was closing in on the championship cup, and Wilf hadn't managed to achieve one goal for his team. They'd become a group of fatigued and demoralized players. A new strategy was needed if he was to turn this around before the final whistle.

He glanced at the pen. He'd better start, because his father's notes were refusing to copy themselves. Once he had a print copy, they wouldn't be covered by his father's spell. At least, it would give him the ability to pass the formula on to the witches. He sighed and began to print the symbols. This would go quicker if he understood what he was writing.

The symbols moved. Then, they rose above the page and swirled around until they formed into a small typhoon above the page. He dropped the pen and it rolled under the table. The symbols then funneled back down onto the page.

Wilf opened his eyes wide and stared at the symbols. He knew how to use them. He couldn't read them, but he could create the spell. He bent down and picked up the pen. The symbols went out of focus and back to their original format. He stared at the page, but it refused to reveal its secret again. Last time, they'd moved as he began to write. Quickly, he scribbled down the first symbol. Nothing moved. He groaned.

"I hate magic," he yelled.

It took what felt like hours to complete a page. He flexed the cramp out of his fingers and paced the room. His stomach rumbled.

The last time he'd eaten had been yesterday. He'd kill for a sandwich and orange juice. They appeared on the table. He gulped down half the drink and then attacked the food. Pushing out his chair, he bumped the table with his leg. The open bottle of juice rocked. He reached out to catch it but missed. The sticky liquid ran over the table, covering the pages he'd written. He snatched up the journal, pocketing it for safety.

"Fuck!" he yelled.

Ink-smudged words disappeared from the pages. He threw the empty bottle at the mirror and it disappeared through it.

Magic. There was nothing worse. He glanced at the half-eaten sandwich. He'd needed it, wanted it, but he hadn't tried to conjure it. He called for the soccer ball, and it rolled over to him.

"Seriously?"

Perhaps, he was trying too hard by demanding his magic obey him. He placed his hand on the mirrored surface. "Open. I need you to open," he said. Nothing happened. His hand stayed on the solid surface.

"I give in," he said and kicked the ball. It went straight through. Now, he'd lost the ball. He leaned against the mirror and stared around the room. He wasn't going to transcribe those pages all over again. This was a total waste of time. His ring flared. The ball came back into the room and bounced next to him.

He banged his fist on the mirrored surface. His hand disappeared through. He spun round and banged on it again, but it had become solid.

"Stop messing with me," he yelled, lashing out a driving kick at the ball that would have sent it and a goalie into the back of the net together. A hole appeared in the mirror where the scorch mark had been. A large quake rocked the room and spider cracks spread from the hole. He pointed at the gap and reached for his magic. A roaring torrent of raw power rushed through him. The mirror exploded, revealing a tunnel with pulsing ribbons of light for walls. He climbed through and came out into a tiled corridor.

He moved cautiously around a corner. He was still in the Wizard Palace. A large crossbeam blocked the remaining few stairs of the grand staircase. Glass covered the floor, and a large crack in the Palace's exterior wall ran from ceiling to floor. Doorframes were misshapen and doors hung at strange angles, ripped from their hinges. Black blast holes decorated the walls at random intervals.

The journal banged against his leg. He needed to get it to safety, but he also needed to rescue Katryna and Myra. Hesitating, he glanced back down the corridor. He couldn't risk the journal being back in Hywel's hands. He focused on the bond.

*Where are you?*

His tattoo tingled. A sensation of being afraid but not terrified swept over him. Taking a step back down the landing, he stopped again. The smart move would be to get the journal out of the Palace and then come back. A desperate longing to see Katryna surged through him. He took another step. The ritual magic was affecting his ability to make the right decision. The journal had to come first. He'd leave it in one of the abandoned buildings near the Veil. It should be safe there until he could collect it.

He dove down a flight of narrow stairs on the right and negotiated his way through the debris covering them. A jagged piece of balustrade caught on his pants, and he grabbed the handrail to save himself from falling. It came away in his hand, and he swayed on his toes trying to recover his balance. Several deep breaths later, his pounding heart slowed enough for him to continue.

A darkened corridor, with buckled tiles, led to the kitchen. He stopped at the entrance and checked inside. A number of servants were clearing away plaster and broken crockery, while others prepared food on cleaned surfaces. The kitchen door stood open, beckoning him, on the opposite side of the room. Pointing at the large potholder attached to the ceiling, he imagined the bolts ripping. The ruby flared, and it came crashing down, missing landing on a small servant by inches. He shook his head in disbelief and slipped across the chaotic kitchen.

"You there! Where do you think you're going empty-handed? Take that bucket with you," a voice shouted. A man dressed in palace uniform pointed at a large bucket full of broken masonry. Wilf nodded and walked over to join the other staff all wearing the same uniform as him. He picked up the handle, went to lift the bucket, but he couldn't get it off the ground. The other servants sniggered.

"Need help?" one asked, pointing at the bucket. Wilf picked up the lightened load and carried it through the kitchen door and out into the yard. A large pile of rubble stood next to a breach in the outer wall. Guards patrolled the hole, scrutinizing everyone coming and going. Wilf emptied his bucket.

Several wizards were using their skills to fill in the breaches with masonry and magic. Another quake sent rubble slipping down the pile. A wooden staircase, used by the sentries, collapsed.

"The quakes are so frequent, I'm not sure we should be using magic," one of the wizards said.

"Nonsense," said another wizard. "The realm won't collapse because we're repairing a wall. It's the witches' attacking the palace that's caused the realm to destabilize."

"I'm not so sure," the first wizard said. "The magic is behaving strangely, not all spells are working as they should."

Wilf surveyed the yard. Guards appeared at a door on the west side of the yard. He didn't think they'd seen him, but clearly it was time he found a way out of here. He continued to scan the yard. Two cloaked wizards, deep in conversation, headed for the gate. He'd follow them out and, hopefully, the guards would think he was their servant.

Carrying his empty bucket, Wilf headed for the main gate and the two guards protecting the entrance. The wizards stopped, and Wilf reached the gate before them. The guards turned around as he approached.

"Where do you think you're going?" one of them asked.

"I'm…" he said, lifting the bucket. His sleeve fell back, revealing the golden shooting star.

"Sorry, Sir," the guard said. "It was the bucket and clothes."

"Well, let me through," he said, swinging the bucket. "We all have to help." The guard opened and closed his mouth, a look of confusion on his face.

Wilf hoped this wasn't going to get him sent back to the locker room, because the look on the guard's face said golden wizards don't act like servants—ever.

Stepping forward, Wilf expected the guard to continue blocking his way, but he moved aside. Wilf forced himself to walk calmly through the gateway and into the street. He struggled against the urge to turn around and check on the guards.

At the first alley, he ducked in and dumped the bucket. Then, he ran, as if heading for an open goal with all the defenders snapping at his heels. He wanted to put as much distance, as quickly as he could, between himself and the Wizard Palace.

Katryna would be safe until he returned. He felt like a traitor leaving her there, but she had Myra. Knowing his stepsister, she probably already had an escape route planned. Although, if he were honest, that would all depend on which side she'd decided gave her the best odds of survival. He patted his pocket containing the journal. At least now, he had the ability to stop the Virus.

# Chapter Thirty
## Joining Wilf

Katryna stumbled, and Myra grabbed her arm.

"Where do you think they are taking us?" Katryna asked.

"This may be our chance at escape," Myra said, keeping an eye on Thiemus' back.

"Enough talking," he said without turning around.

Katryna followed Myra down the corridor, away from the grand staircase. She maneuvered around the masonry, glass, and broken furniture.

"Bloody witches," one of the guards said, spitting at Katryna's feet. "I hope they pay for the damage they've caused." She stepped back, crunching through glass from a large arched window, all that remained in the frame were jagged edges.

They halted at the top of the servant's staircase, and Myra went ahead. A plank of wood lay across the gaping hole where the last two steps should have been. Katryna looked down into the black depths as she crossed. The plank wobbled, and she paused trying to regain her balance. One of the guards grinned, his foot resting on its edge.

"You do know she's Wizard Hywel's daughter, don't you?" Myra said from the safety of the ground floor.

Thiemus raised an eyebrow. "They know who she is." He turned to the guard. "Enough."

The guard removed his foot.

"Come on. It's fine," Myra said,

Katryna took the last few steps and grabbed onto Myra's arm. She stood silently next to Myra, avoiding looking at the plank. Her heartbeat raced and her legs felt so weak she wasn't sure she could move.

"This way." Thiemus hobbled off to the left. Wails and groans came from inside several rooms she passed. The ground rippled under her feet, and the walls undulated as a quake ripped through the building. Katryna held out her arms, trying to balance. Coving fell from the ceiling. Floor tiles cracked and buckled under the pressure.

"Argh," yelled the guards. A large piece of plaster broke free from the wall and landed on top of them. Thiemus lost his footing and pitched to the ground.

"Now." Myra grabbed Katryna's arm and pulled her along.

"Stop," a guard shouted. His boots crunched through the debris as he gave chase. A door stood open at the end of the corridor. Katryna and Myra ran through it, out into the yard, and dove behind a large barrel as the guard came to a skidding halt.

"Have you seen two witches?" he asked.

"Too many witches. Look what they've done."

"No, I mean… Hey, I was talking to you." The guard's voice faded.

Katryna glanced round the barrel. Wizards and servants milled around, some helping repair a breach in the wall, others trying to raise a wooden staircase by the gate.

"How are we going to get out of here?" She edged back into the shadows. They'd never make it through all those wizards. She ran her clammy hands down her skirt.

"We're a bit conspicuous," Myra said. "I don't see any other witches in the yard. The rest of the guards are going to come racing through that door at any minute." Myra glanced left and right, scouring the yard.

"I can try changing our clothing." Katryna pointed her fingers at Myra. It had to work. A puff of black smoke rose from her fingertip. She tried again, and again.

"Some of the Palace's protection spells must still be in place," Myra said, grabbing hold of Katryna's arm and pulling it down. "The building over there is a laundry. There's bound to be something we can use."

Katryna's legs refused to work. She would be captured, and she had no wish to learn how Thiemus dealt with escapees. Her hands trembled and she clasped them together.

"What are you waiting for?" Myra's eyes narrowed. "You can't hide in the shadows forever. We need to move."

Katryna took a deep breath and pushed off the wall. Keeping a step behind Myra, she clung to the building's shadows as they rounded the yard. Glancing back at the servant's entrance, she bumped into Myra.

"Pay attention." Myra pushed Katryna into the laundry.

The air was thick with moisture and the smell of detergent. Redundant water channels, leading to a central drain, interrupted the chipped tiled floor at regular intervals, a testament to the age of the building. Large industrial washing machines and dryers lined one wall. The whirling sound of the machines was deafening. There were dry cleaning pressers, laundry sleeves, and ironers on another wall. A large conveyer belt hung suspended from the ceiling, filled with laundered apparel.

Myra pressed the control. Items moved along the belt. She stopped it at two robes and passed one to Katryna.

"Should we get out of here, or would you rather quiver here in the shadows?" Myra said, frowning.

"You don't have to be so mean." Katryna squeezed her eyes.

"Sorry. I'm not used to having someone with me." She gave a weak smile.

"I'll try not to be a burden," Katryna said, stepping back into the yard.

Myra kept close to her. "Act as if we're deep in conversation and don't care about what's going on around us," she said. "But walk slowly. If there's another quake, and the guards at the gate are distracted, then let's use that."

"I hope it happens soon. My legs are quivering. It's hard not to break into a run."

"It's taking me all my self-control not to bolt for it too," Myra said.

She ambled along towards the gate. Her head was inches from Myra's, although her gaze roamed the yard. One shout, and she didn't think she could restrain her longing to sprint for the exit.

"The guards are here. I can see them." Her fingers grabbed Myra's arm, tight.

"Have they seen us?" Myra released Katryna's fingers. Myra kept a steady gait. Her eyes fixed on the main gate.

"I don't think so." Katryna looked over her shoulder again.

"Stop glancing back," Myra said. "There's a servant walking towards the gate. He seems to be watching us." Myra stopped in front of her. "Let him go ahead of us. When he's talking to the guards, we'll walk through."

Another section of stairs tumbled to the ground. Katryna flinched and bit her lip. The servant approached the gate and the guards stopped him.

"I think that's Wilf," Myra said.

"Where?"

"Shhh. You'll attract attention screeching like that," Myra said. "The servant is Wilf, and they're letting him leave the Palace."

"Come on. We don't want to lose him."

Myra grabbed hold of her arm and slowed her down. "Act more like a wizard." The guards saluted as they passed.

"Look! Wilf's going into that alley." She went to run, but Myra held her back again.

"As a general rule, wizards don't run," Myra said. Her walking pace quickened to gold-medal speed as she made her way to the alley, but Wilf had disappeared.

"He's gone. He didn't know wizards don't run," Katryna said, placing her hands on her hips.

"Do you still have a connection with him?"

"It really only lets me know if he's alive. I can't ping his location."

"What about the marking?" Myra's tone was sharp enough to slice glass. "That has to have its own connection as well. You want to give it a try?"

"I suppose." Katryna's cheeks burned as she rolled back her sleeve to reveal the golden shooting star.

"Try adding a little magic to it," Myra said.

"Thank you. I'd never have thought of that." She huffed, placed her finger over the star, and closed her eyes. A mist formed around her. "I think he's heading for the Veil."

"Are you sure?" Myra asked.

"I wouldn't have said it otherwise." Katryna took a deep breath and calmed her jittering nerves. Myra was trying to help. "He might be trying to get the journal back to Mathowytch."

"The Veil will never let him pass." Myra pinched her lips.

"But you can go through the tunnels."

"Me?" Myra took a step back.

"Yes. Come on. We need to catch him." She set off at a run, Myra's footsteps pounding behind her.

Bewildered wizards and witches wandered around, stopping to talk to anyone who would listen. Several buildings had collapsed in the quakes and the roads were blocked. Cries could be heard from people trapped under the rubble. Katryna fastened her hood tightly whenever they passed patrols, but the guards didn't seem interested. They were more occupied with stopping looting or trying to help trapped citizens.

"There's Wilf." Myra pointed down the street.

Katryna picked up the pace again, trying to catch him.

He turned as she approached, then looked both ways, as if about to bolt. "Wilf," she called.

He stopped, and she flung herself at him. He held her close and their lips met. They both stepped back. Katryna's cheeks radiated heat.

"You're safe." He put his hands in his pockets.

"Do you have the journal?" Myra asked.

Wilf paused and furrowed his brows. "It needs to go to Mathowytch."

"Myra can take it. She's the only one who can travel through the tunnels," Katryna said.

"Let's get to the Veil first." He gave Myra a long stare. "This route is blocked." He gestured to several buildings that had been razed to the ground. They turned and began walking down the street until they found a cleared road leading off towards the Veil.

"It's only a couple of streets further," Myra said. "I entered Mathowytch through the tunnels."

They walked passed deserted buildings and turned down a path. Tendrils from the Veil stretched across the street. "Be careful not to touch any of those strands," Myra said. "I saw a guard burned by them."

Myra edged along the side of the buildings. The tendrils recoiled as she went. They darted at Wilf and Katryna like vipers. Myra stepped protectively in front of them and the tendrils shrunk away with a whimpering sound.

"It's this one." Myra stopped outside one of the buildings.

"How do you know?" Wilf twisted the ring on his finger.

"I remember this window. It's the only building that has one. I know this is the entrance to the tunnels." Her words tumbled over one another. "I've still got my talisman. So unless I take a wrong turn, the journal will be safe."

"And while you're keeping the journal safe, what are we supposed to do? Wait for the next patrol to pick us up?" Wilf said.

Katryna glanced from Myra to Wilf. "It was my idea she take it," she said.

"Hmm," he said. "It's a moot point, because the journal is of no use without me. The words only appear for me. That's why Hywel needed me to transcribe it."

Myra raised an eyebrow. "He didn't mention that piece of information."

"Does it matter?" He pressed his lips together and glared at his stepsister.

"Then, we'll have to take our chances in the tunnels and hope the Veil doesn't destroy us," Katryna said, placing her hand on Wilf's arm.

Myra's bark of laughter echoed off the buildings. "The Veil will never let a wizard travel through it, or someone with wizard magic. You'll end up losing the journal."

"Is that why you brought us here? So you could finally acquire the journal?" Wilf asked.

Myra took a deep breath and released it. "It's the only way I know to keep it safe."

"The safehouse," Katryna said, waving her arms. "I traveled under the Veil from there."

"Hywel knows where the safehouse is. That's the first place he'll look," Myra said, shaking her head. "How do you think he knew you were in Kureyamage?"

"You told him, you mean," Wilf said.

"Of course I told him where the house was. That's how I could come back to find you." Myra paced.

"Glad you didn't say rescue," Wilf said. The muscles in his jaw tightened.

"Stop it. I don't know what's going on between you two, but this isn't the time or place," Katryna said.

"We have to use the tunnels." Myra stepped towards the window.

"I still have my talisman." Katryna pulled the amulet out from under her collar.

"I don't. It was destroyed in Hywel's Advancer." Wilf's shoulders relaxed. "I suppose the bond might be enough to protect us."

"I'm willing to try if you are." Katryna twirled the amulet. "What do we have to lose?"

"Would you like a list?" Myra said.

"We have to take the risk," he said.

"But…" Myra began.

"Do you have a better plan?" Katryna cut her off. The dusk added to the Veil's grayness, and shadows crept towards them. She shivered at their unnatural movement. Myra walked over to the small bricked-in basement window and, without a backward glance, stepped through.

"That looked easy," Wilf said. "Do you want to go next?"

"You go."

"Coward." He grinned at her, walked over to the window, pressed his foot against it, and slid out of sight. Katryna placed her hand over her chest. Her heart raced, and she swallowed twice before stepping through.

The bricks' consistency changed to a gel that sucked her inside. She told herself several times to relax, and the undulations moved her into the tunnels. A globe materialized. Myra and Wilf stood apart, waiting for her.

"That wasn't so bad," she said.

"Reminded me of Oobleck," Wilf said.

"What?"

Myra lifted her talisman, and it glowed purple. Katryna's turned golden.

"I don't know what that means," Myra said. "Doesn't it have to be purple?"

"There's only one way to find out." Katryna wanted to go home and find her mother. "Do you know the way through the tunnels?"

"I think so, but last time Nipits guided me," Myra's voice sounded muffled by the dirt walls. A path emerged from the darkness.

"I hope this is the right one." Katryna's voice quivered.

"So do I," Wilf said, squeezing her hand. "There's only one way to find out."

# Chapter Thirty-One
# In the Tunnels

Wilf let Myra lead the way, with Katryna trailing behind. Indistinct shapes formed and vanished in the mist on both sides of the path. He had no desire to meet them. His journey to Kureyamage was still vivid in his memory. A small globe bobbed along in front of Myra, casting strange images on the floor.

He squinted, rubbed his eyes, and glanced back at Katryna. He could see her clearly, but the air around Myra changed, thickening. She started to disappear as the mist swallowed her.

"Myra, stop."

A second pathway emerged, inch by inch, on the right. Myra continued. She couldn't hear him. He ran forward to catch her, but the mist swirled to form an impenetrable wall. The light faded. He caught hold of Katryna's hand.

"Myra's disappeared. We're on our own." He peered into the gloom.

"There are two paths. Which one should we choose?" Katryna's voice trembled.

He could hardly see her features. He concentrated on forming a globe. His ring flared, but the spell wouldn't form. A high-pitched scream filled the air.

"I don't think I should try magic again in here," he said.

"Let me try."

A small globe materialized next to him.

"We'd better get moving." He squeezed her hand. "It won't be long before a squad of wizard guards are on our tail."

"They can't come down here. The Veil wouldn't let them," Katryna said

He glanced around at the thick, gray mist. "I don't think it's going to let me go through either. You should go. Make your own way through."

She held his gaze. "I'm not going anywhere without you. Besides, I don't think I'm a witch anymore. So, if the Veil lets me though, it must let you."

"You have a talisman, I don't. It doesn't make any sense to risk both of our lives." He released her and took a step backward. "Magic me another globe and then go."

"No," she sobbed. "I won't leave you here alone. You might need my help."

"Katryna, please."

"No. You're stuck with me." She took a deep breath. "We don't know why the talisman is golden, but it must have something to do with our bond."

"I'm not happy about this. It doesn't feel right."

She began to lead the way down one of the paths. The light from the globe reflected back off the thick layer of mist surrounding them. Shadows moved in the haze, never revealing their true form.

"I don't want to know what's lurking behind there," he said, aware that his palms were sweating. "I'm getting the feeling that we're being watched. Do you think it's only opaque on this side?"

The path narrowed, and Katryna let his hand drop. He wiped it down his pants. She took several paces in front of him.

"There is no one down here but us and Myra," she said, leaning forward slightly.

"That's what I thought the last time we walked through the Veil." He shivered at the memory of the clawed hands grabbing him.

"The enchantment is stronger above ground."

"Here, there won't be any spirits?" A howl sounded and Wilf spun around. His breath coming in quick, short bursts.

They trudged along in silence. The sound from their feet deadened in the swirling mist. Cackles and screams penetrated the quiet from inside the Veil. Each time, his heart raced and his muscles tensed.

"It's taking a long time to reach Mathowytch. The journey seemed shorter last time."

"That's because we were running to escape the spirits," she said. They lapsed back into silence. The sounds from inside the mist grew louder.

"It's eerie down here," he said. "And those sounds aren't helping. You would expect to smell dampness and the air to taste stale, but there's nothing. Do you think the Veil is robbing us of our senses?" He was babbling like a rookie trying to impress the team, but couldn't stop.

"You're certainly making less and less sense, if that's what you mean," she said.

"Ha ha," he said.

A rumbling noise, like a wave of defenders bearing down on them, broke the silence. Wilf spun around looking for shelter. A thick roll of mist swept down and consumed him. It invaded his mouth, nose, and ears. He gasped and grabbed at his throat. He couldn't breathe or swallow. The mist was trying to suffocate him. Then, it was gone.

Katryna stood, looking dazed. "What happened?"

"I think the Veil tried to kill me." Wilf bent over, coughing.

"Then you'd be dead," she said.

"Let's keep moving before it decides to come back and finish us off next time."

He took a step and stopped. A weight clunked against his chest. "Look at this." He held up a talisman hanging around his neck.

Katryna looked all around. "But it's red."

"Yours is now purple."

The mist rolled in again. "Run," Wilf shouted, pushing forward down the tunnel. Tendrils snapped at his ankles as he ran. The path divided again in front of him. Katryna held out her hand to him and he grabbed it. He faked a turn to the left and then dove down the right path of a long, gray-walled tunnel. Kathryn stumbled, and he half-carried, half-dragged her until she regained her balance.

"I can't do this for much longer," she said, between gasps. "My legs are tiring."

"Don't talk, just run. Don't take your eyes off the goal."

A spiral of mist clung to his ankle, fouling him, and he tumbled. He let go of Katryna's hand as he fell. Her momentum took her another few paces, and he watched as the mist filled the gap between them.

"No. Wilf." Katryna yelled, and then only silence and darkness filled the tunnel. The Veil released him and opened a new pathway for him. It glowed in a strange half-light.

"Where are you taking me?"

Deafening silence surrounded him. He could either go where the Veil allowed or stay there. Glancing around, he didn't see a third option. Staying where he was could get him killed sooner.

His steps were heavy, and his feet dragged as he followed the new pathway. After everything they'd been through, to come so close to evading the wizards and bringing the formula to the witches. It was ironic that, after he'd been forced to accept magic, it was a witch spell that prevented him now.

"I'm trying to help the witches of Mathowytch," he yelled. "Why are you stopping me? The wizards are about to gain control if I don't reach the Council. You'll be just a wisp of history."

He struggled on. If it had been a proper wall, instead of an enchantment, at least he could have punched and kicked it.

A figure appeared and floated towards him.

"Myra? Katryna?"

"I am a guardian." The figure had the shape of a woman, but she remained slightly out of focus.

"A guardian?" He held his palm up, and his legs buckled.

"There are four of us, we are the Veil."

"Are you here to lead me to Mathowytch?" Wilf rubbed his hands down his pants.

"That is not possible. Our duty is to protect against wizards, and you are a very powerful wizard. We would have destroyed you, but your strength seemed divided when you entered."

"The bond. I share magic with a witch. You let me through last time." He tripped over his words, and his body flushed with heat.

"At that time, you were told never to return, but here you are."

"I'm helping the Witch Council."

"This we are trying to determine," the guardian said. "My sisters are protecting travelers through the tunnels. They will discover if you speak the truth." She leaned forward. Her hollow eye socks glowed. "Or if you mean them harm."

"Can't you ask the Council?" Wilf became intently interested in the ground at his feet.

"The lines of communication have been lost. The realm is weakening. We are struggling to maintain the integrity of the Veil, but there are wizards at the border." She turned and looked off into the distance.

"Then, we need to hurry and get me to Mathowytch." He took a step forward, but tendrils of mist grabbed his arms and held him.

"This we cannot do. Our sole purpose is to prevent wizards from entering Mathowytch."

"But I've been there before," he said. "Isn't that why you gave me a talisman?"

"The talisman is why we haven't destroyed you, yet. It should have turned black, not red." The figure turned, as if listening. "Red for warning, black for death."

"So?"

The guardian held up her hand.

"You are attached to both of the young witches. One is a kind of sister to you. The other is your mate and has... wizard magic. What trick is this?"

"That's what I've been trying to tell you." Wilf tugged at the tendrils holding him.

"The wizards are firing at the Veil." The figure took a few steps away from him. "The spell is weakening. One of my sisters has fallen. There are only three guardians now. I must go."

"Wait! Help me get to Mathowytch."

The figure started to retreat back into the mist.

"Don't leave me here." He strained against the strands of Veil still holding him. The figure waved her hand. The tendrils withdrew.

"I will leave you a path. It's all I can do. The Veil will decide." The figure merged with the mist and disappeared.

He moved cautiously as the slope grew steeper and led deeper into the tunnels, away from the surface. He turned a corner, and the trail opened out into a large cavern with a chimney of light shining down onto an underground lake. Boulders covered the beach next to the lake. As he approached the lake, the boulders stood.

Witches. A lot of them. And they all turned to stare at him. The Veil had decided to destroy him. He touched the journal in his pocket.

"Wilf." Katryna ran down the path towards him. Picking up his pace, he ran to meet her.

"I thought I'd never see you again," she said, hugging him. He swung her in the air, and she laughed. He put her down and waited for the witches to make a move.

"Stay behind me," he said.

"What are you talking about? These witches all have the Virus and have been abandoned down here. This is where I was sent."

"They don't look very friendly." He folded his arms across his chest and widened his stance.

"They're frightened. You're a wizard."

"It's you," one of the witches pointed at Katryna. "You're the witch who got her power back. Why are you back here? Relapse?"

"Why have you brought a wizard here?" another witch shouted.

"The Veil is failing," Katryna said. "We are trying to get to Mathowytch with the formula to cure the Virus."

Noise bounced around the cavern. Wilf held up his hand, and the witches quieted.

"How do we get into Mathowytch from here?" he asked.

"It's that path," Katryna said. "But there's an enchantment on it that prevents anyone leaving from this side."

The witches shouted over each other. "It kills anyone who tries," one of the witches yelled from the back of the crowd.

"If that's the only way out, we don't have a choice." He twisted his ring. He'd need full control of his magic here.

"Why should we trust you?" another witch yelled.

"I'll go," Katryna said. "The witches need you to survive."

"No." He grabbed her arm. "We all go together. We have to take these witches out of here."

"It's a trick," someone said. "This wizard wants to destroy us."

"We want to save you," Katryna said. "The witches have abandoned you here to die. With the quakes getting stronger, this cave could collapse. The whole realm may not survive."

"Why?" another witch shouted. "What use are we?"

"The wizards are massing on the border. They will attempt to storm and take the city." Witches broke into groups.

"We should start moving," Katryna said. A tall, curvy witch walked towards him, her long red hair fell in waves to her waist.

"We will help you," she said, her voice deep and seductive.

Wilf felt a sharp pain in his side from where Katryna elbowed him. He closed his mouth and cleared his throat. "Thank you," he said, trying not to focus on her full, red lips. She smiled, and he swallowed.

"I know she's beautiful, but you really shouldn't stare at her like that," Katryna said. "It's embarrassing."

"She is." He stopped himself in time. "Sorry."

The witch kept pace with Wilf as they started up the path. He could feel the enchantment at the top of the slope. The spell crackled and fizzed when he approached. His ring blazed and his tattoo itched before his focus shifted, revealing strands of light crisscrossing the tunnel, blocking their route. This would take a team effort.

"We need to do this together. I'm still having difficulty with control," he said, placing his ringed finger on Katryna's tattooed hand. She pointed, sending a long blast of red magic. The strands resisted, absorbing the power and glowing as they expanded. A humming noise grew to a shrill whine, and the strands exploded, sending pieces of rock hurtling around the cave.

He led the way into the tunnel. It twisted and forked several times before it brought them to a flight of stairs.

"At the top of the stairs is a door that leads into the Council chambers," the red-headed witch said.

Wilf took the steps two at a time. The group of witches followed. He stopped at the large steel door blocking their progress. "I'll need your help again, Katryna."

"How?"

"I'll give you control, and you can direct my magic." He placed her finger on his shooting star mark.

"I'm not sure how we did it last time."

"You're a very smart witch-wizard." Wilf smiled and gave a quick kiss on her cheek. "I trust you." A murmur from the other witches grew louder.

"They're nervous," she said. "There's never been a female wizard before."

"First time for everything," he said.

She placed her hand on the door. The steel door started to glow a faint pink color, which deepened to red and spread outwards from Katryna's hand. Wilf closed his eyes and tried to concentrate on slowly feeding energy to Katryna, like a faucet on a half-turn. A trickle flowed from him to Katryna. She controlled it. So, he turned the faucet to increase the flow.

"Too much," Katryna said, gasping. Beads of sweat stood on her forehead. Her face scrunched up in pain.

"I'm sorry." He struggled to reduce the flow.

"Better," she said. The fingers of her outstretched hand looked swollen, a blue tinge to them.

The door buckled and then melted, leaving a hole large enough for them to walk through. "Where are we?" Wilf asked.

"Down that corridor is the Council meeting hall," the red-headed witch said. "Down that corridor, and then up one flight, are the libraries and laboratories."

"Come on." He kept hold of Katryna's hand and pulled her along.

"Shouldn't we let the Council know we're here?" she asked.

Alarm bells rang out.

"I think they know. Let's start with the scientists, before guards arrive to lock us up," he said.

Katryna let go of his hand. "You're faster than me. Go." He rocketed off down the corridor, trying to locate Degula Spack's office like a ball struck for a winning penalty.

Degula lifted her head when he burst inside. Wilf took the journal from his pocket and waved it in front of her.

"I can transcribe the formula for you," he said, panting. "How soon will you be able to start production?"

"That all depends on her." Degula pointed at a witch in the door. Wilf spun around. Myra stood with her arm wrapped around Katryna, her fingers resting on Katryna's throat.

"That's very good of you," Myra said. "Please, don't let me stop you. Degula, could you please give Wilf paper and a pen?"

Degula rifled through her desk drawer until she brought out the writing implements.

"What are you going to do with this?" He sat down and opened the journal. The formula appeared on the page. He pointed at the page. A copy of the formula rose from the journal and transferred to the paper. He was exerting a lot of control in not reaching for Myra. Narrowing his eyes, he glanced up at his stepsister.

"How can you do this?"

"Ermentrude infected my brother," she said. "I'm returning the journal and formula to him and Hywel."

"You understand this realm is dying. It's impossible to save it."

Myra edged Katryna forward and picked up the paper. "Not now." She placed it in her pocket, never taking her eyes off him. Her fingers remained at Katryna's throat.

"That will save witches who have the Virus. It will even prevent anyone else from contracting it, but it won't save this realm. The damage is too great," he said.

"He's right," Degula said. "The rest of the Council is down at the Veil, trying to bolster it. Let me produce that vaccine."

"Please, Myra," he said, the urgency in his voice heightened by the dangerous situation. "Don't do this."

"Give me the journal," she said.

Wilf picked up the journal but kept his eyes on Myra.

"It's of no use to you. Why take it?" He turned the book over in his hand. "What don't you want me to know about you?"

"Hand it over." She tightened her grip around Katryna's neck until the younger witch made a gurgling noise.

"There are a large number of witches outside in the corridor. How are you planning to escape?"

"Witches," Myra said. "They came from the underground cave. They have no magic." She stepped forward. "Katryna, relieve Wilf of the journal and place it in my pocket."

Katryna hesitated.

"Do it," Wilf said. Katryna's eyes pleaded with him. A sensation of calm washed over him through the bond.

Myra dragged Katryna back to the door and out into the corridor, Wilf stalked after her, but the escape route was blocked by the red-headed witch. Myra wriggled her fingers and Katryna collapsed. Then, she sent a bolt of red magic spinning at Wilf as she dashed down the corridor. Wilf cut to his left, dodging the blast that ripped through the wall. She sent a blue bolt of magic at the red-headed witch. The witch collapsed and Myra disappeared down the stairs.

Wilf knelt beside Katryna. She was breathing. A large bruise spread across her neck. She opened her eyes.

"Go after her," she rasped.

He sped down the corridor in pursuit, sprinting down the stairs and racing along the next corridor. Witches screamed as they saw him running. He dodged random blasts of magic sent spinning towards him. Guards appeared and shifted to mark him. Cutting hard to his left, he dodged the blue blots aimed at him without breaking stride. He gained on Myra as she headed out of the council building.

More guards came running. Not having time to stop, he raised his ringed finger and produced a soccer ball of white magic. He pictured it as a free kick and took two short steps, then, he sent a hard right-footed cross driving down the corridor. The empowered ball knocked the guards to the ground. It would have been an impressive goal. He weaved around the unconscious guards, out of the building, down the steps, and through the plaza. Myra was far in front of him. The guards had cost him precious minutes, but he continued to chase after her. She couldn't leave with his journal.

# Chapter Thirty-Two
# Back in Hong Kong

Myra sped down the street. She had no plan or idea where she was heading. Two large buildings collapsed. Dust clouds filled the sky, and she could taste grit in her mouth. Witches wandered around, looking dazed, or sat on benches, rocking backward and forward.

A witch grabbed at her. "I can't find my cat. Have you seen my cat?"

Myra pushed the witch aside but slowed her pace, checking the buildings and the road behind her. Alarms sounded. Three witches mounted on broomsticks headed up into the sky. Green lights flashed and fissures opened. More witches abandoned Mathowytch before the Veil collapsed and wizards poured across the border.

A large, cat-like animal, the size of a horse, pounced on an elderly witch, biting her head off.

"Watchers are in the city," a thin, white-faced witch whispered. "We're all going to die."

A trolley bus burned in the middle of the street, the smell of rubber and hot metal added to the acrid air. Myra left the main avenue and dived down a side street. Her fingers caressed the book in her pocket, the feel of leather reassuring to the touch. Once she reached the Veil with the journal, she would feel safe. She snatched back her hand as the lock snapped at her fingers.

Rounding the corner, she stopped. The Veil, no longer a dense wall, had a gossamer sheen, and Kureyamage's buildings appeared as threatening as the wizard guards lined up, waiting to reclaim Mathowytch.

The witches from the Council stood, hands joined, trying to support the Veil's magic, even as it collapsed. A group of witches stormed a warehouse. Flashes from blue energy bolts appeared in the windows. Then, the building vibrated and disappeared.

Myra turned another corner, leaned against the wall for support, and waited for the Veil's total collapse. Her heart raced and she wiped sweat from her brow. Pulling out the paper she'd taken from Wilf, she frowned. The symbols were unrecognizable, but Hywel would be able to decipher them. She'd earned her right to stay. He'd save Thiemus, and she'd be free of them both. Her life would be her own to control.

Myra folded the paper and replaced it. Hywel would be in the first wave of wizards coming through to claim victory over the Mathowytch witches. Standing up straight, she crossed her arms. This was going to work. It had to. Hywel could take the journal and refuse to let her go. He might still have a use for her as a spy. She ran a hand over her itchy eyes. No. She wasn't thinking straight. When had she last slept? Reaching into her inside pocket, she took out her last vial of elixir and downed the contents. Her hands stopped shaking seconds later.

In the middle of the road, Wilf slid to a stop. She edged back into the building's shadows. He glanced around and then dashed to the circle of Council witches. Leaning in, he spoke to Akuna and touched her shoulder. The Head Witch placed her hand over his shooting-star tattoo. Akuna nodded. The Council began to chant again, and this time the Veil began to thicken.

"No," Myra shouted. She sent a blue bolt of magic at Wilf. It bounced off him, but he turned to stare in her direction. He'd learned how to use his magic. Hywel thought he could control Wilf, but his Advancer had changed Wilf into a very powerful wizard. He could shield himself while aiding the rebuilding of the Veil, which suggested he had access to a vast amount of magic.

A quake vibrated the buildings around her, and a large crack appeared in the road. She stumbled the first few steps away from the buildings and edged closer to the Veil. Her legs moved automatically, her mind racing. She could make a dash through the Veil before it was fully rebuilt. She took a deep breath, but Kureyamage disappeared again. She groaned. She shouldn't have hesitated. A heaviness settled in her stomach. She had to remain calm and think.

The Council kept their circle, but Akuna released Wilf. The warehouse next to her started to vibrate, and then it disappeared. Portals. She could use them and send a message to Hywel from wherever she arrived. Wilf turned and walked in her direction. "Give it back, Myra." His voice echoed in her head. She glanced left and right, and ran for the next warehouse.

A ball slammed her between the shoulder blades, and she fell forward through the warehouse's entrance. She tried to move, but the ball felt like a heavy kettlebell on her back, pinning her to the floor and trapping her arms beneath her.

"The journal answers to me." Wilf's voice vibrated in her head. The book inched out from her pocket until it leaped free. Then, it floated out of the warehouse. Tears rolled down Myra's cheeks. The floor rippled underneath her and the walls spun. The ball bounced off her back as a blinding surge of yellow light filled the warehouse.

Myra struggled to her knees. A group of 20 witches pushed past her and headed out the door. She used the doorframe for support as she rose to stand. The warehouse stood on the edge of a river. Newer buildings stood in rows along the street, all with perfectly manicured green spaces and parking lots.

Myra staggered along the street and looked at the road sign— Shing Wan Road. A green taxi disappeared around the corner. She was back in Hong Kong.

"Fantastic," she said. "Bloody fantastic."

"And after all your hard work."

Spinning round, the world tilted. She gasped, holding her head until she could focus on… "Seldan! What are you doing here?"

"Escaping before the realm collapses. The same as everyone else." Seldan stepped forward, her hands behind her back, out of view.

"I thought you'd been captured in the palace attack," Myra said.

"I left before the end. Brought someone with me whom I've been keeping safe." Seldan nodded over to a slumped figure sitting on the ground. The figure raised her head.

"Ermentrude," Myra said, widening her eyes.

"I didn't intend to bring her along, but we were hiding out in the warehouse." Seldan shrugged.

"But why?"

"Insurance." The witch brought her hands forward, palm side up. "Never know when you might need some."

"So now what?" Myra couldn't believe she'd managed to land in another fire-and-cauldron situation.

"That depends on you. Do you have the formula?"

"I might have." Myra raised an eyebrow.

Seldan smiled. "You and I make a great team. However, first you need to contact Hywel. Tell him you have it and Ermentrude."

"I do?"

Seldan might be as slippery as eating egg noodles with metal chopsticks, but Myra was an expert.

"Then, he can treat his infected wizards, not to mention your brother. When they set up a colony here, we can be part of it. I'm tired of living with only witches," Seldan said. "Can you contact him?" Myra crossed her arms at the challenging inflection in Seldan's voice.

Having Seldan, Ermentrude, and the formula could get her back in Hywel's good graces. And returning to the Magical Realm anytime soon seemed out of the question. It might be a good idea to throw her lot in with Seldan. It would certainly be an advantage to have the old crone as a bargaining tool, except Wilf would probably come to rescue her. And she didn't want to meet him again without help.

"Why would you want to join with Hywel?" Myra asked.

"If the Realm collapses, his biome technology will be the only access we have to magic," Seldan said. "Do you want to live here without magic?"

"What are biomes?"

"It's a top-secret project the Wizard Council has been conducting. We happened upon the information when we intercepted one of their test portals. The concept is fascinating, if it works."

Myra bit the inside of her cheek and glanced at Ermentrude. "Yes, I can contact him from the store in Wan Chai." Myra nodded at Ermentrude. "She seems docile."

"I've been feeding her prison brew, reducing her ability to access magic. The last dose was an hour ago, and I don't have any more," Seldan said. "We should be safe, for now, but I'm not sure how the portal affected her."

They each took one of Ermentrude's arms and helped her to stand. "How do we get around in this place?" A tight smile played on Seldan's lips.

"MTR—public transport. Like your trams," she said. "But, it's going to be difficult with her in this condition. It will attract attention."

"Leave that to me," Seldan said. They turned the corner.

"We're in Sha Tin." Myra recognized Shingles' Chuen Road and the Shing Run River. "It's about 50 minutes to the store from here."

"We'd better hurry then," Seldan said, wriggling her fingers. "You can let go. I've put her under a compulsion spell." Ermentrude's eyes blazed.

The streets became busier as they neared Tai Wai Station, and they fell in step with the commuters going through Entrance 'A'. Myra led them to the east rail link that would take them to Hung Hom. "We'll need to take the Cross Harbour Tunnel bus." Myra produced three Octopus cards. "You'll have to use one of these to travel."

"This is how you get around in this realm?" Seldan asked, in a disgusted tone. "Give me a broom any day."

"I'm sure most people would agree with you, but that's not an option."

The train doors opened, and passengers surged in, pushing, shoving, and jostling each other to get seats or a better standing position. Seldan raised her fingers, but Myra put a warning hand on her arm. Keeping the witch in check would be like slowing a bolt of magic—impossible.

"You can't do that here," Myra said. "There are cameras everywhere, and you don't want to be caught performing magic." Seldan shrugged and dropped her fingers.

Myra grabbed hold of Ermentrude's other arm and steered the witch onto the train. They hung onto the handrails. She shouldn't have threatened Katryna's life, but there hadn't been any other option. She wouldn't have hurt her, not intentionally. And she couldn't believe she'd sent bolts of magic at Wilf. If she'd left him alone, she'd still have the journal, but he'd been helping to fix the Veil, stopping her escape from Mathowytch. Her fingers searched around in her pocket for a vial. She couldn't be out of them. It wasn't possible. There had to be more elixir in the store. She glanced out the window and counted down the rest of the stops to Hung Hom Station.

"We need to catch that bus," Myra said, pointing at the Number 101 double-decker bus already filling with passengers. She ran ahead and stood in the doorway, preventing the bus's doors from closing. The bus driver yelled at her in Cantonese, waving his arms at her to get off the bus. Ermentrude and Seldan climbed on, and the doors hissed closed.

The bus ambled along the road and then crawled along in the congestion towards the Tunnel's entrance. "I can see why you hate living here. It takes so long to travel anywhere." Seldan stared at Ermentrude. "We need to help this bus along."

"That's impossible," Myra said. "I've tried to control the flow of traffic before, but there are too many vehicles to be able to move them all. Once we enter the Tunnel, the traffic will move better."

"I hope so." Seldan crossed her arms and leaned back.

The bus inched forward. Then, it entered the bus lane and moved freely through the Tunnel.

"We get off here," Myra said. "It's only a short walk up the Wan Chai Road, and we'll be there." They disembarked from the bus and Seldan grabbed hold of her arm.

"The brew will be wearing off. We need to hurry. A simple compulsion charm isn't going to hold her. I'd rather not have to take her on when she's fueled by anger and magic," Seldan said.

"It's going to take around ten minutes to get there," Myra said. "Do what you can."

Seldan nodded and sucked in her lower lip. "Let's get moving."

Myra led the way past the temple, to the gift store. She wriggled her fingers and the boards disappeared from the door. It creaked open.

The smell of humidity, mold, and dust stung Myra's nose and she sneezed. She stepped over the broken pottery and fallen racks until she stood in front of the communication mirror at the back of the store. Taking a deep breath, she took out her compact, flipping it over in her palm several times before shrugging and opening it. A crack ran across its surface.

"It might not work," she said, showing Seldan.

"We won't know if you don't make the call, will we?" Seldan pushed Ermentrude to the floor, next to the counter. Myra placed the compact in the larger relay mirror and imaged Hywel.

"Myra? Is that you? The image is blurred," he said.

"I have a copy of the formula and Ermentrude," she said in a rush.

"Where are you? Kureyamage?"

"Hong Kong. I accidentally transported in one of the witches' warehouses."

"Back in that realm. Do you also have Katryna? Or Wilf?"

"No. Once I had the formula, I left. I knew you'd want it urgently."

"Hmmm," he said.

"How's Thiemus?" Myra asked. Her stomach tightened.

"Your concern would be touching if you hadn't played a role in his infection. I'll be with you shortly. Don't do anything until I arrive." The screen went blank.

"I need to make another prison brew for Ermentrude." Seldan glanced round the store. "Do you have any supplies?"

"In Reginald's workshop, but only Wilf can enter."

"Then, we'd better tie her up until Hywel arrives," Seldan said. "I hope he doesn't take too long."

Ermentrude let out a long groan.

# Chapter Thirty-Three
# Vaccine Production

The journal lay open on a workbench, and a copy of Reginald's formula lay next to it, written on a yellowed parchment. Degula picked it up and wriggled her fingers. A second copy appeared next to it.

"Take this to Kureyamage. See it reaches the Wizard Council." She handed a copy to a witch in a brown uniform.

"What are you doing?" Katryna's voice sounded strained, and her eyes screwed up with pain.

"Stopping the spread of the Virus." Degula gave the messenger witch a talisman and travel pass.

"This was always your plan?" Wilf held his clenched fists close to his body. Fire raged through him, and his palm itched, longing to be released. "That's why you sent me to Kureyamage."

"The Realm's survival is paramount," Degula said. "Negotiations were stalled. The witches' holding onto Mathowytch, given the current situation, isn't a viable option. There have only been a handful of new witches born, or arrived, in Mathowytch since the Veil's creation. Soon, there won't be enough of us to run the city, let alone defend it."

"But you did more than that. You helped spread the Virus among your own kind." A golf ball-sized bolt fizzed in his closed hand. He gritted his teeth against the pain of holding the magic.

"Did you have the backing of the whole Council, or was this a solo project?" Katryna asked, crossing her arms.

"There are a number of us, not the whole Council, but enough." Degula wriggled her fingers and ingredients flew to her from around the room. A black cauldron settled down on the bench.

"All this death and destruction has been for what?" he asked.

"Do you think seats on the Wizard Council matter now, that the realm is collapsing? We have to pick our fights," Degula said. "I don't understand this final ingredient."

"Why should we help you?" He struggled to contain the power building in his palm. The ball grew to the size of a tennis ball. He took a deep breath, hoping to dissipate some of his anger.

"I thought Katryna might like a dose of the vaccine before you leave to chase after your stepsister." Degula ran her finger along the formula and then wriggled them at the ingredients, which lined up in order. Wilf swallowed hard. The magic in his hand reduced back to a golf ball size but sizzled loudly.

Degula raised an eyebrow at him. "Are you going to enlighten me or blast me?"

"Do you remember when you interviewed me before you sent me through the Veil to Kureyamage?" Wilf opened his fingers. The magic floated in a wisp to the ceiling and fizzed out.

"Yes." Degula tapped her fingertips on the bench. The ingredients began to jump into the cauldron.

"You took one of my memories and projected an image of a flower from the outfit my mother used to wear. That is your missing ingredient."

She turned to the shelving and lifted down a bunch of wild peapod flowers. "To think it was here all the time." Degula shook her head. "A common weed."

"It's all just politics." Katryna placed her hands on her hips. "Sorry you were infected, but we've struck the best deal we can and now we'll just surrender?"

Degula wriggled her fingers over the cauldron. It grew a lid and started to whirl like a centrifuge. "I'm not apologizing, if that's what you're looking for. My role is security, and that's what I'm doing, making the Realm secure." The cauldron stopped and the lid disappeared. A vial floated out and into Degula's hand.

"Do you want this or not?" Degula asked.

"She wants it," Wilf said. Katryna glared at him. The building shook. Books, jars, and scrolls fell off the bookshelves.

"Fine," Katryna said, rolling up her right sleeve. The star on her left hand glowed. Akuna entered the laboratory.

"We don't have time to make more vaccine here. The building isn't safe," Degula said. "We can use the last of the portals to transport the infected witches to the Real World and make it there."

"Does it work?" Akuna moved closer to Katryna.

"We'll know soon." Degula injected Katryna. She made another copy of the formula and handed it to Akuna. "This is insurance in case anything happens to us. Wilf, will we be able to use your father's workshop?"

"Yes. Is that where all the warehouses go? To Hong Kong?" he asked.

"There are four gateways: Hong Kong, London, New York, and Mumbai. The portals can be assigned to any of the gateways," Akuna said. A witch stood in the doorway, waiting. Akuna handed her the formula. "Make more copies."

The corridor appeared blocked with witches wanting Akuna's advice or instructions. "The workshop may not be the safest place if Myra went back to Hong Kong," he said.

"Do you really think she will go back there?" Katryna asked.

"She'll go back to the store, but she can't get into the workshop," he said.

"Have you seen my mother?" Katryna rubbed her arm at the injection site.

"Ermentrude? No," Akuna fastened escaping strands of her wiry, gray hair back into its jeweled clasp. "I haven't seen her since she left for Kureyamage."

"But I thought Seldan brought her back here." Katryna held the Head Witch's gaze.

"Whatever made you think that?" Degula packed a small black bag with various herbs and vials.

"Seldan took over control of the spy ring and sent Ermentrude back to Mathowytch," Katryna said, standing in front of Akuna.

"That witch is part of a breakaway radical faction," Akuna said. "She has no alliances here anymore. It wouldn't make sense for her to transport Ermentrude here."

"You don't think my mother's still in Kureyamage?" Katryna asked. "I should have searched the safehouse when we were there. She might be trapped in one of the upstairs rooms."

Wilf took Katryna's hand. "We'll find Ermentrude, I promise."

"First, we need to get to that workshop and start production of this vaccine," Degula went to the cupboard and brought out two brooms.

"I'll organize the sick," Akuna said, heading for the corridor. "The Veil didn't like us adding wizard magic to it. I don't think it will survive much longer. Hopefully, it will give us enough time to evacuate Mathowytch."

"Where will you go?" Katryna asked.

"Out of the Magical Realm," Akuna said.

"But the balance?" Wilf asked. "This realm won't survive."

"I know," Akuna said, leaving the room.

Wilf and Katryna stared at each other. He'd thought he was helping stabilize the Veil, but he'd destroyed it. "This will be the fastest way to travel." Degula handed one of the brooms to Katryna.

"Me? But I've never traveled the Thermals before," Katryna said, meeting Wilf's eyes.

"Just follow me," Degula said. "I'll open the fissure. You'll be fine." Katryna hesitated, but Wilf squeezed her hand. She sat on the broom, and he jumped up behind her.

"I hope you've taken a passenger before," Wilf said.

"All the time," Katryna replied.

He placed his arms around her waist. Her body trembled, and the broom rose off the ground and wobbled.

"You sure?"

"Yes, Now, be quiet, I need to concentrate." She readjusted her grip on the handle. The window opened and she followed Degula.

"Ready?" Degula hovered outside the second story.

"Sort of," Katryna said.

Degula shot off into the sky, and Katryna kept pace. A blaze of green light flashed across the sky and a fissure opened. The older witch spurted forward. Wilf felt Katryna increase her speed, trying to catch Degula, but his added weight made it difficult.

Degula sped into the fissure.

"We're not going to make it," he said into Katryna's ear. The fissure began to close. The broom gave a lunge forward and they entered.

"That was close," he said.

Ribbons of light flashed around them. Katryna hunched low on the broom. Specters appeared, and she blasted them. Long, hooked tendrils reached out for him. She dodged around a large mass.

Wilf could just make out the silhouette of Degula ahead. Another fissure opened, and the witch vanished through it. Touching the broom's bristles, he added his magic to it. The broom bucked and jittered. He bent over, and the broom bounded forward at twice the previous speed. They broke out of the Thermals and into the cloudy Hong Kong sky.

The familiar smells of humidity, tropical vegetation, and mold hit him as they slowly descended onto Tai Wang Street. The gift store stood in front of them, boarded-up except for the door.

Degula went to open the door, but Wilf stopped her.

"I don't think we're the first to arrive."

Katryna used her magic to silence the doorbell, and they entered. Dim light from several globes left lots of shadowed spaces.

Wilf trod carefully over the debris-covered floor. Katryna and Degula left their brooms by the door. He signaled for them to go down the aisle on the left and right. Taking the central route, he hunched down and crept forward. A bundle sat huddled in front of the counter. Calling up his magic, he approached. The bundle moved. Ermentrude raised her head. She appeared tied and gagged, and she gestured towards the back of the shop, where the Mage's Crystal had stood.

Katryna sent a loosening spell, and Ermentrude's bonds slipped off her. She rose slowly, using the counter for support.

"Seldan and Myra are back there," she said in hushed tones. Wilf nodded. Degula joined them at the counter. Katryna embraced her mother.

"We have guests," he whispered. "Ermentrude, can you and Katryna hold them while I take Degula down into the workshop?"

"I think so, but my magic is limited," Ermentrude said.

He led the way to the closet, opened the door, and motioned for Degula to enter. Katryna and Ermentrude stood guard on the door. Footsteps crunched towards him. A blast of blue magic hit the doorframe.

"Go." Katryna fired back.

Wilf placed his hand over the black knot on the wood paneling. The runes and staircase appeared as the entrance grew. Stepping with his left foot, he ran down the staircase. Globes flickered into life as he went. He entered the workshop. The journal flew out of his pocket. It landed on the wooden table. Reaching for it, the ruby flared on his ring as his hand made contact with the binding. The front cover banged open and paper turned.

"Fantastic." Degula glanced round at the fully-equipped room. "Your father has combined a wizard and scientific laboratory. It's amazing the equipment he has."

He stared at the letters appearing on the page.

*Biomes—there are several situated around Hong Kong. Wilf, you will need to start the chain that will collect energy from the Magical Realm to help rebalance it. The following pages explain how the process works.*

"I can't do this now."

The journal banged shut and locks snapped into place. He placed his hand on the binding. A click came from each lock.

"Seriously, you'll have to wait," he said.

"What was that?" Degula asked.

"Nothing," he said. "I think I can be of more use upstairs."

Degula waved a dismissive hand at him. She was already gathering ingredients. Wilf ran back up the stairs.

Ermentrude stood, braced against the wall. The witch had been hit, but she was still sending swirling blue blasts of energy.

"Glad you could join us," Katryna said.

"Where are they?"

"Myra is trapped over by the communication mirror." He grabbed Katryna and jerked her towards him. A blast of red magic hit the wall where her head had been.

"They're playing for keeps," she said. "Seldan is behind the counter."

"But why are they here? Neither of them can enter the workshop without me."

"Myra was calling for reinforcements," Ermentrude said. "Hywel is on his way."

"Hywel?"

The door flew open, coming off its top hinge. "I think he's arrived," Katryna said. Ermentrude stepped forward, but Wilf put his hand on her shoulder.

"Leave him to me," he said. "Hywel," he shouted.

"Wilf." A red blast hit the floor in front of him.

"Enough," Hywel said. "Myra. Seldan. Cease firing. I'm sure we can work this out without anyone else being hurt."

"There's nothing to work out," Wilf said. "It's too late to prevent the collapse of your realm."

"That is true," Hywel said. "But the Wizard Council is never going to let you survive."

"What do you mean?" Katryna said.

"Wilf's power is one of the reasons the quakes increased. He draws too much energy. One of the unexpected side effects of that little machine of mine."

"He can learn to control it," Katryna said.

"None of that matters," Wilf said. "Did you know he murdered my mother?" He glared at Ermentrude.

"That was a long time ago." Hywel moved further into the store. Wilf clenched his fists and could feel the energy building in him.

"Wilf, no," Katryna said. Wilf raised his hand and pointed it at Hywel. Seldan sent a red blast at him. He blocked it and sent back a large blast of blue that knocked the witch off her feet. She slammed into the shelving and slumped, unconscious, to the floor.

"You have no control," Hywel said.

"That took a lot of control. It was only blue, not the killer red she sent at me," he said.

"You killed Yan Shuai?" Ermentrude asked.

"To prevent my father from helping the witches and warn him next time it would be me."

"I knew Griselda sent reports to Hywel on Reginald's activities." Ermentrude glared at her estranged husband.

"And Myra?" Wilf was aware that his stepsister had moved closer.

"Your stepsister decided to take over her mother's role after Griselda left," Ermentrude said.

"Such a vivid imagination." Hywel paced along the central aisle.

"Did you kill my father too?" Wilf stepped in front of the wizard

"That was all Myra's idea," Hywel said. "I had no wish for Reginald's evaporation. He was still needed."

"How could you kill our father?" Wilf asked.

"He wasn't mine," Myra stood next to Hywel. "But it was an accident. He found me trying to read his journal. I think that's when he placed that last enchantment on it. I didn't mean to kill him. I thought he was going to attack me."

"Enough of this. Do you still have a copy of the formula?" Hywel asked.

"Yes."

"Thiemus will be delighted." Hywel took a step back. "I think it's time for us to leave."

"No." Wilf sent a blue blast at Hywel. It hit the wizard in the chest and he slumped down.

"I'm sorry, but…" Myra sent a blinded flash of magic at Wilf. He staggered back, holding his eyes. She ran for the door, picking up a broom as she went. Swinging it in front, she jumped on, kicked off the ground, and floated up into the air.

Wilf stumbled out of the store and tried to grab her leg, but she was already out of reach. "I'll find you. Don't think I won't."

"I know," she said. "But that will mean you have to travel back to the Magical Realm, and I'm willing to bet that's not going to be an option for very long." She rose higher and hovered. "I want freedom to follow my own destiny, instead of everyone manipulating me. Leave me in peace, Wilf. Freedom is worth fighting for."

Wilf picked up the other broom and held it to Katryna. "We need to go after her." Ermentrude finished tying up Hywel and came to join them. She took the broom out of his hand.

"We know where she's gone and she's no threat without Hywel. The Wizard Council might be grateful to receive the formula, but they're never going to give a young witch any power or influence." She wriggled her fingers and the broom went back into the store. "Let her go and save Thiemus. We have more pressing issues to resolve. Firstly, to treat those infected by the virus, and then help stabilize the realm," Ermentrude said.

"You're a little behind on information." He watched a fissure open in the sky. "The Wizard Council already has a copy of the formula, provided by Degula, and the Veil is destroying the realm."

Katryna linked her arm through her mother's. She looked pale, and beads of sweat glistened on her forehead. The beginning of a wart showed on her chin and her nose looked longer.

"And I don't know if I'm a witch or a wizard." She held out her hand and examined the extra wizard knuckle. "I've access to both forms of magic. It's so strange."

Ermentrude slumped against the doorframe. "I'm going to need a large cup of brew for this story. What have you children been up to without my guidance?"

"That's a completely different tale," Wilf said, taking hold of Katryna's hand. It could be the bond he shared with her, or the danger they'd been through together, but he wanted her to stay close to him. He was even prepared to accept her mother—a little.

Wilf stared back up into the sky. He hoped Ermentrude was correct about Myra, because he would find her wherever she went.


# THE END